Killer C

Simon Maltman

To shalene,
Hope ya enjoy it,

all the best,

Simon

KILLER CASTING

Part 1: The Vulture

Chapter 1

A light drizzle had already begun by the time Joe stepped outside. It had started earlier than forecast. The door to the bar swung closed behind him, silencing the hubbub within. Outside it was replaced by the noise of a few cars running along the wet main road of the small town of Patterson. Joe allowed his act to disintegrate; his smile fell away and twisted into an angry scowl. He pulled up his collar and hurried away along the sidewalk.

Stupid. Stupid and careless.

He scolded himself for allowing his plan to evaporate so easily and spectacularly. His whole body vibrated with frustration as he strode past pedestrians and other folk milling outside the few bars still open in the quiet town. It was a little after ten. It would be almost midnight by the time he drove back to the city. He walked a block away to the almost empty parking lot. He clicked the fob for his dark blue Honda CR-V a few steps away, peeled off his damp raincoat and tossed it in the back. Joe hauled himself inside, gunned the motor and pulled out of the spot.

Three weeks Joe had spent planning this murder. It had been tried and tested many times and should have been easy. But not tonight. Joining the traffic, his expression remained unmoving, fixed in a controlled fury. It had been months since his last kill. He was so close, but now it had become another dead end. There had been several recently – too many. He felt like a jilted lover, lying frustrated next to an object of desire. Or a junkie returning to his squat empty-handed. There were many ways he set up his murders. Sometimes he liked finding a suitable mark online and picking them up through a manipulated meet-up in a bar. It was one of his favourites, particularly when it had been a long stretch since a kill. It took time, but usually paid off. On this occasion he had waited patiently for almost four months. He found women through Facebook, friends of friends of friends. At least five times removed; that was always the rule. There had been several

1

possibilities, but this one appeared the most promising. Gillian Morcombe was a few years younger than him at thirty-four. Moderately attractive, working in retail, she had recently broken up with her boyfriend of half a year. Joe had learned everything he could about her likes and interests and had researched them all thoroughly. He had his many strands of potential conversations all rehearsed.

It started off very promisingly. His alleged love of the Yankees and modern jazz had been well received. When her two work friends moved onto another bar, she had chosen to stay with him as he had hoped. It was all running along nicely. He presented himself as a little shy and geeky. He pitched it just right. He could sense it, like a fisherman just before a bite. Joe had always known that he was attractive to women – just shy of six feet, with thick brown hair and dimples. His voice was deep and his face appeared warm and open when a carefully-crafted smile was fixed securely upon it. And then out of nowhere, the chance was gone, dead in the water. Just as he was lifting over fresh drinks for them, she draped her arm over his neck, pulled out her iPhone and snapped a picture of them. He wanted to wring her neck there and then. Instead he attempted to smile sweetly. He couldn't risk the picture having been automatically saved somewhere, even if he tried deleting it from her phone later. Soon afterwards, he abruptly made his excuses and left.

Ruined.

Thinking again about it now, playing the night over, his brow sweated, his hands gripped the wheel tighter. The heater was making the car too hot; his mouth was dry and tasted foul with the remnants of cheap watered-down beer. Suddenly Joe pulled out of the traffic and down a side street. It was a small town and very few people were out beyond the main street. The prowling thrum of the engine did nothing to quell his thirst. He drove on through the now pouring rain, aimlessly, frustrated. A silver BMW passed him before he turned the Honda at the end of the block and started along the road parallel to a kids' play park. There were no other cars about. A lone figure walked along up ahead in the opposite direction, about fifty metres way, struggling against the rain. It was a woman, perhaps mid-forties, carrying two bags of groceries. Joe's eyes set, deciding instantly. He slammed down the accelerator pedal to the floor and swung the wheel, mounting the sidewalk. The growl of the engine and skidding of the tyres over the curb made the woman stumble and anxiously half turn around.

He held the gas down to the metal.

She never had a chance.

The car crunched over her and he slammed on the brakes, skidding to a halt up ahead, half the tyres hanging over the curb. The car idled, the wipers swishing away the driving rain, as he searched all around. Nobody was anywhere to be seen. It was deathly quiet. As he threw the car into reverse, he had already started to giggle.

Chapter 2

Jessica awoke with strands of her hair stuck to her face. Sunlight was creeping through her thin blinds and there was a whiff of vodka on the air. She swept her red locks to one side and groaned. Sitting up, Jessica squinted, then rubbed at her eyes. She looked around her simple, but neat little bedroom. The morning sun threw a glare as it bounced off her purple walls.

Had she made a fool of herself last night?

No, she'd only had a couple of drinks. But the vodka hung heavily in the air. It wasn't even her usual drink.

And those three rounds of shots.

She shuddered at the memory and her stomach remembered them too.

Even just a couple of drinks always made her feel like this; half hungover. *A lightweight* – that's what her friends had always called her. Last night had been somewhat of a special occasion and she had enjoyed indulging a little more than usual. It had been a celebration party – the official launch of her new documentary, her first as primary director. The funding had recently all been secured – enough to get started at any rate. The team had all gathered together in a trendy bar in The Village called The Narrows. As far as she could remember, it had all gone well.

'Jesus,' she said, sitting up, her head throbbing. She lifted up her compact mirror off the bedside table and regarded herself. 'Yuck!' she said, sticking out her tongue and tossing the compact back into her handbag. It was true that she didn't look her best – but it couldn't diminish her natural, unassuming beauty. Beneath her red bangs was a pretty face; thin, pointed and almost elfish. She was average height and kept in shape, with a good figure. She pulled on her dressing gown and traipsed through the apartment. It was on the small side, but decent for being in the heart of Alphabet City. As soon as she opened her bedroom door, her eager cat rushed in and began to whine loudly for food.

'Alright Eddie,' Jessica said bending down to pet him. 'Good morning. Breakfast time again?' The little black-and-white cat meowed shrilly in response. 'Alright, let's see what we've got.'

Jessica headed straight for the coffee maker in her kitchen-diner and flicked it on. Eddie complained that she hadn't attended to him first. She poured out dry cat food into a bowl. As she set it on the floor, Eddie nudged her hand out of the way to get at his breakfast. Jessica stood back up, cocking her head as her mobile began to play *Walk This Way'* from the other room. Jessica hurried back to answer it, grabbed the phone, and fell back onto the warm bed.

'Hiya Lucy.' Her voice was hoarse.

Did I smoke last night?

She didn't think so.

'Well? Sore head, chick?' Lucy asked, her voice warm and playful.

'You could say that. What about you?'

'Aww you know me – I'm hardcore.' She gave a throaty chuckle. 'Actually – I'm just home.'

'What? Ohhhh,' Jessica said with a dramatic gasp. 'You hussy – did you go home with that guy we met... whatdya call him?'

'Brendan.'

'You're such a slut!'

'I didn't say I did anything.' Lucy's voice hadn't changed since high school. It was the kind of cliché *Mean Girls* accent. But she wasn't a mean girl. It was just the voice she had, there wasn't any affectation to it.

'Well, did you?'

'Yeah,' she said with a giggle.

'Then you *are* a hussy!'

'How dare you! That's no way to talk about your Assistant Director.'

They both laughed.

'Maybe more like the assistant to the director Luce, or the chief camera operator.'

'Okay Michael Scott, I'll take that I guess. I'll be your Dwight.'

They chatted casually for a few more minutes. Jessica was glad to see that her coffee was ready when she was finished, and headed back into the kitchenette. The aroma was inviting and she began thinking what there might be to eat. Eddie had eaten his breakfast and was now plucking the side of the sofa with his claws. Jessica tutted and shook her head before curling up on the sofa beside him. He jumped up on her lap as she rotated her body so that she could open her laptop bag. She pulled out a copy of her shooting outline and held it in front of her. She took a sip of her coffee through pursed lips. Too hot. She set it back down and began to read. A sense of pride and excitement surged through her as she read the working title:

Death in New York: A murder that shook America. Fifteen Years on.

Chapter 3

Joe still made it home before midnight, though only just. The traffic on the outskirts of the city had been heavy enough for a Thursday night. It seemed like every yellow cab was out on the streets whenever he weaved through downtown. Thankfully he knew the city inside out, having lived in and around it all his life. Once he had closed the door on his apartment, he was able to begin to relax. The kill hadn't been the most satisfying, but it had offered him a degree of pleasure. Just not enough to make up for the wasted planning on what should have been a long and satisfying night. He had planned to go back to her small house in the town and spend time, several hours maybe, before death would finally arrive. Those were always the sweetest of kills. Like a cat toying leisurely with a dying bird.

He boiled the kettle and leaned against the worktop, waiting to make a cup of instant decaf coffee before bed. A kill was better than no kill. But still it felt more like a night with a world-weary prostitute than a passionate lover.

His Brownstone building had been cheap eight years ago, but since then the area of Cobble Hill had seen regeneration and gentrification. Rent control had still kept his monthly bills down. The apartment had a kitchen-diner, one bedroom and a bathroom. The landlord had paid to refurbish it a few years before and it had already been a good size and finish compared to a lot of places in the city. Joe took his coffee into his bedroom and switched on the lamp. The room was painted a dark navy with fashionable blinds on the window. It was simply furnished, but tidy. He had turned on the heat and now the radiator started rattling as the water pumped through the old copper pipes. Joe set the coffee on his desk and selected a worn notebook from the small shelf. He flicked to the current page. All of the previous pages were lined with handwritten entries. After his first few kills in his early twenties, Joe knew that he would continue killing for as long as he wasn't caught. He hoped that would be never and if he were careful, it should be. Killing was something that Joe would never give up.

Other folk had smoking weed, or gambling, extreme sports. Joe had killing. He had realised early on that it would be easy to forget particular murders after many years, as some were already beginning to become muddled in his memory. But he was also intelligent enough to know it would be unwise to ever have a list that could be easily interpreted by the police if it ever came to it. He made very brief entries that would hopefully remind him of some of the details if he couldn't recall it. One example was:

FNY022002- standing for FEMALE, NEW YORK, FEBRUARY 2002.

He dared not put on paper any more information than that. It was a small risk writing anything at all. It wouldn't be like cracking the Enigma Code to work out its meaning either. But many of his murders looked like accidents anyway and there was nothing within these entries that could ever convict him of anything. He lifted up a black biro and entered his new kill beneath the others. Number thirty-six. He hopped onto his bed and searched through social media on his phone. Soon enough he had found a news item mentioning a hit and run in Patterson. The woman was dead before paramedics made it to the scene. She had been found by a couple taking their Alsatian puppy for a late-night walk. Patterson PD suspected a drunk driver and were apparently following up on a number of leads. Joe knew that was likely to be bullshit. Nobody had been around to even see his make of car. His tyres wouldn't give much away. He doubted there'd be any CCTV catching it either. He always had fake plates on the Honda when he was on a mark. It wouldn't be the only death on the roads that night and he knew there wouldn't be many resources put into it. He clicked off to his lock screen of a cartoon bat with bloodied fangs. He set the cell phone and mug on his bedside table, then lay back and closed his eyes. He breathed out and let his body untense. That would do for now. Tomorrow he would work on something much better.

Chapter 4

Jessica took the subway from Alphabet City into Queens. She checked emails on her phone while listening to Joe Rogan on her headphones. She was in a good mood. The partial hangover had passed and the excitement about the documentary being launched exhilarated her. The train was busy, but she managed to get a side seat by herself. She bounced off the train at her stop and scurried up the steps and out into the sunlight. The city was heating up, turning into a fine, crisp fall day. It was a short walk to the Starbucks for her ten-thirty meeting.

Patrick Falk was already seated by the window. She gave him a little wave as she joined the queue inside, ordering a caramel cappuccino. Patrick was the primary producer for the documentary and one of the main funders. They had known each other for several years, involved in many projects together as Jessica worked her way up within the industry.

'Patrick, honey,' she said, greeting him, leaning in with a kiss on his cheek.

'Jessica, you look wonderful. Especially after last night,' he said, raising a bushy eyebrow. Patrick was a mammoth of a man: tall and with an enormous belly to match. It was a stomach that even Orson Welles may have been embarrassed by. In his early sixties, his blue eyes were still beady and sharp, his manner always easy yet commanding.

'I wasn't that tipsy, was I?'

'No, not at all my dear. I'm just teasing. I had one too many whiskey sours myself.'

'I think it went well, didn't it Patrick?'

'I thought so too. It was a great turnout. Nice to see such an interest in the project already. And the team you've built around you – it's impressive, a fine production crew.'

'Aww, thank you – I'm so pleased. They'll make me look good. I've been careful with the money – your money,' she said, patting her hand on his arm. 'But I wanted to spend the largest part on using the *right* people.'

'Very sensible too. I have every faith in you Jessica,' he said, picking up his double expresso with his large paw. 'We have the opportunity to make a very good film.'

'I hope so too.'

'I know it's your first as director, but all those films as assistant, never mind your years as a grip and what not, you know how to run a production from the ground up. I hope this will be the first of many.'

'I think we have everyone we need. It's a small crew, but if we can get one of the big companies to buy it, we've the chance to form a great little production company.'

'I would love to see that. I would.' He sipped his coffee and a smile played at the corners of his mouth. 'But first we must get this little show on the road. Now, I had a call from David Mercer's defence attorney this morning.'

'Really?' Jessica said eagerly, edging forwards in her chair.

'Mercer says he'll meet with you.'

'Oh my fucking God!' she squealed. 'Sorry,' she said, placing a finger to her mouth.

'That's alright,' Patrick said, waving his hand with an amused chuckle. 'It's great news, isn't it?'

'Amazing. It's the missing piece. We can really tell this story now.'

'We can, and you're just the person to do it.'

After saying their goodbyes, Jessica hopped onto another train and travelled the few stops to get to the office. She was trapped between a teenager with an odour issue and a snoring security guard, but she didn't care. She listened to a best of Bill Withers album on Spotify through earbuds. She caught herself nodding in time with the music, but she couldn't care less who saw her. She loved nothing better than old soul and funk records. And when she was in a mood like this, with the sun shining, there was nothing better.

'Hiya Jimmy, are you well?' she said after getting off the train, stopping at her favourite hotdog stand along the street.

'Doesn't matter much, nobody would listen anyways,' he said

with a twinkle in his eye.

'Aww, I'd care, Jimmy.'

'Well that's why you're my favourite customer.'

Jessica walked on, balancing the scalding bun as mustard tried escaping out the bottom. The sun was now shining brightly, the sidewalk dry, and much of the grime washed away for now. Leaves lazily turned over, under the feet of commuters, rolling towards the gutters. The skyscrapers above shone like newly-polished glass. It was the time of year that Jessica loved best. Another block and she was there.

Jessica had hired a modest office a few months earlier as the production had begun the various planning stages. There had been several potential subjects at the start. The Mercer case had nosed ahead as the unanimous best option and she was glad. It was the story she most wanted to work on. The story she had felt most compelled to tell. Once enough funding had been sourced, she started renting the small office beside it as well. That would be where most of the interviews would be filmed. It would be easy to make it look good enough as a backdrop and it would be always set up correctly for sound and film. Then there was the added bonus that everything else to do with the production was right next door. The offices then took over the whole third floor of the seven-storey building, knocking a wall in between rooms and also using the little bathroom and kitchenette down the hall. The other tenants in the building mostly kept to themselves – a jumble of call centres, insurance brokers and computer repair companies.

'Morning Stan,' she said, smiling warmly at the heavy-built security guard.

'Mornin' Miss Kinney, now were you just eatin' a hotdog by any chance?' he said, tilting his head playfully.

She smiled, her eyes widening. 'Oh God!' She dabbed at the side of her mouth with a tissue, smearing off the stray mustard. 'Thanks Stan.'

'It wouldn't do for the boss to be goin' in like that,' he said with a deep chuckle, holding the door for her.

Jessica took the elevator up to their floor, straightening down her purple blouse and checking her makeup on the way up.

'Hiya guys.'

'Morning Jessica,' said Bev as Jessica walked into the little open office.

'Hi Jess,' said Charlie.

'Do you never get hangovers?' Jessica said, looking towards Lucy with her fresh- looking face and full, blonde hair.

'Not really, chick,' she said, smiling.

'I had a great meeting with Patrick there. I'll tell you all about it. Are you guys good?'

Jessica went and sat down at her desk as they chatted together for a few minutes. The room was painted white with film posters on the walls of past productions some of them had been involved in. On one wall was a white board where some of the planning for the documentary was done, with various post-it notes and photographs pinned up. Jessica was a fan of getting input from everyone and capturing ideas in as interactive a way as possible. She had geeked out on a number of management books before starting the project.

Her desk was along the back wall. On the left was a desk shared by the others. There was a seat against the wall on the right beside the door leading to their second office. Bev was the office manager, working part-time, an old hand in the industry. She was a large woman in her early fifties, with still smooth, black skin, purple horn-rimmed glasses and an easy manner. Charlie was in his mid-forties, hailing from Canada originally. He still wore his hair in *curtains* that were now beginning to turn from blonde to grey. He was the second camera operator and sound engineer. Like everyone on the production he wore many other hats too, whatever needed doing on a given day. Lucy was sitting off to the side, drinking a can of soda.

'So team, I have some good news,' Jessica declared with a broad smile.

'I like good news,' Bev drawled, peering over her glasses.

'Spill,' said Lucy.

'Go on then – stop building suspense – you're not Hitchcock yet,' Charlie said, setting down his mug and pushing his chair back from the computer.

'Okay, okay,' Jessica said with fake indignation, pressing her hands together as if in prayer. She paused. 'We've got an interview with David Mercer.'

'Brilliant honey-pie! I never doubted you,' said Bev.

'That's awesome, Jess,' Lucy said.

'It's Patrick's doing, really. He's much more sway with these things than I'd have.'

'Still – that's terrific news,' added Bev.

'Good job Jessica,' said Charlie, 'So, what do you guys reckon, is he guilty then? Cops sure as hell thought so. The jury too,' said Charlie.

'I don't think so,' Bev said, rubbing an eye beneath her lenses. 'That man never did those things. I just don't buy it. Usual police up to their old tricks. Watch any of those other true crime things, they're always at it. Planting evidence and what have you. Once you start this picture Jessica, my bet is you'll think the same. What do you think Jess?'

'Right now?' Jessica said, flicking a stray red hair from her brow as she puffed out her cheeks. 'I'm on the fence. I really don't know. He might be innocent. I'm happy to be convinced either way. I suppose that's a good starting point for what we're doing.'

'Guilty as sin,' Charlie said, with a wry smile.

Bev rolled her eyes dramatically, throwing in a glare at Charlie for good measure.

'You're a piece of work Charlie,' Bev said half seriously. 'You're always thinking the police are just these nice guys, out protecting the public. I guess some of them are, it wasn't like that in my neighbourhood.'

'Just cause I'm not some woke woolly liberal, it doesn't mean I'm a right winger. Heck – I'm from Canada!' he said, exaggerating his natural accent.

'Keepin' my eye on you,' Bev said, tipping her glasses back up the bridge of her nose.

'When are we going to see him then, Jess?' asked Charlie.

'Tomorrow afternoon,' Jessica said slowly.

'Jesus, that's quick sweetie. He thinkin' we gonna get him off then?' said Bev, with a chuckle.

'Yeah maybe,' said Jessica, holding down the standby button on her laptop. She pursed her lips, turning to Charlie.

'The thing is Charlie, Patrick says only two of us can go. This first time anyway. Frig, the guards wouldn't be keen on a whole pack of us busting in anyway, I'm sure.'

'So you're taking Lucy?' Charlie said with a hint of irritation.

'Well, yeah - she is Assistant Director. Sorry Charlie.'

'Sorry Charlie,' Lucy said, looking worried.

'It's okay.'

Bev looked a little awkward, began fidgeting with a few sheets.

Charlie took a sip of his black coffee, looking a little sullen.

'Just I thought you'd at least want me there doing sound,' he added, looking away.

'I would if I could. It's just we're not allowed more. But we can handle it okay. Hopefully there'll be plenty more interviews - maybe we can soften him up some. David needs convincing, the prison too.'

'Fair enough,' Charlie said standing. 'Just popping to the john,' he said, heading out though the hall.

Bev took off her glasses and wiped them with a tissue, fixing a look on Jessica. Jessica smiled thinly and shrugged. Lucy chewed on her lip.

'Aww don't take any notice of Charlie,' Bev said. 'You know what he's like. Always getting his panties in a twist over something.'

Chapter 5

'Joe, I need you to go and help Andy with the delivery. There're a dozen pallets just been shipped in. Pronto.'

Joe lifted out his cell and clicked the pause icon on the player. He liked listening in headphones while working. He listened to a lot of True Crime podcasts. He was halfway through one about a book called *Hitman: A technical manual for independent contractors*. In the nineties, a former Motown record producer used the book and an amateur hitman to murder his wife and child for a trust fund. It wasn't long before the police caught him and sent him to prison for the rest of his life. Joe had scoffed at the rookie mistakes he had made. The book was banned, but Joe had found a copy on eBay a few years before. He'd gotten a few tips from it, but mostly it reaffirmed his view that most killers barely had two brain cells to rub together.

'Okay, cool.'

'Cool,' Lewis mimicked, rolling his eyes before strutting off. *What a douche bag.*

Joe turned and made his way up the rickety wooden steps to the first floor of the warehouse. He dug his fingernails into his knuckles.

Joe had worked in the warehouse for a mechanical tools distribution company for several years. The monotony and routine of the work suited him. He didn't need to earn a lot of money. His parents had left him a decent inheritance when they died in a car crash when he was thirteen. Money was never much of a pressing concern, nor something that he thought much about. Though not a primary motivation in his murders they also brought him in a sizeable amount of cash now and again. One thing that wasn't so good was when Lewis had been promoted above him to foreman. Younger than him and previously at his level, but always a bit of a prick, and Joe now found him to be unbearable. The paltry promotion had gone to his head. Joe spent so much of his life pretending to be someone different, someone other than himself, it was at times a strain to have to do it in work as well. Most of the time it was okay. Much of the time was spent working solitarily unloading pallets, stacking boxes, labelling products. He could pass himself well enough, but had the self-awareness that he was regarded as somewhat of an oddball.

'I'll go start up the forklift if you grab the pallet truck,' Andy said, passing him on the stairs. Andy worked part time putting himself through college; he was alright.

'You got it.'

Joe went up and clicked off the lever on the trolley and rolled the cumbersome thing across to the open doors. The double doors led to nowhere but a forty-foot drop. The engine of the forklift spluttered into life below and soon a pallet stacked high with tools wrapped in pallet wrap was raising in the air towards him, suspended on two long prongs. Joe fixed the truck between the cross section of wood as it slid over the lip on the edge of the building, and let off the brake before pulling the pallet free and heaving it into the warehouse. He flicked on his iPhone to a local news station, a beep sounding in his ear buds. Joe unloaded the rest of the pallets over the next hour, listening closely. There was another mention of the hit and run the previous night, but it was already further down the news items and the details were even more scant.

'What you listening to – One Direction?' came a voice loudly beside him. His body went rigid. He fished out an earphone and turned to Lewis's sneering, chubby face.

'Yeah, something like that,' Joe said dryly.

'Go on for your lunch now Joe, good job,' he said, patting him on the back. Joe felt like a puppy being offered a fresh chew toy.

'Okay Lewis.'

Joe usually sat in the cramped, dilapidated kitchen for lunch, but he needed to get out of there today. He went for a walk around the block, letting the tension ease out of him. He had hoped to be on a high today, but that wasn't to be. Never mind Lewis, he was still sore after having to settle for a quick kill the night before. He could usually go for a few months between killings, but not this time. The hit and run hadn't brought all that much satisfaction. It was just a sticking plaster. It was like paying for a hooker and just staying for a cup of coffee. He smiled at the thought. It would be fine, there was always another, better kill to be had. He walked on, heading towards the little shop at the corner where he could get a sandwich and a soda. Yes, he'd go out and try one of his favourite, tried and tested murders. One of the safe bets that didn't take a whole lot of planning. Tomorrow, maybe. He'd spend the evening getting ready, preparing. It wouldn't need all that much thought. That would be something nice to look forward to.

Chapter 6

The next day and Jessica woke up feeling anxious. It was a big day. She pushed it to one side and got on with her routine of making a coffee and giving her cat some attention. Even if he mostly just wanted the food, she was glad of the company. She met Lucy in the morning and they checked over all of the equipment and loaded up the travelling gear into the van. They just packed what they could easily manage between them: one camera, a few mikes, one boom, a laptop and a bag of notebooks.

'I reckon we're all set, chick,' Lucy declared, shutting the rear door on the black van. Jessica had invested in a second-hand Ford Transit van when the first of the money had come through earlier in the year. She didn't need a car in the city, but for filming she certainly couldn't lug gear on the subway.

'I think you're right.' Jessica gave a little nod and ran a hand through her hair. 'Thanks for all the help, Luce.'

'You're welcome,' Lucy said, giving a theatrical curtsey. Her long blonde hair fell over her face and she swept it off her fine, pretty features. 'So, first things first –I'm taking you to lunch.'

They grabbed a sub and soda in a nearby street cafe, before buying a take-out coffee for the drive.

'Nervous?' Jessica asked, pulling out into the traffic.

'A little. You?'

'Yep,' Jessica said with a forced laugh. 'It'll be fine.'

Her brain was working overtime, going over and over all of the questions she wanted to ask. She willed herself to settle down. This was just the first interview. Hopefully there'd be more. The most important thing was for it to go well. To make a connection. Sometimes she hated the need to gain trust in a subject so that their story could be *mined* for a production. But she believed in doing it in an ethical way. She was a journalist first and foremost. What she strived for was the truth.

It was less than an hour's drive to Sing Sing; the notorious New York prison. The conversation died out as they drew close. Formerly, it was home to executions for convicted murderers, sent "up the river" from the big city. There was no longer a death penalty in the state, so the many violent offenders mostly now lived out their days there. As the van slowed and approached the impending gates of the complex, Lucy gave Jessica's arm a little squeeze and they shared a *holy shit* expression. The old dilapidated Victorian section they passed was long disused and after several security checks, they were waved across to the main car park. With some difficulty, they made their way to the reception building, lugging all of their gear with them. The austere middle-aged black lady on reception gave them a half smile after informing them of the various rules for visitors. They sat and waited anxiously on wooden chairs in an echoey hallway, their gear propped up next to them.

'As a teenager my Mom always said I'd end up some place like this,' Lucy whispered.

'Mine said I'd end up in the funny farm,' said Jessica, returning the conspiratorial smile.

The receptionist came over and handed them some paperwork and asked if they wanted a coffee, but wasn't too enthusiastic in the way that she asked. They declined, signed the disclaimers, then handed them to the assistant warden when he came across to greet them. He wore a brown suit over his thin build. There was still brown in his hair too, though he must have been at least sixty-five. He was courteous, but vaguely frosty as he talked them through the various rules again. As he marched them through several heavy security doors with his pass key, Jessica's stomach began to flip Olympic-level somersaults.

This is what you wanted.

Come on now, you're a professional, you're not gonna screw this up.

The next two doors were metal barred entries, manned by burly, armed prison guards. The heavy key clicked in the locks like in every prison movie Jessica had ever seen. The guards on the other side nodded to them coolly as they passed through and the bars were locked behind them. Lucy looked even more anxious than Jessica and she flashed her a few encouraging smiles.

'Just in there, ladies,' he said, finally letting them into a small, blue-painted meeting room. 'I'll let you set up. Hopefully I'll see you afterwards. Take care.'

With that, he was gone. The door shut behind them with a thud.

'Jesus, was he *trying* to freak us out?' said Lucy.

'Yeah, maybe,' Jessica said, raising an eyebrow. She checked her watch. 'Okay, let's get set up. Over here, I think.'

There was one plastic-coated table in the centre of the room. On the far side, away from the door, were two chairs. One chair faced across from them. There was another seat behind, to the left of the door. A window on the back wall overlooked the car park. Part of their van could be viewed through the bars. They set to work. First they mounted the camera up off to the side, behind the table. They carefully trailed the microphone lead across the floor and set the free-standing boom behind at the other long end of the table. Jessica booted up the laptop as Lucy ripped off pieces of Scotch tape and stuck a few strips over the trailing wires. After a few minutes of testing, they let the camera roll and sat down in their chairs. Jessica rubbed her sweaty hands along her trousers. It was very quiet. There was an occasional shout or loud conversation, somewhere far away, down the vast hallways housing the prison population. They both searched in their handbags, brushed their hair in tandem and then checked their make-up. Then they sat together in silence, looking towards the frosted glass in the door in front of them. A few minutes passed. Then two sets of feet echoed along the hallway beyond. The footsteps stopped outside the door; two grey outlines stood talking in hushed tones.

'Here we go,' Lucy said breathily.

'We'll be fine,' Jessica said, her voice dry. She cleared her throat.

A beep and then a click from the lock cut through the quiet and the electronic LED flashed. The door opened.

Chapter 7

'Hello? Yes?' The voice on the buzzing intercom was elderly and thin.

'Hello Ma'am. My name is Clarke Ferguson. I'm a technician with City Gas, number one three two, zero zero. We've had reports of a leak in your building.' Joe's voice was confident and professional.

'Oh... oh my. Is it serious?'

'I hope not, Ma'am. We think we have it pinpointed, but I'm gonna need to take a reading inside your home, just to be sure, if that's okay with you?'

There was a pause, then the noise of muffled breathing from the other end. 'Well... ah, yes I guess that's okay. Third door along the hallway. I'll buzz you in, dear.'

'Thank you. This shouldn't take long,' Joe said, trying not to sound too pleased.

There was a dull beep and Joe pushed the tall wooden door open.

He made his way along the hall, carrying a plain black sports bag. He was dressed in a blue-and-white top and black trousers, with *City Gas* embroidered on the polo shirt. Joe knocked the door and it was immediately opened by a thin white lady in her seventies, dressed in a cream blouse, black skirt and navy cardigan. Faded costume pearls hung around her neck.

'Afternoon Ma'am, thanks for letting me in.'

'That's alright,' she said, still holding onto the door, her face uncertain. 'Have you some ID, you know my niece always says I should ask...I uh...'

'Of course,' Joe said evenly, raising a hand and setting the bag down. He pulled out one of many fake ID's he owned from his trouser pocket. She gave it a cursory glance with embarrassment, then ushered him inside. 'Come on in.'

'Thank you,' said Joe. He smiled widely, picked up his bag and went in, closing the door behind him.

'Is in here okay?' she asked, sweeping a frail hand at her little living room. There was a musty damp smell inside; all the windows were shut and the curtains part drawn. The room looked as if it had been preserved since the 1980's, with striped, cigarette-yellowed wallpaper, an old shag rug, and cut glass everywhere. Family photographs in colour and black and white covered the mantelpiece and mahogany sideboard.

'In here will do just fine,' Joe said, licking his lips and getting down on one knee, opening up his bag.

'Would you like a coffee, young man, the kettle's just boiled?' she asked, peering down.

'No, don't trouble yourself,' he said quickly, rustling through his bag.

'If you're sure. I'll have a cup anyways.'

The small kitchen was through the back door. She stood and turned towards it, taking a few steps. Joe rose to his feet behind her, a wrench gripped in his right hand. He took two quick steps and whipped it up above his shoulders. She began to turn. Then he brought the wrench crashing down, burying it in her skull.

Chapter 8

'Ladies, thank you for coming.'

Jessica and Lucy got to their feet.

David Mercer bowed his head as he stepped into the room, dressed in an open blue shirt tucked into black trousers. His hands were cuffed in front of him.

'Thanks for having us in,' Jessica said awkwardly, her hands fidgeting together.

Settle down for God's sake.

David nodded with a guarded smile.

Lucy chimed in saying, 'Pleased to meet you,' in a quiet voice.

The burly, ruddy-faced guard, with a belt that Batman would be jealous of, came in behind David. His eyes hovered over the room, his broad face expressionless. Then he shut the door and took a seat beside the entrance.

Everyone sat down.

'I'm very pleased to meet you both. Patrick Falk spoke very highly of you, Jessica, and your team,' David said, gesturing his cuffed hands towards Lucy. His voice was very deep, friendly, but authoritative. He was over six feet tall, black, with a shaved head. He was solid, but not overweight. In his early sixties, he looked well. But there was a tautness to his features, something like granite that weighed heavily on him.

'Thank you, David. All we want to do is hear your story and represent the facts as best we can,' Jessica said, gesturing with her moist palms open on the table. 'Thank you for sending back the signed agreements. Everything is on *your* terms, you call the shots.' She winced inside at the choice of words, but she was at least getting into her groove. 'We will of course represent whatever you tell us as honestly and thoroughly as we can.'

'Thank you. I appreciate that. And I'm sure that you will appreciate that I have had several offers to speak on camera... about what happened. Not all were from... well, persons who I would feel comfortable doing this with.'

'I get it. Thank you for giving us this chance,' Jessica said, smiling warmly, then scribbling a few lines in her notebook, mostly just to continue to settle herself. The team had watched the court footage of David's trial and his failed appeal many times. They had also trawled through the various news reports, many not complimentary towards him. It was unnerving to be suddenly here with this person. To be thrown into a pressurised meeting with him. He seemed familiar, yet so much about him still unknown to Jessica.

'I hope that I don't come to regret it,' he said. His mouth remained parted, his eyes vacant for just a moment. Then taking a breath, he said, 'I am an innocent man. I recognise that everyone is *innocent* in Sing Sing, but I assure you that it is the truth... in my case.' He paused, looking a touch flustered for the first time. 'Do you believe that?'

Jessica shifted in her chair, returning his gaze. She sucked in a lungful of air. 'I'll be honest with you David. And that's something I'll do from now and always. I don't know.' She felt Lucy's eyes on her, with her own nervousness behind them. She continued on, 'I don't know you... not yet. I'm more than willing to accept that there is an even chance that you have nothing to do with these killings. I'm certainly not convinced by the arguments that were given in court. If I come to believe the jury was wrong, then I will do my darndest to help you.'

He gave a clipped chuckle and his lips rested into a thin smile. 'I guess I can't expect any more than that, it's fair. That'll do just fine. Shall we begin?'

Jessica smiled and leaned over the desk and turned to a fresh page. She outlined how she would first like to discuss an overview of the case against him. Then they would dissect this and at each meeting dive deeper into each area. If that was agreeable to him. He said that it was. Lucy double checked the recording equipment. The guard re-crossed his legs and told them in a low, even tone that they had half an hour remaining.

'Okay, thanks,' said Jessica, sitting upright, her hands clasped together. 'I know this is all going to be very tough to talk about, Mr Mercer. I also appreciate that you've had to do this many times before. But please, if you can, tell me about what you found on that day, exactly as it happened.'

'Alright. I'll do my best.'

Lucy went over to the camera and checked the angle, before slipping on a pair of headphones and giving a thumbs up.

'Okay then,' Jessica said. 'Where was it that you and your family lived, let's start with that?'

David leaned forwards heavily in his chair, took a deep breath and began.

'We lived in Cold Springs, out in the suburbs of the city. We'd a nice town house, nice street, good neighbours. It was a quiet place, you know?'

'And who lived there with you?'

He breathed out heavily again. 'It was me, my daughter Ashleigh,' he said, looking away towards the window, 'and my wife… Roseanne.' He cleared his throat, then glanced sadly towards the feet of the boom stand.

'And what happened exactly when you arrived home on November fourth? What time did you get there, who was with you?'

'I uh… got home from work early, about three thirty. I was by myself. My wife was still at the office.'

'You worked together, your own realty business, isn't that right?'

'Yes, it was our family business.'

'Okay, please go on.'

David awkwardly scratched his forehead with his cuffed hands.

'I used my key and went inside. There was nothing – well nothing *obviously* the matter. I didn't know if my daughter would be home from school or not, sometimes she would be. Sometimes not. I called up but… there was no response.' His eyes glistened and he licked his lips. His voice became a little hoarse. 'I went into the kitchen, fixed myself a coffee. I assumed she had gone to the library or something. After, I don't know, maybe ten minutes, I went up the stairs. I was gonna get something from our bedroom. Ashleigh's room was the first on the left at the top of the stairs.'

He paused, obviously becoming emotional. Jessica and Lucy both looked towards him sympathetically, encouragingly.

'It's okay,' Jessica said. 'Take your time. Do you need a glass of water or something?' she said, looking past him at the guard, who looked back in a non-committal way.

'No, I'm alright. Thank you. Okay... I guess I wanted to double check Ashleigh wasn't home, maybe asleep or with her headphones on or something. I knocked on the door, then went inside.'

The room was filled and charged with a weight of emotion in his voice.

Jessica forced herself to keep a suitably professional and neutral tone, but it was hard. 'What did you see when you opened the door?' Jessica asked softly.

'Ashleigh was on the bed, her boyfriend was beside her – Will.'

His face was contorted with grief. A tear dripped down his face and across the thin layer of stubble on his chin. 'They were both... dead. There was...' he took in a sharp intake of breath, 'there was blood everywhere.' His low baritone quivered.

'What did you do?'

'I ran over to them, I think I cried out something, I don't know. I pulled her up into my arms, God, it was horrible, just horrible.' He shook his head, swallowed hard. 'I knew she was dead. She had to be. There was just so much blood. Will too. But I searched for breathing anyway, I checked for pulses, both of them. I was in a state... shock I guess. It didn't seem possible, it couldn't be real. I must have lay there for I don't know, a few minutes. Then I ran out crying and phoned 911.'

Jessica gave him a pained smile, nodding sadly towards him. He looked ten tears older suddenly, his face showing every iota of his deep wounds.

'Thank you,' she said. 'Thank you for going through it all again. Can I just ask a few more questions and then we'll leave the crime scene for today?'

'That's okay... yeah,' he said, blinking away a few tears, then nodding his head sombrely.

'Lucy, do you want to continue here?'

26

'Yeah… sure,' she said, looking up from her own notebook, trying to sound chipper.

'Mr. Mercer, David… did you see any weapon left in the bedroom?'

He shook his head. 'No, nothing that was obvious.'

'The prosecution argued that William's body had not been moved from where he was killed. They think he was killed in the bedroom along with Ashleigh. But you dispute that?'

'Yeah, that's what I think now. I didn't know it at the time, hell I couldn't get my head round any of it. But yeah, I guess we'll talk more about the blood spatter and everything later. I don't think he died there… in her bed.'

'Thank you, that's great,' Lucy said with a reassuring smile. Then she turned to her partner. 'Jessica?'

'Thanks Lucy, thank you David. David, why is it you think that William's body was moved?' Jessica pressed.

He shook his head, straightened his back. 'The killer wanted to frame me. Make it look like I busted in there and went nuts or something.'

Jessica nodded, her face hard. She knew she needed to push further, but she didn't want to alienate him either. More than that, she wouldn't enjoy asking as one human to another.

'I'm sorry to have to be so invasive, do you mean that the narrative would be you found them in bed together, became angry and murdered them?'

He took in a breath of the stuffy air, his face growing irritable. 'Yeah, I guess that's what some would say happened. The prosecution said it. That seems to be the lie that the jury bought.'

'Again, I'm sorry to have to ask, but do you know if your daughter and her boyfriend had a sexual relationship?'

He pursed his lips as beads of sweat formed on his forehead.

'I don't know, is the honest answer, or at least I didn't. I mean – they tell me now that she had sex that day.' He looked towards the window again, adjusting himself in his seat. 'Listen – I'm a man of the world, I guess I expected that she probably was. She'd been seeing him for a few months and was a sixteen-year-old girl. It wouldn't have been that much of a shock, I guess.'

'But it wouldn't have been pleasant to walk in on,' Jessica said.

David's face hardened further and he tilted his head, looking Jessica in the eye. 'But I never walked in on anything like that. I walked in on them dead,' he said, raising his voice a notch.

Jessica nodded and made another note in her book. She felt sick.

David glanced around to the guard and jerked his head. 'That's enough for today,' he said. Then he turned back to the women, his body deflated. The cordial atmosphere had now evaporated. 'I'm done.' He stood up abruptly and the guard rose immediately. Jessica got to her feet and started to protest gently. The guard opened the door and David hurried out muttering, 'Goodbye ladies.' They both walked out. The door closed loudly behind them.

Jessica thumped the table with a fist. 'Stupid!'

'Hey, you did good, Jess. You have to ask these things.'

'Not good enough. One question too many. Just one.'

Chapter 9

Joe was back home a few hours later. He treated himself to a Chinese takeaway. Joe had worked up quite an appetite. He sat in his living room eating, watching a few old sit-coms he had watched many times before. Despite his tiredness, he felt great. More than great. Recharged. His *soul* felt good. The old lady had been easy to silence and overpower. There was no fight in her from the first blow. Sometimes he preferred it when there was. He had toyed with her for over an hour before finishing her off. Then Joe had sat with her for a few minutes, enjoying the moment and the peace. He had been careful and of course had worn gloves and clothes that would be disposed of. Before leaving he threw bleach all around to kill any other DNA evidence. He shook the place up some and pocketed a few obvious valuables. It was an obvious murder, but would hopefully be viewed as yet another robbery/ homicide. Then he quietly slipped out again.

Joe scooped up the last of his chicken in black bean sauce and set it down beside him. He stretched out, like a satisfied tomcat, sipped a beer and searched the local news on the TV, then on his phone. No mention yet of the murder. She mightn't even be found for some time. That's how it went sometimes. It was okay. He felt sleepy by nine o'clock, worn out. Everything had gone well; it should satisfy the needs for some time. Before climbing into bed he took out his journal and jotted down the fresh entry.

Chapter 10

'I hope I haven't pissed him off,' Jessica said, pulling the van out onto the freeway. It was approaching rush hour and the roads were crammed.

Lucy shrugged. 'Listen Jess, he's gotta expect to be asked some difficult questions. It goes with the territory.'

'I know – but I suppose he'd prefer if I had trodden lighter. I don't know.'

'Maybe, but when he goes back to his cell and thinks about it, he'll see it for what it was. I reckon he'll see that you were upfront with him, you weren't blowin' smoke up his ass. He'll see you're trying to be impartial.'

'Yeah, I guess. Thanks Luce.'

'It's his first experience of being interviewed like this too. Okay if I have a smoke out the window?'

'Yeah, go ahead,' Jessica said.

Lucy plucked out a cigarette from a fresh pack, stuffing the cellophane into the bin in the dash.

'What did you make of him?' Lucy asked.

'He seemed, I don't know… nice? That seems a bit of a stupid word. I don't know. I guess he was just upset at the end, I get it. He didn't strike me as a brutal killer, that's for sure – but heck look at Bundy?'

'Yeah, I'm not sure. He came across well. But I'm still on the fence,' Lucy said, blowing smoke carefully out the window. 'He *seemed* a decent man. But I reckon he's got an edge to him.'

'Maybe. But if I'm honest, on first meeting… I kinda found myself believing him.'

That night Jessica curled up with Eddie and a bottle of red wine in her living room. She flicked on Spotify to her Bluetooth speaker and shuffled on a soul and funk playlist. Gill Scott Heron began singing about *The Bottle*. New images flashed across her screen muted in the background on her small flat screen TV. She had made a stir fry and put the rest in the fridge for tomorrow. She tucked her feet under herself on the sofa and flicked through Facebook absently. Jessica let her mind tick over and re-run the interview with David. All in all it had gone well. It was only natural that David would find the first interview difficult. She had enough experience and confidence to feel that she would be able to keep it all on track.

She felt herself relaxing; she knew that it was best to focus on the positives. She checked her personal emails, replied to a few. Then she remembered to drop her Mom back home in Oregon a text. She needed to be a better daughter. But things had been so hectic. Bill Withers sang about his *Grandma's Hands* and Jessica sang along gently with the parts she knew. It was one of her favourites. Growing sleepy, she continued flicking through her messages. Her ex-boyfriend Tim had forwarded her a "funny cat" video on Whatsapp. They had been broken up for over a month, and it hadn't been all that serious to begin with. They hadn't been together very long. She just sent back a laughing emoji. That would do alright.

Jessica yawned, startling Eddie.

'Don't so jumpy, little man,' she said tickling under his chin. 'Oh to be a cat?'

Jessica was looking forward to a change of pace over the weekend. She'd do a little work, but not too much. She already had plans to catch up with a few girlfriends. Monday would be a big day when they would be going through the applications for amateur actors for roles in the docudrama aspect of the documentary. She had initially gotten the idea for doing that after being impressed with the documentary *Casting Jon Benet*. She liked how using local actors who were aware of the case and lived in the vicinity brought an extra dimension to the film. A half hour later and she was dozing on the sofa. A last cup of decaf and then she would drag herself off to bed.

Chapter 11

Joe spent Saturday morning strolling around Central Park. He took the subway across town and entered via the museum side. Autumn was in full swing and there were leaves everywhere – more than could ever be picked up by the team of park groundskeepers. Once they had all dropped, the task would become easier. Joe preferred it once it was more orderly again, everything as it should be. There was a chill in the air and Joe pulled his brown suede coat close to him as he walked on along the path. He ambled along The Mall, the thin, tall trees all hanging inwards, making up a natural walkway. Or as Joe liked to think of it: a gauntlet. He liked spending free days sauntering through Central Park. He enjoyed the scenery and the personal solitude. It didn't matter how many couples, joggers or drunks were around. He could just block them all out. Sometimes he'd listen to a podcast, blocking the outside world further. The natural world was okay, but not the rest. Community, society, friendship. They were terms he understood and things he manipulated to his own purposes. Maybe everybody did. But he was never part of them. Joe walked on, breathing in lungfuls of the fresh air. Here it felt much purer than anywhere else in the city.

He'd had always had a fascination with other serial killers. Even before he had become one himself. He pored over books and devoured the many documentaries on streaming services.

Joe stopped by an empty row of benches. Every time he visited the park, he thought about *The Couplet Killer*. A prolific murderer in the eighties, he stalked New York, making girls disappear without a trace and leaving cryptic messages on benches in Central Park. Joe patted the bench and walked on. He bought a coffee from a vendor, and a packet of potato chips.

The plaques had long been removed, but Joe knew which ones represented victims and he chose to sit down on one such bench now. He flicked through social media on his phone, then browsed some of the recent news stories. Finally there was a piece about the killing the day before. The NYPD considered it to be motivated by theft. They were allegedly following up on several leads. If it were true, Joe was confident that none of them would have anything to do with him. He knew that throwing bleach around the place wouldn't have been the mark of a crazed junkie, but protecting his DNA was his primary concern. Just as he was finishing his coffee, another news item caught his eye. Joe set his half-drunk coffee beside him and held his phone with both hands. A small production company in the city was making a documentary about the Ashleigh Mercer murder. Some of the gutter presses at the time had dubbed it the *Deadly Dad* murder. Joe's pulse quickened and he felt intense excitement course through his body. He read on. They were commencing production very soon and were also looking for amateur actors to take part in the documentary, playing characters from the case.

Jesus.

Joe looked away from the screen and stared up at a nearly bare tree with a wide grin.

The killing had been one of Joe's first. It was also the first time that he had successfully framed somebody else for one of his murders.

Could I?

Chapter 12

Monday morning came all too soon. At nine thirty the whole team were assembled in the office. After a brief staff meeting, Bev started into the various admin work to be done while the other three went into the adjoining room. Jessica wanted to get started on shortlisting prospective actors. She could have just done it with Lucy, but thought it would be good to include Charlie as well.

'So, is everyone all sufficiently caffeinated?' Jessica said, patting the pile of printed applications.

'Yep, all good to go,' Lucy said, raising her cup, 'and I've had my first cigarette of the day already – trying to cut down though.'

'Good, good,' Jessica said.

'Let's find the next Brando then,' said Charlie, running a hand through his hair.

'Okay, good. So, just to recap. We need somebody to be our detective– our DS Stevenson. We need an Ashleigh and a William.' She looked down at her notes. 'Then we need a smattering of witnesses, neighbours; they're not as crucial. They can also fill in for background scenes. That's about it, isn't it? If we can cover all of that we should be sitting pretty. Anyone I've missed?'

Lucy's brow furrowed, thinking. 'No Jess, I think that's everyone.'

'What about the killer?' Charlie said, chewing on the end of a Sharpie.

'Well, remember, we talked about that before? Those scenes will just be very blurry, atmospheric. It'll only really be an outline. Sure, one of the extras could do that.'

'Yeah, I suppose,' Charlie said, his eyes narrowing. 'I could do it if you like,' he said, shrugging.

'Yeah, cool,' said Lucy, 'What d'ya think Jess?'

'Yeah, thanks Charlie, that could work too. Though you might be doing the sound or second camera.'

'True, though I wasn't needed for that yesterday,' he said with a look Jessica wasn't sure was fully good humoured.

'That couldn't be helped unfortunately, like we talked about,' she said, shutting it down, 'Anyway, we can cross that bridge later. Let's get having a look at these.'

Jessica passed out copies of the applications and headshots.

'There's only thirty altogether,' she said. 'We should get through them all by lunchtime. Then maybe make a decision this afternoon?' she said, her voice raising in a lilt.

'Sounds like a plan,' said Lucy. 'Them knowing we can only pay expenses has hopefully kept numbers down.'

Jessica nodded in agreement, leafing through the first form. 'Yeah, as long as they're good and can offer us plenty of availability.' She began studying the first page closely.

'That may have been a mistake,' Charlie said, with apparent wisdom. 'We might have narrowed it down too much already.'

'Well we'll see,' said Jessica, trying not to sound too dismissive. 'It came down to something we simply couldn't budget for anyway. Let's see who we've got here,' she said, bringing the conversation to a close.

They drank their coffees out of their plastic cups and spent the next two-and-a-half hours working their way through the forms, discussing each one in brief detail, before compiling a shortlist. They broke for lunch. Jessica had ordered them in a platter of sandwiches and another round of coffees. They chatted with Bev next door and she filled them in on any calls they had missed. Then they reconvened and whittled the applications down further. Another two hours and they were done. The room had taken on a mustiness of stale air and coffee. Lucy had gone for another few cigarettes and the dusky odour from her clothes added to the mix. They were all tired, but pleased with their work. It had gone more smoothly than Jessica had thought, especially after the strained beginning. The discussions had never become too heated. She recognised Charlie was getting a little irritated a few times and she let a couple of additional applicants through to the interview stage, mostly to appease him.

'Well guys, I think that's about us. I think we've done good work there. I'm excited about the list we've got.' She looked down at her top sheet. 'So, for Stevenson we've got three good candidates. We've two to interview for Ashleigh, two for Will and... er...

seven to cover the smaller parts. Great stuff guys, thanks for making it all go smoothly.'

'Great stuff, Jess,' said Charlie, stretching and leaning back in his plastic chair.

'Yeah, great job everyone,' echoed Lucy. 'We've all earned a few glasses of vino tonight... oh yeah, and I've got a date,' she said, smiling and pulling a face.

'A new guy?' asked Jessica, raising an eyebrow.

'Yeah,' said Lucy with a wink.

Charlie shook his head with a half-smile. 'You're gonna need to move to a new city soon, the pool must be runnin' low by now,' he quipped.

'How dare you,' said Lucy, landing a playful punch to his right arm.

'Oww!'

They reconvened back in the main office, Lucy and Charlie going to their computers to check emails.

'Bev, here's the final interview shortlist,' Jessica said, handing the bundle of paperwork to Bev. 'Have you time to send out an interview schedule today? If you can't, the morning should be fine.'

'No sweetie, I'll get it done. I was gonna start later in the morning if that's okay. I've got the damn dentist at nine. As long as I don't forget my phone again. Left the damn thing again last night and had to get the bus back over.'

'Oh dear, that's a pain. Yeah, great – thanks Bev. You're a star.'

'Yeah, I know,' she said, peering over her glasses, the large white beads around her neck ratting against her desk as she chortled.

'It's true. Let's see, they were all told to keep Wednesday free. If we get the first one in at say nine fifteen, we should get them all through – twenty minutes each and ten minutes in between. You two okay staying a bit late if it runs over? My shout for burritos after? You too, Bev?'

They all nodded in agreement.

'That's settled then. Thanks again everyone. I've got a really good feeling about what kind of film we can make here. Maybe even something quite unique.'

Jessica could have had no idea how right she would be.

Chapter 13

Joe was working in the warehouse on Monday afternoon, pulling the late shift into the evening. He was working on the second floor, while Andy and Pete were downstairs wrapping pallets with Lewis. Joe was in the middle of stacking five hundred boxes of angle-grinder wrenches into columns when his phone pinged in his pocket. He pulled it out. An email from the production company. He tensed.

'Thank you for submitting your application. We are delighted...'

Yes!

Joe had been invited for interview. He clenched his left fist and gave it a little pump in the air. On Wednesday morning he would be given an interview with three members of the team. He was thrilled.

'Good news?'

'Oh, Lewis... um, yeah.' Joe hadn't heard him come up behind him, a podcast still playing in his ear buds.

'That's good. These boxes ain't gonna stack themselves.'

'Yeah, sorry. It was just a quick text – I've a break soon anyway,' he said evenly.

'So long as you get this finished before the end of the shift,' Lewis said with a patronising smile.

'Yes Lewis, that won't be a problem.'

Fuck that guy.

Lewis raised his eyebrows, then went off down the steps whistling, swinging a tape gun.

'Dick,' Joe said under his breath. He re-read the email. Lewis being an ass couldn't dampen his good mood. He drafted a quick, polite response to somebody called Bev, informing her that he was very pleased and would look forward to seeing them then. He had been hopeful that he would get an interview. His CV was impressive. Of course, none of it was true. Nothing apart from his name and address. He had put down about working part time in the warehouse too and the details for them. He figured it was par for the course for a struggling to actor to have a menial job. But almost everything else was a lie. He had listed credits in several amateur companies on the outskirts of the city at real life halls and theatres. The companies were all fictional. But he did go to the trouble of building several free blogger sites for them each. He had copied and pasted text from real groups, changing the plays, group names and dates. For good measure, he sprinkled his name in various places on the sites. He also added a contact number for each one, the same numbers he had put down on his form. They were for burner phones, of which he had several. He had been thorough and evidently it had paid off.

He savoured the task now of preparing for the interview. How sweet it would be if he could attach himself to a film about one of his own murders. The notion was almost too thrilling to bare. He had no actual acting experience, but that didn't worry him. They were only looking for amateurs anyway. Who had more real-life acting experience than Joe?

Chapter 14

'Could you tell us in your own words how you would approach this role?'

Jessica leaned forward in her chair. It was the third interview of Wednesday morning. Lucy and Charlie flanked her on either side in the second office. The air-con wasn't working properly and it was unseasonably warm. The windows were open fully, giving some respite from the sharp perfume of the previous applicant and the sweating armpits of the present one.

'Yeah, certainly,' said the man in front of them. He looked older than his headshot suggested and not quite as handsome. He spoke as if carefully sizing up each word. His answers hadn't been very good so far and the lengths of his responses were making the panel feel impatient, collectively willing the interview to go faster. But Jessica knew how these encounters felt and was always compassionate when she was on this side of the table. He gave another long-winded answer that didn't offer them much of what they wanted to hear. She tried to look attentive, though she found herself listening more to the stream of traffic from outside.

'Great, well thank you very much, Peter,' said Jessica, trying not to sound too abrupt. 'I think we have everything we need. I really appreciate your coming in and thank you for your time. We'll let you know.'

Jessica stood and went around the table and opened the door. Peter remained seated for an awkward few moments, smiled without his eyes, then made his way to the door.

'Thanks again. Bev will see you out.'

Jessica closed the door and turned to the others, making a cringing face.

'Well we haven't found our detective yet,' whispered Charlie.

'Nope,' agreed Lucy. 'That was a little painful.'

'Okay, do you guys need a few minutes or will we fire on ahead? We're about twenty minutes over time already.'

'I'm okay to crack on,' said Charlie.

'Me too, can I grab a smoke after the next one?'

'Sure thing, thanks guys,' said Jess, standing and pouring a fresh glass of water and positioning it in front of the empty seat.

'Right, fingers crossed for this one. I'll go get him.'

She opened the door and peered into the outer office. Bev was on a call and a young black girl was seated opposite her, fidgeting with her sleeve. She was early, or maybe they were just late. Beside her was Joe. He had gelled his hair into a semi-quiff and was wearing a smart black suit with a faint blue stripe on the jacket. He had an open-necked blue shirt underneath. His legs were crossed, his black shoes well buffed, a beam of sunlight bouncing from them.

'Joe Ament?' Jessica asked, looking towards him.

'Yes, that's me,' he said with an easy smile, getting to his feet. 'You must be Jessica,' he said, offering his hand. 'Pleased to meet you.'

She shook hands with him, Joe offering a light grip. 'Please come through,' she said with a smile.

He seems nice. So far, so good.

Jessica introduced him to the panel and outlined the interview format and the general housekeeping. Joe nodded along attentively, making eye contact with each of them and giving a little nod as they were introduced to him.

'Nice to meet you all,' he said warmly.

'Okay, now we've got all that out the way, we'll get started on a few questions,' said Jessica, looking down and leafing through her sheets. 'Right Joe, so please tell us a little about your experience and what you've learned from your acting career so far.'

'Thanks,' said Joe, raising his eyebrows and offering another little smile. 'I've been acting for around five years. I came to it late enough, taking classes a little before I turned thirty. An early midlife crisis maybe,' he said with a short laugh. 'I was always a big film fan and decided, it's now or never. I've been fortunate enough that companies/producers have found me to be of use to them and have liked what I've done. The last year or two I've been in regular work and have begun to progress onto being offered some meatier roles. I feel my skills have vastly improved and I'm enjoying it more than ever. I'm not deluded into thinking I'm gonna be Brad Pitt, but I hope to continue moving on in the right direction.'

Jessica nodded at him encouragingly.

Quite a good answer.

She checked her notes. 'Joe, you were recently featured in a production of *An Inspector Calls*, isn't that right?'

'That's right.'

'Could you tell us a little about that?'

'Sure,' he said eagerly and went on to give a well-rehearsed and engaging answer, about his apparent performance in a leading role.

The panel all gave him reassuring nods and they each scribbled down notes as he went.

'That's great to hear, a nice answer thank you, your passion really shines through,' said Jessica. 'We'd like to record a short piece of dialogue if that's okay,' she said, raising a finger towards Lucy.

'Yes of course, I'd be pleased to,' said Joe, as Lucy crossed and switched on the camera positioned off to one side.

'Part of the film will have the actors in non-speaking scenes,' Jessica continued, 'with voice overs and the like at the same time. But there will also be dramatized scenes and your character has probably the most lines out of anyone.'

'Okay good, sounds great,' he said, clearing his throat and accepting the sheet of dialogue that Jessica passed across.

'Awesome. Okay, so I'll be playing the part of a sergeant. We're having a conversation in the precinct about the case. You good to go?'

Joe glanced down at the page, then looked back at Jessica, holding her stare and smiling lightly. 'Yep, I'm all set.'

Jessica leaned back in her seat and crossed her legs, balancing her own copy over one knee.

'What did you make of him?' Jessica had lowered her voice, speaking in an urgent tone.

'Who? The father?' asked Joe, trying to get into character, rolling his shoulders.

'Yeah... I mean - he's gotta be our number one, right?'

'Maybe. He did have their blood all over him. Had a motive too, I suppose.' Joe sounded confident and quite authentic.

'You suppose?' Jessica said, allowing some incredulity to creep into her voice. 'No offence sir, I walk in on my daughter like that – there's no tellin' what I might do to him.'

'Well Sergeant, we ain't investigating you,' Joe said slowly, trying to give off an air of natural, honest-to-god authority. 'Every man's innocent till proven otherwise. Let's see what the facts tells us. The SOCO's are going in now, let's see what they've got for us too.'

They continued to run through the scene. Halfway through it and Jessica knew she was going to offer him the part.

Chapter 15

'Pass me a soda would you, Luce?' Charlie asked, gesturing across the table.

'There you go.'

'Thanks. Geez – these wraps are spicy.'

'You should try my extra hot chili beef,' Jessica said holding the burrito aloft, raising one eyebrow.

'No thanks – not for me,' Charlie said, pulling a face.

'So y'all got some good people today?' Bev asked, pulling the plastic top off her Mex salad bowl. She pushed some paperwork to one side. 'Salad. Damn – those wraps look good. But I can't afford another visit to the dentist – don't wanna rip out my new crown.'

'Yeah, I'd think not, poor thing,' said Jessica, wiping grease off her lips with a napkin. 'Yeah, we did. We've most of them whittled down, haven't we?'

'Yeah,' nodded Lucy. 'We sure did.'

'And we even all agreed, too,' said Charlie, raising a playful fist. Lucy and Jessica shared a knowing smile.

'Good job guys,' said Bev. 'Suppose you're gonna want me emailing out to everyone today on a half-filled stomach?' she said, her beady eyes dancing behind her lenses.

'Tomorrow will do just fine, thanks Bev,' said Jessica, smiling back, using a wipe on her hands. 'When I get home, I'll ring all the successful ones this evening as well.'

'You know I was particularly impressed with one guy,' Charlie said, pontificating, holding up a ketchup-soaked fry, 'The guy we got for the detective – Joe. I think he's gonna be great.'

Lucy nodded, while distractedly texting on her cell phone.

'Yeah, I think he should be okay,' Jessica said slowly. 'He's got great experience. It's the most important role really.'

'He sure does, right?' said Charlie. 'I mean – his CV blew the other guys out the water.'

'That's true. I mean – I like him and all. I think he was the best one. There was… something I wasn't sure of.' Lucy shrugged. 'I dunno,' she said, smiling and brushing a few crumbs from the table. 'I'm probably just being fussy, it's probably nothing.'

'It was a long day,' said Lucy, setting her phone down. 'It's all becoming a blur. But I think he was good. Compared to the others, it's a no-brainer.'

Jessica made her calls once she was settled at home and cosy on the couch. She'd got wet in a downpour walking from the train. She was actually glad of it cooling her down. She stripped off and took a shower, then got into pyjamas and settled down in the living room. She'd be glad to get the calls over with and settle down properly for the evening. She rang Martha Peters who'd got the part of Ashleigh, and Jed Gorman who'd got the part of her boyfriend. Then she rang Joe. He sounded very pleased and was incredibly gracious and courteous. There was no good reason to have any doubts about him. Bev said she'd phone the couple of successful candidates, who they'd only be using occasionally, in the morning. Jessica cosied into the soft fabric of her sofa, pulling a blanket over her cold toes. It had been a good day. She had this. All was going well. She watched a dark true crime doc on Netflix before bed: *The Couplet Killer – Murder And The Park.* A busman's holiday, and one of the few she hadn't watched. It was okay. But her sleep that night was not. She was restless and anxious. Maybe it had been the show, or maybe it was something else.

Chapter 16

During the interview, Joe had felt something akin to elation. It was surely his greatest performance. Not so much the scene itself, but everything. He had imagined the kind of person they would want to pick and he had *become* that person. As the interview went on, he had wanted it more than anything before. When Jessica phoned and offered the job, it wasn't so much a surprise as a vindication.

The following week and Joe was due to have his first day 'on set.' There would be some external shots of him walking around and a few interviews filmed in the second office. It would be further along when they would be hiring a set for the internal murder scene shots. That would be really something.

He was feeling good about it all, feeling positive. He stopped for a stack of pancakes at a diner he liked, and had two cups of coffee with it. He wore a simple jumper and jeans, as he had been fitted out for his own uniform, which he would be receiving later. He took the train across town and got off early, choosing to walk a few blocks. He breathed in the city, the smells, the dirt. It was a cold day, no sun to speak of, and it was as if the towering skyscrapers were veiled in a grey Perspex. Nothing looked quite right and nothing felt quite real. Joe was used to his plans generally coming off well, but he could hardly believe that he had managed to get himself cast in a film about one of his own crimes. Every time that little piece of self-reflection popped into his head, he savoured it, chewed on it. But it still made everything feel a little strange, a little off. He had no end goal in mind, he just wanted to be part of it, experience it, get off on it. Licking a stray drop of syrup from his finger, he cast his mind back again to the original crime. Ashleigh had been one of his favourite kills. He had had his eye on her for some time. Yes, she was beautiful and he supposed he *desired* in that way too. But it was more than that. It was the first time he could remember that his overpowering fantasy had been to kill somebody in particular, that he just had to have her. He had killed several times before, but this was the first time he had such an extreme urge for a specific person and managed to follow through on it. And it had felt good, so good. He didn't care much for killing men one way or another, but the boyfriend had been a bonus. He hadn't planned it as a frame-up either, but the idea presented itself and he went with it. The boyfriend had arrived while she was still warm, soaked in her own cooling blood. He had to be taken care of, that was for certain. One thing could be said for Joe, he was always the pragmatist.

The four members of the team he had met were all there already on his arrival at the office. They made him a coffee and talked with him about their production plans for the day in high spirits.

'Now, wait'll you see what we've got for you,' said Lucy with a playful grin. She reached under her desk and pulled out a full police suit in a transparent plastic case.

'Oh wow,' he said with a chuckle. 'Officer Ament reporting for duty,' he said, giving a little salute.

'You'll need this too,' Jessica said, lifting up an imitation gun and holster from her desk drawer.

'Whoa!' he said putting his hands in the air. 'Scary stuff.' He crossed the room and took the gun from her. He held it in his hands. It sure did feel pretty real. Looked good too. He shot a look at the group in front of him. He pointed the gun at Jessica, then at each of the others in turn. A fantasy flashed through his mind of plugging a hole through each of them. 'Thanks, this is all great,' he said, fixing a casual smile on his lips.

'The men's room is just down the hall Joe,' Charlie said, pointing.

Joe regarded himself in the rest-room mirror. He smirked. He pulled out the gun and gave it a spin around his fingers, before taking in his full reflection. He banked the thought that a suit like this could come in handy. It'd be a risk using it for a mark, but boy would it be fun.

His return to the office brought a little smattering of applause. Jessica took him into the second room and went through the plans for the day while Charlie and Lucy got the equipment ready.

'First off, we're just gonna get some stock footage of you. We'll film you walking up and down the block, really just walking mostly. Then we'll have you get on like you're speaking into your radio set. Okay?'

'Okay, sounds fine.'

'Then we'll come back in and film a little in here. Alright, let's get going, the light's better now.'

Joe rode down in the elevator with the other three, now in full uniform, complete with hat, radio and belt carrying his imitation gun and cuffs. A few office workers eyed him up as he strode through the reception area. He enjoyed the sensation. The old security guard tipped his cap as he walked past him.

'We've got some extra protection today,' Jessica said to him as they passed by, giving him a little wave.

'I'll always take any help I can get, Miss Kinney,' he replied.

Outside, Charlie and Lucy were quick setting up the two cameras. Lucy operated one on a tripod, out of the way beside a trash can. Charlie held a smaller camera on his shoulder as he moved about the sidewalk, testing the lens. Jessica said a few words into the camera before flashing a sheet of paper in front of it with some numbers written on it in black marker.

'That's us good. Right Joe, off you go,' she said, moving to the side beside Lucy. At first Joe felt quite foolish walking up and down the sidewalk. He got strange looks from most of those that he passed, particularly with Charlie following close behind, keeping his camera trained on him. Joe felt rigid, all bunched up in his new clothes. He knew he needed to relax, or at least appear to. Or maybe he was meant to look tense. He tried to loosen up anyway.

'Okay, that's great Joe. We need to be some shots of your shoes on the ground,' Jessica said, jogging over to him.

'Okay, no problem.'

'Charlie,' she said waving an arm of instruction, beckoning Charlie closer. Joe set off again slowly as Charlie shot his shoes passing over the flagstones. His shoes strode over old decaying gum now, exposed by the sunlight. He glared down on the dirty, rain-soaked sidewalk. Joe turned at the end of the curb past the office building, then walked back again. He looked over to Jessica and she have a thumbs up. 'Keep going, it'll look good. Very noirish,' she said jovially.

'I told you I was a pro,' he shouted to her with a chuckle. He walked to the opposite corner and Charlie kept his camera on his heels, sometimes backing away, sometimes appearing to be framing a puddle as Joe squelched through it. When Joe got to the end of the block, he turned again and gave a little half jump and spun round and walked on again playfully.

Is this what actors spend their time doing?

Piece of piss.

He looked up towards Lucy and saw her grin, making eye contact with him for a second. He noticed for the first time that she was really very attractive. Then he banked that thought and reminded himself that he didn't need to add in any other complications. Not for the time being at any rate. The truth was, he had no real plan for what he was doing. But the whole experience was pleasing him very much. How stupid these idiots would feel if they ever found out the truth. But Joe was certain they never would. Nobody would. He had proven himself over and over again. Cops, lawyers, journalists – nobody had ever been even close.

Jessica wrapped up the takes of the shoes, then they set up a block further away and repeated the whole thing again. A light rain began to fall and the team quickly packed up and agreed to take fifteen minutes or so. Joe walked around the corner to a drugstore and bought coffees for everyone, bringing two cardboard carriers back inside. He nodded to the security guard with a cocky flick of his head, then rode the elevator back up to the office. Bev was typing on her computer. Through the middle door he could see the others setting up the cameras and microphones again.

'Well aren't you a sweetie,' Bev said, peering over her glasses, smiling.

'Just doing my bit. You guys seem flat out – I'm sure you could do with a caffeine hit.'

'Always dear, always.'

The others gratefully received their styrofoam cups and Joe sat down, sipping his, watching them set up. With their backs turned from him, he allowed himself a sly smile. How did things turn out so good? Here they were asking to be part of filming the story of one of his murders and they had absolutely no clue.

'Okay Joe, that's us almost ready,' Jessica said, getting off her knees, breaking him from his private reverie.

'Great,' he said, pasting his public face back on.

'So, we're gonna try a little improv. I'll ask you some questions about the case. In the documentary this will be a piece to camera as if you're answering questions at the time or a little after the case gets going. We'll see what comes out. If you can just be as natural as you can. We'll cut out me asking the questions in editing. I'll start off slow. Did you get a chance to familiarise yourself with the notes I emailed you – all of the nuts and bolts of the investigation?'

'Yeah, I know the case pretty well now I think.' He supressed the urge to smile wider.

'Okay great. Good to go, guys?'

Lucy gave a thumbs-up from behind the camera and Charlie did the same, sitting off to the side with a set of headphones on.

'Good. So, detective, I guess it was a pretty horrific scene you found that day?'

'Yes… yes it was,' Joe said, grappling to pull himself into character. 'I'd never come across a scene like that before. Chilled me to my bones. My partner damn near threw up afterwards.'

Jessica nodded and smiled that he was on point. Joe felt elated.

'I'm sure it was hard for you, going in there. What exactly did you find when you entered the house?'

'My partner and I arrived at the house – Mr Mercer's residence. He was pacing around by the door – highly agitated. His face was full of horror, wet with tears. He said he'd found his daughter and boyfriend, dead in her room. My partner stayed with him while I went up the stairs.' Joe paused for effect and stared into the camera lens. He tried not to react as Jessica stared back at him, looking pleased. 'Miss Mercer's room was the first on the left. Boy, it was awful. I'd never seen anything like it.'

'Great Joe!' Jessica said enthusiastically. 'That's spot on. Can you remember the way the bodies were positioned from the notes?'

'Yeah, I think so.'

'Okay, take your time. Talk us through the scene, just like you were doing – sombre, reflective – but professional.'

Joe nodded. He licked his lips and pictured the actual scene as he actually remembered it. It made him feel excited, jubilant. He tried to hide it.

The monologue seemed to go well. They did a few more takes, which Joe found rather tedious, but he did his best to give it enough enthusiasm. They took some more footage of him sitting in the chair, staring into space, or sipping from an empty mug. They took more close-ups of his feet too.

What's with all the shots of my feet?

Then Jessica declared that that would do them for the day. She appeared pleased with him. It wasn't what he was here for, but he welcomed it.

'Really great stuff Joe, that was perfect. If you want to change down the hall, I've a few calls to make. We're all grabbing a drink after work, feel free to join us if you like?'

'Oh yeah? Em… yeah thanks – sounds swell, I'm up for that.'

'Great – just sit out there with Bev when you're done, we won't be long.'

Chapter 17

'Well, what did you reckon?' Jessica asked after Joe had left and shut the dividing door behind him.

'I think we got some good stuff,' said Charlie, slipping off his headphones.

'He did real good,' agreed Lucy, standing up and taking out a pack of cigarettes.

'Yeah, I'm pleased, well done everyone.'

'I'm just going for a quick puff,' said Lucy, walking with Charlie to the door.

'I'll go check my emails,' said Charlie. 'You doing that call with Patrick now?'

'Yeah, he spoke with David's attorney. Should be a three-way call with him and Patrick.' She checked her watch. 'Then we can go grab that drink. I'd better get set up actually.'

Jessica went out to the ladies' room, used the toilet and touched up her lipstick and dragged a comb through her hair. She went back into the large room alone and set up the little conference call speaker/microphone unit on the table. It was old fashioned, but served its purpose. Patrick wasn't one for Skype or Zoom at any rate. Jessica flicked through a few emails on her phone before the device began to chirp. She pressed the call button.

'Hello, this is Jessica.'

'Hi Jess, it's Patrick,' came the rich baritone.

'How are you, Patrick?'

'I'm good – you?'

'We're all good here. Just finished some filming with our guy playing Detective Stevenson. He's called Joe Ament, it went well, really well.'

'Great to hear Jess. I'll have to swing by for some of the filming. Drop me a few dates and we'll get something in the diary.'

'Will do. Is David coming on the call now?'

'Yes, should be. His attorney said it was all arranged. I'm just waiting on us being patched through.'

'Okay, brilliant. What about the real D.S Stevenson – still no dice there?'

'No. The NYPD has all closed ranks on us. Nobody wants to talk to us, never mind be interviewed. They know that we'll cover the criticism and allegations against them. Their PR team have all but blanked me.'

'Pity. It'd help the credibility of the documentary.' She breathed out and it made a little hiss from the speaker. 'Oh well, we've still lots of other witnesses on board. There's Mrs Mercer, a couple neighbours and the defence team. There's still a chance the prosecutor will talk to us?'

'Yeah, it's on the table, the prosecutor's office are at least still taking my calls,' he said with a throaty chuckle. 'We'll have to see. I'll keep following up on Stevenson too, him being retired and all, you never know.'

'Thanks, I appreciate you being so involved Patrick, I know how busy…'

'Connecting you to the US Prison Service now, please hold,' came a distant, robotic voice, cutting her off mid-sentence.

They waited, their breaths echoing with a crackle through the speaker. Then there was a click and a muffled rustling.

'Hello?'

'Hello, is that David?' asked Jessica, rubbing her sweating hands along her skirt.

'Yes, hello Jessica.'

'Hi David, good to hear you, thanks for taking our call. Patrick's on the line too.'

'Hello Patrick.'

'Afternoon David, how are you?'

He made a little click in the back of his throat. 'I'm doing okay. Jessica – it was nice to meet you last week. You and er…'

'Lucy,' Jessica suggested.

'Yeah. I'm glad we had that meeting. I'm sorry if I got a little, well… emotional.'

'No apology necessary, David. It's totally understandable. You did great,' Jessica said and really meant it.

'Well thanks. I know it's not going to be easy.'

'But you're happy to continue, David?' broke in Patrick.

'Yes, yes I am.'

'Great David, thank you,' said Jessica. 'When's good for you for us to come again?'

'Well, I'm here all the time,' he said drolly. 'If you can square it with the warden, I'll meet you whenever you like. Next week, say?'

'Sounds fantastic. We'll get right on it,' said Jessica.

'Good. Look, they're telling me I have to go,' David said, distracted.

'Okay, thanks David.'

'Thank you, David,' said Patrick.

'Thanks both, take care.'

There was another click and then a dead tone.

'You still there, Patrick?'

'I sure am. That was good news.'

'Yeah, I'm quite relieved actually. I'd hoped I'd made a good enough impression on him.'

'Never in doubt, Jess.'

. . .

'Drinks on me. First one anyways. What can I get ya?'

They were in a bar two blocks away that had become a favourite haunt. An Irish pub with tricolours, good whiskey, old advertisements, traditional music live on the weekends and decent pints of Guinness poured from a keg underneath the bar. It had a pleasant, upbeat atmosphere. It wasn't the kind of Irish pub where folk went to annihilate their problems with drink and start a fight while they did it. Joe helped Jessica with the drinks while Lucy and Charlie went in search of a table. Bev had gone on home – she said her husband would burn the apartment down if he tried to cook for himself. Jessica wasn't quite sure if she had meant through incompetence or anger. She chatted casually with Joe as they waited on their drinks. The bar was half full and there was a mix of lively chat and noise from a soccer match on the widescreen televisions. They joined the others at a table they had found in a snug corner with an early picture of U2 on the wall next to a charcoal drawing of Van Morrison.

'So, how'd you find it, Joe? Enjoy it okay?' said Jessica.

'Yeah, it was great. I mean, I hope what I did was okay?'

'Absolutely, you did super. Cheers,' she said, clinking glasses with him. Lucy and Charlie joined in with a 'cheers.'

'Sláinte,' Joe said, nodding at the surrounding Irish paraphernalia.

The conversation was easy as they started in on their drinks. They all chatted casually about politics in Washington and about a new reality show featuring celebrities and their cats. They inevitably moved back to talk about the documentary. Joe only stayed for the one drink, made his excuses, then slipped out. Jessica's eyes lingered on him for a few moments as he left. There was something about him that she found mildly unsettling, but she was stumped as to what it was. Maybe it was just that he appeared very guarded. Sure, everyone was different, weren't they? She caught Lucy staring after him too, a blank expression on her face.

'What?' she said, turning to Jessica.

'No,' Jessica said, pointing a finger at her playfully.

'What?' Lucy said again, raising her hands.

'You know what,' said Jessica.

'Hey – I've a date tonight already.'

'Yeah, tonight,' Jessica said pointedly.

'Jesus. Aww Lucy,' Charlie said with a shake of his head. 'Right, who's for another?'

Chapter 18

Joe took a last bite of his sub, then stuffed the greasy paper in the trash. His fingers were stained a reddish residue from sweet chili sauce and with a strong oniony aroma. He pulled out a tissue and wiped them over, before throwing it in the bin with the rest of the sub. He sighed, feeling tired. He needed to get his head straight. It was Thursday afternoon and he was meeting the team again, this time in Central Park. The sun was out, heating up a breezy fall day. The coldness in the shade was a reminder that winter was on its way. He entered the park through the east side and found it easy to spot them already waiting on a bench up near a fountain.

'Hi guys,' he said raising a hand and jogging over to them. They caught up together as Joe helped them with their equipment, setting it up over by a quiet grassy area. He had worked an eight-to-eleven short shift in the warehouse before collecting his uniform from Bev, changing, then carrying his work clothes in a holdall.

'Sorry you had to make a detour to pick up the uniform,' Jessica said, nodding at his outfit.

'Don't worry, it was no bother.' The truth was he was tired, rushed and overheated.

'We were out filming with some of the rest of the cast in The Village,' said Jessica. 'Sorry there wasn't time to go get you.'

'No probs.'

'You could always just keep the uniform at home if you like – might save you time the next day.'

'Yeah, sounds good, thanks Jessica.'

Jessica went over the plan for the afternoon's filming with him while the others set up the shot.

She took a sip from a take-away coffee. 'You okay for a drink Joe?'

'Yeah, I'm good – not long after one.'

'Okay great, I'll just down this and we'll get started.' Jessica looked past him, taking in the angles for filming. 'Y'know there was one of those "couplet" benches over there – you remember "The Couplet Killer". From the eighties?'

'Oh yeah,' Joe said, as if struggling to recall.

'I was part of the crew for a doc about him a few years back.'

'Yeah – I think I mighta seen that.'

Jessica nodded. 'A real sicko – crazy bastard.'

'Was he crazy?'

'Well you kinda have to be to do stuff like that don't you?'

'Not necessarily.'

'Either that, or just pure evil.'

'I guess he had his reasons,' Joe said.

Jessica crinkled her forehead. 'I don't think those girls' families would think so.' She watched Joe purse his lips.

Joe had forgotten himself for a moment. That wouldn't do. 'No, I mean… of course – terrible thing,' he said.

'You guys ready?' Lucy said, coming over and shooting Joe a wide smile.

Joe felt Jessica's eyes lingering on him from the side.

'Yeah, for sure,' said Joe.

'So, we've got this big brick for ya,' Jessica said, handing Joe an old Nokia cell phone. 'If you just improvise something roughly around the script I sent you. We'll take a few shots of that. You remember it okay?'

'Yeah, got it,' Joe said quietly.

'Okay, let's try a take. Charlie'll follow you walking over to that tree there,' she said, pointing. 'Just make sure you come around the far side of Lucy's boom and she'll pick you up when you lift the phone and start talking. Okay?'

'Sure.'

Everyone took their places. Jessica shook a page with a filming number written on it in front of the camera, then stood back. 'Go ahead.'

Joe began walking towards the trees stiffly, looking down at the ground.

'Cut,' said Jessica. 'Okay Joe, just relax. Start walking like you're just on a stroll. When you get to the tree we'll add a ringing sound later. Just lift out your phone like it's started chirping at you.'

'Okay, yeah, sorry.'

'Okay, rolling.'

Joe felt irked. He wanted it all to go as smoothly as the last time. He wasn't used to being ordered around and feeling unsure of what he was doing. Sometimes he got bossed around in the warehouse, that was different, but he sure didn't like that either. He set off again, a little less stiffly this time, looking all around him. He stumbled over a bulky bundle of tree roots.

'Sorry... lemme start again.' He jogged back to his starting position and flashed a questioning look at Jessica.

'Okay, take your time. Rolling.'

Joe set off again, visibly chewing on his lip. He looked down at the ground carefully, working his way around the roots, but going too far to one side.

'Joe you're out of shot,' Jessica called, her voice stiff.

'Am I? I don't think so?'

'Yeah, you are,' Charlie shouted over, looking up from his camera, jogging back to place, shooting a quizzical look towards Jessica.

Joe watched Jessica as she read over her sheets, her face a frown.

'D'ya want me to start again?' Joe said, looking and feeling uncomfortable.

'No, let's pick it up from by the tree. Just move a little to your left. Yep, that's it. Let's take it from the phone ringing. Rolling.'

Joe nodded to her, then looked off into the distance, concentrating hard. There was quiet for a few moments, as some children ran in the background towards their mother on a picnic rug. A flock of birds flew between two trees. Joe stayed still, poised.

'Joe, the phone,' Jessica called sharply.

'Shit, yeah- I forgot. I was waiting for the ringing. Sorry. 'He paused awkwardly, annoyed with himself, then fumbled the phone out from his pocket.

'Hello? Hi... yeah it's me. Yes, uhuh. Oh, right – that's news to me... unhuh.'

'Cut!' Jessica shouted a little louder than she probably intended. She headed across to Joe at pace.

'What now?' Joe said shortly. 'I mean, was the boom in again or something?' he said, correcting his tone.

'It was a just a bit... well you were kind of stumbling over it,' Jessica said with a worried expression Joe found patronising.

'It's hard, ya know, when there's nobody on the other end.'

'That's acting, buddy,' Charlie said, approaching them, setting his heavy camera down, meaning it to sound light-hearted, but receiving a dark look from Joe. Inside, Joe began to seethe.

'It's okay, we're in no rush, Joe,' Lucy said, stepping out from her camera. 'Take your time.'

Joe nodded, running a hand through his hair. 'Sorry, I'll try again,' he said tensely, his face reddening. He just wanted out of there.

'Do you need to take a minute?' Jessica asked, trying to sound casual.

'No... no I'm fine. I'll get it. I'm maybe just a bit tired. I worked an early shift this morning and am in again tonight. I must be a bit distracted... sorry,' he said, the word catching painfully in his throat.

Jessica held his look for a moment. 'Let's all take five, sure.'

'I'll get us some coffees,' Lucy broke in, switching her camera onto standby.

'Thanks Luce,' Jessica said, turning around and pulling out her phone. She scrolled absently, walking away as Charlie began talking with Joe. He stared after Jessica as he mumbled his responses to Charlie, not really listening to him. Joe couldn't afford to screw this up. Not when it had only just begun. He thought it'd be easy. It was only god-damned walking. And talking into a cell phone. He could do a good enough job surely to please these egocentric assholes. He just needed to gather his thoughts.

I wish this prick would shut up for a minute.

He zoned out further, calming his body.

He would get this job done. And he would squeeze every drop of pleasure that could be savoured. And maybe after, he'd teach them all a lesson.

Chapter 19

Joe dug the box cutter into the pallet wrap and slashed it through to the wood. He pulled out the next box and tossed it onto the growing pile. He had been working through a bundle of pallets by himself on the third floor since the start of his second shift. At least it was quiet. Only Lewis was left in the warehouse with him and he was downstairs in the small wooden office. Joe had been breaking up pallets and boxes for over an hour and he hadn't calmed down any.

Stupid. Damn stupid.

The filming might have improved slightly and he'd left on okay terms with them all, but he knew he had still messed up. He was too used to feeling confident in most things that he did. He was sure he could handle a little amateur acting role. But he had felt out of his depth, he had floundered. And worse than that he wasn't able to hide it. He had been pissed off, and it showed.

He picked up a pile of empty boxes and began slashing them open with his sharp box cutter.

Careless. Unprepared.

Things had been feeling off kilter for a while. First off the recent Facebook murder had gone sour stratospherically, and now this. He could usually handle whatever life threw his way, and whatever web he had created. But he had slipped up. He had been enjoying the whole thing too much, the delight of it. It had made him sloppy, overzealous. And that stupid, arrogant bitch Jessica. Who did she think she was? Clearly displeased with him, didn't like what he had said, looking down on him. He would show her. He would do whatever he pleased. If she really knew what he was like, *really knew*, how she would cower before him. But he had been too at ease, lowering his guard – that was true. When she mentioned "The Couplet Killer", why hadn't he just agreed with her?

Stupid. Unnecessary.

She had given him such a strange look. A questioning look. He hadn't liked it. It was if she could see past his mask. Perhaps just a tiny piece. But how could she? He knew it was stupid to fret about it anyhow. Nothing could be done. But nevertheless, it had put him off his game, made him question himself. And then he had been flustered. Flustered! Him! That wasn't his style at all. And he hated her for it.

Joe stacked the pile of boxes he had just cut and flattened, then gave it a cursory kick and walked over towards the open hatch. The city beyond was dark. There was a thin mist hanging in the cold evening too. He took in a long breath of cold, fresh air. It cooled his lungs, sending a tingle through his body. He pulled out his phone and looked for any new alerts. There was an email from Lucy. It had a Dropbox file of some of the shoot from earlier on and a chirpy message saying that he had done well. Christ, he could do without her sympathy. He clicked on the link and began watching a few takes of himself speaking to camera and walking through the park. It wasn't as bad as he thought it would be, but it wasn't good enough either. He sighed.

'Fucksake Joe, on your cell again?'

Joe nearly spilled the phone from his hand. 'Jesus,' he said, stumbling.

Lewis folded his arms across his overalls, tilting his head and regarding Joe with an unpleasant expression.

'Really – I'm sick of tellin' you to get off your damn phone.'

'It was just for a second,' Joe said slipping the phone back into his trouser pocket. He felt anger bubbling up and hadn't the inclination to hide it. 'I'm pulling my second shift of the day, and it's nearly done, ease up like.'

'Ease up?' Lewis said incredulously, now setting one hand on his hip, walking around behind Joe, his back to the loading door. 'I'm your boss, Joe, if you hadn't noticed.' He made a meal of checking his watch. 'You've nearly fifty minutes left of your shift and I'll tell ya when you're done.'

'For God's sake,' Joe said, shaking his head. He kicked a box to one side and pulled out his box cutter from his pocket, fidgeting with it in his right hand.

'You'll treat me with respect Joe,' Lewis groaned, his tone still hostile. 'I don't know what's got into you lately, your attitude.

You're not pulling your weight. I'm gonna need to discuss this with the other managers.'

Joe took a step towards him and absently flicked out the blade full on the box cutter. Lewis took a step back, glancing at the knife for a moment.

Joe squinted his eyes, glaring into Lewis's. 'My work is just fine. And you're not a manager, you're a supervisor at best.'

'I'm your *line manager*,' Lewis said, his voice hard. 'Give me any more crap and you're on a verbal warning.'

Joe moved towards him and Lewis shuffled backwards away from him, looking again at the blade. His expression was less sure, nervous even.

'Why not make it a written warning Lewis, you jumped-up little prick,' Joe said, advancing further. Lewis took another step away, glancing behind him to check he wasn't too close to the open door. He was now a yard from it. Joe slowly raised the blade, pointing it at him. 'Yeah, make it a written warning, you do know how to read and write okay, don't you?' His voice was low, nasty. If Jessica at glanced behind the mask, it was now cast aside and thrown on the dirty floor. The dark ugliness within him was now displayed across his face. He took another step closer.

'Listen Joe, there's no need to get angry,' Lewis said, raising his hands submissively. 'Let's all just calm down some.'

'Angry? Who's angry?' Joe said. He raised the blade again and made two slashing movements in the air. He smiled incongruously, his eyes full of quiet rage.

'Just put down the knife, okay?' Lewis croaked, his throat dry. He kept his hands raised.

Joe looked confused, then lifted the box cutter and eyed it as if had leaped into his hand without his knowing. 'This?' he asked, raising his voice, shrugging.

Silence.

'Is this scaring you?'

Suddenly Joe threw the knife down on the floor beside Lewis. It made a clang and Lewis gave a little jump, accompanied by a yelp. Joe smiled cruelly at the now terrified Lewis. Joe's eyes bore into him until he broke eye contact and looked down at the dusty floor, trapped.

Then all at once, Joe leaped towards him, grabbing his right arm and pulling it up his back. Lewis gave a frightened yell and was rocked off balance. Joe dragged him towards the open door, accompanied by the sound of a sickening snap of his arm as Joe pulled it up further.

'Stop Joe, shit... stop!'

He made a keening noise as Joe pulled him to the very mouth of the door. Tears started to stream down Lewis's cheeks and he pissed his pants. Joe gave his arm a further twist and there was another snap. Then he let go, the arm swaying limply. Lewis's eyes lolled vacantly in his head. Then he grabbed Lewis by his shirt, bunching a handful in his fist, before launching him off the side of the building. Lewis cried out as he fell the three storeys, soaring through the air. He made a huge thud as he landed on the gravel below. His limbs were sprawled out at impossible angles as his head hung back, blood pooling out from under his neck. And then he was still.

Joe stood panting, watching from above, exhilarated; his body tense and on fire, all his senses overloaded. Then he stepped back into the warehouse and looked down at his hands.

'Fuck!' he screamed and kicked the box cutter, sending it scuttling across the wooden boards.

Chapter 20

Jessica had gone back to the office after the shoot to catch up on some admin. Bev was there with her 'til around five, then Jessica worked on for another hour before locking up. After switching off her computer, she waited as it closed down, thinking back on the day. The filming had gone just well enough in the end, but it had been strained. It had given her more questions about Joe than answers. What was his deal? At times he was seemed an altogether different proposition from the first day. Was he going to be difficult to work with? She had to be able to rely on him. There was certainly some sort of edge there she hadn't detected before. She could do without having to work with a *huffy* extra. But he had got it together in the end. It was as if he was more inexperienced than he was supposed to be. That wasn't what had bothered her the most. It was the question over his attitude and some of the things he said. Maybe she was overthinking it. She closed the laptop screen down and switched off the lights.

She took the train three stops, and got off to swap to another onto West 19th. She trotted up the subway steps as the aroma of the street forced its way underground: a mix of motor fumes, sweat and cigarette smoke. A bustle of commuters moved against one another, jostling and pushing.

'Jess!'

'Oh… Paul.'

It was her ex. He had been about to pass her before he stopped, wide-eyed, causing some congestion on the stairs. People continued to push past them, glaring as they did so.

'How are you Jess? Just finished work?'

'Yeah – you too?' she said, nodding at his backpack and his still damp hair. Paul was a lifeguard at two of the city pools. Jessica felt her face flush and her hands were clammy. Paul looked good. Really good. Carl Perkins would have called him a *tall handsome man.*

'Yep, it was a late one. Look – you maybe don't wanna, but I was gonna get a bite – do you fancy a quick coffee or somethin'?'

'Em…' She didn't know what to say. She could have made up an excuse but didn't. 'Yeah, sure… that'd be nice.'

Ten minutes later and they found themselves in an old-school Italian café. It wasn't one they had ever visited when they were dating. They sat opposite each other at a window table, steam rising from their hot coffees. After a stilted few minutes, Jessica found the conversation turn easy, comfortable.

'So tell me, how's the movie coming?'

'Documentary,' she corrected, raising an eyebrow.

'Sorry your worship,' he said playfully.

'God, don't start calling me that again,' she complained, feeling a little uncomfortable. A huge Star Wars fan, Paul had tried to indoctrinate Jessica to the ways of the Jedi. It hadn't been very successful. She'd liked The *Mandolorian* okay, particularly Baby Yoda. *Andor* – not so much. But to Paul's dismay, she never warmed to the originals. She'd given up on Star Wars halfway through *The Empire Strikes Back*. But she did find the interplay between Han and Leia enjoyable, such as the way he called her "Your Worship." It had become a pet name of theirs.

'It's going okay. Pretty good actually. There's a good little team we've got there. We've even got David Mercer on board with it.'

'Really? That's great, Jess. Have you met him yet?'

'Yeah – the other day.'

'What was he like?'

'Em… well- he was nice.'

'Nice?' Paul asked incredulously, mimicking her.

'Well yeah – he seemed like *a nice man*. I guess I don't have much of a handle on him yet. It's early days – but the feeling I have about him – I don't think he did it.'

'Really?'

'Yeah, that's my gut.'

'Okay, cool. I don't really know enough about it all to judge. I'll sure watch your doc when it comes out though,' he said, smiling earnestly.

'I hope you will.'

'So what's it gonna be like? What's the tone? I watched a few crime shows recently – catching up with a few I'd missed here and there. There was one about *The Night Stalker* and one on Bundy. Some dark shit. Hard going.' He picked up a teaspoon and swiped a bit of froth off his cappuccino and put it in his mouth.

'It's not gonna be like those,' she said raising an eyebrow again, before taking a sip of her own flat white. 'Seriously though, I want it to be something much more... real.'

'Fair enough. And what were you doing today? Were you interviewing anyone?'

'No, not today,' she said, her face straightening, reflecting. 'We were filming with one of the amateur actors. There's some parts that are gonna be dramatised.'

'How did it go?'

'Em... well – it wasn't the best actually,' she said with a little laugh.

'Oh?'

'I mean... it was alright. It's just... one of the guys – he was great at interview but... I don't know.'

'Interviews can be that way. People aren't always all that they seem. I hope it works out okay – maybe he'll improve.'

'It's not even really that. I'm just not all that sure about *him*.'

Jessica didn't know why she was being so candid with Paul, she hadn't really meant to be. She supposed she had just felt the need to unload to *someone*, and here was Paul, somebody close, but also apart. Jessica wound up the conversation, finished her coffee and said she needed to get going. Paul looked a little disappointed, but smiled warmly as he gave her a brief hug goodbye. She said she'd be in touch.

Back home, Jessica snuggled up with Eddie and another cup of coffee. Her mind was in a whirl. Between Paul and Joe, she had many questions. But she knew she was too tired to answer any of them tonight. And tomorrow would be another busy day. She took a book to bed and soon she turned out the lights and tried to go to sleep. A few pages from Lawrence Block helped distract her. Eventually her mind did as it was asked and she slept solidly. But it was a night full of black, intangible dreams.

Chapter 21

The next morning and Joe was back in the warehouse, waiting in the downstairs office. What a night it had been. Minutes after Lewis's fall, Joe had got himself together and had his story clear and straight. He called 911, pitching his voice with just the right amount of shock and horror. Then he hurried down the two flights of stairs and over to Lewis. Nobody was around. No one seemed to have heard or seen anything. He looked down at the ground. Lewis's body was a mess. Joe stretched across the tangle of limbs and pool of blood and felt for a pulse. Nothing. Then he had waited. Five minutes later and an ambulance roared up the gravel path towards the warehouse. Joe had staggered over to it waving his arms, his eyes glistening with tears he had forced out. Two paramedics had jumped out and worked with Lewis before lifting him up onto a gurney. To Joe's horror, Lewis was still alive – just. One of the paramedics put a hand on Joe's shoulder and told him he didn't think he would last as far as the hospital.

But they'd do their best.

Joe had nodded, no words available to him.

A minute after the ambulance left, a cop car roared into the car park. Joe was now functioning on pure adrenalin. He hurried across to them and explained how the ambulance had just gone. He also gave him the version of what happened, which he would have to repeat many times again throughout the night. He explained that Lewis and he had been stacking boxes near to the open door. Lewis stepped back at one point, slipping on his box cutter that he had just set down, skidding backwards and out the open door. Joe had scrambled to grab him, but it had all been too fast. Joe squeezed out a few more tears for good measure.

He went in the car with the NYPD and was interviewed several more times back at the station house. He had time in the back to think, to gather himself. He felt that he had dealt with the sudden pressure well and had made a decent show of playing the 'innocent and upset work colleague'. They were thorough, but had seemed to buy the story okay. That would be good enough if Lewis woke up. Before they finally sent him home in the early hours of the morning they informed him that Lewis had been put into an induced coma to give his body a chance to cope with the trauma. But they didn't expect him to last until morning.

Joe had tried to go to bed after writing the new addition into his journal. There was so much to think about, to digest. His thoughts were a jumble of fears and plans. He must have dozed a little as he was woken at seven by a call from Mr Madden, the warehouse and company owner. Although not due to be in work, he had asked under the circumstances if Joe could come in immediately for a debrief and to offer him any emotional support. There wasn't much in the way of emotion in the offer.

Joe made it in for eight and was now seated with a take-out coffee, waiting for Mr Madden to come in from the outer office. He had been on a call seated beside two of the managers when Joe arrived and had waved him to go into the little annex room. The adrenalin was still coursing through Joe's body. He hadn't felt his senses lower much since the previous night and wasn't even aware of his body's tiredness yet. It was a literal haze. The door swung open and Madden heaved himself inside the tiny room, pushed out the chair opposite and sat down. He was a huge man – tall, but the overriding feature was his massive stomach. He was incredibly obese, though his face wasn't anywhere near as fat is it should have been, with only one large roll of flab hanging over his collar. His nickname among the workers was *slug*. He wasn't around the actual warehouse much and didn't associate with his general workforce. Joe could count the number of times on one finger that he had ever spoken to him. That morning. Madden was now towering in front of him, his fried breakfast still on his breath. He was dressed in an expensive-looking black suit with a red trim. Jimmy was in a woollen navy jumper and black jeans.

'Thanks for coming in Joseph… er Joe,' he said, peering down at a bundle of sheets.

'No problem sir.'

Madden gazed at him, his face set, his voice very deep and imposing. 'A terrible business, terrible. We're all very sorry that this happened. We have a very high health and safety record here, as you know.'

'Yes sir.'

'*Mr Madden* is fine, Joe. Now, I know you spent many hours with the police last night. I sent Bert down last night too and he provided additional information to the police department. Of course, we're keen to investigate this incident thoroughly ourselves.' He paused and placed his large hands palm down on the table in front of him. 'Hence, this,' he said lifting one hand again. 'If you will, one more time, please tell me exactly what happened.' His small, probing eyes settled somewhere on Joe's face. Joe tried to focus and get into character. But he was so very tired.

'Yes, of course Sir, er... Mr Maddden. Em... I was working upstairs – on the third floor. Lewis came up to give me a hand with some of the boxes. It was close to finishing time and we were getting tidied up. Lewis had set his box cutter on the floor. A minute or two later he was stepping backwards and slipped on it. He fell backwards and... well that's when he fell... all the way.' Joe did his best to sound clear, yet grave.

Madden shook his head. 'A terrible thing. Terrible. It was definitely Lewis who had left the knife on the floor?'

'Yes, it was. It was just one of the shared box cutters.'

'Uh huh,' he said absently, jotting down notes with a fountain pen. 'And what happened next?'

'I uh... well I was shocked. I couldn't believe it. I looked down at him, he looked awful. Then I ran down the stairs and went to him. I checked his pulse. I couldn't find one. Then I called for an ambulance.'

'Okay, fine, fine. Now let's rewind just a little, shall we?' He shuffled his pages, wriggling his massive bulk as he did so. 'There hadn't been any messing around upstairs I take it? No fooling about, anything like that?'

'No, absolutely not.'

'Good. You'll forgive me having to ask these questions. And there wasn't any altercation between the two of you?'

'No, of course not. Sorry, I mean – definitely not, Mr Madden.

Lewis and I were work colleagues... friends.'

'Of course, of course. It's just... Well, I was speaking with the detective in charge and he mentioned some irregularities in the injuries.'

'Irregularities?' Joe's stomach gave a little flip and he pressed his palms down onto his knees, straightened up his back.

'There were of course many broken bones, sadly for Lewis. In both arms. But it was *unusual* that there were two upper breaks in his right arm. Apparently, it was odd that the fall caused these due to the way in which he landed.'

'Oh.' Joe licked his lips and shrugged, attempting to look confused. 'I don't know about that. The way he fell though Mr Madden, it was an awful fall. His body was battered around. He hit off a full pallet of boxes down there too below before finally hitting the ground. I guess that's why he had so many breaks.'

'But you didn't actually see that happen, did you?'

Joe paused, licking his lips again. 'I just surmised from how he looked when I looked out through the hatch. It would make sense.'

Keep to as many facts as you can, he reminded himself. Tiredness was beginning to creep in further and the general feeling of being severely under par.

Don't get caught out in a lie.

'Yes, quite. Now, was it unusual that the door was left open? Should it not have been closed, given that you were not using the forklift at the time, I understand?'

'We had been using it just before and might have needed to lift out a few more pallets before we finished. It isn't the usual practice to close it inbetween use.'

'Mmmmm, maybe it should be,' Madden muttered thoughtfully. He made a few more marks on his page.

Joe's confidence was growing again. He seemed to be buying it okay. Joe was due to meet Jessica and the team later for a coffee and to plan out the next few weeks of filming.

How the hell am I gonna do that?

Somehow he'd have to get himself into the right frame of mind for it.

'I assume that given the chance, Lewis would corroborate all of this fully?'

Joe gave him a quizzical look, briefly rubbed a hand over his face. 'Yes, I mean if it had been possible. But... Lewis is dead. I understood that he was in a coma last night and was slipping away?'

'No, Lewis is very much still with us. The doctors had induced the coma, but his body is responding very well. Impossible to know how his brain is, you understand. They are allowing him to slowly come out of it. He's still unconscious, but they hope he will wake up in a day or two.'

Joe swallowed hard. 'That's fantastic news.'

Chapter 22

Jessica and Lucy spent the morning filming with Martha and Jed – the two actors playing Ashleigh and Will. They followed the pair around Manhattan, getting shots of them walking around the city holding hands, embracing. It would be all good pick-up shots for during voice overs and for flashbacks. Jessica was pleased with their progress and sent the two on their way just before lunch, happy with what they had in the can. Jessica had needed to operate the second camera herself. Charlie's mother in California had had a fall and he'd taken a plane out that morning to go and visit her. He promised he'd be back before the end of the week to film with David Mercer. Sing Sing had agreed to let them bring two cameras to the next interview with up to three team members this time. Charlie was particularly pleased about this. Jessica had told him to take whatever time he needed, but hoped he'd be back for the interview.

'Lunch time, Jess?' said Lucy.

'Abso-flippin'-lutely. My shout.'

They stopped off at a little diner where Jessica loved the pancake stacks. They both wolfed down a portion, dripping in pure Canadian syrup, followed by coffees.

Lucy checked her watch. 'I guess we'd better be off soon – we meeting Joe at two?'

'Yeah- don't worry – it's only about a five or ten minute walk from here. We'll leave the van and come back for it, sure.'

'Sounds good. Time for a quick smoke?'

'Of course – you go on ahead and I'll settle up.'

'Thanks, Jess.'

A light drizzle came on as they walked the block to the other café. It was a large Starbucks and they saw Joe seated at a table near the counter with a large mug of coffee in front of him. He looked deep in thought. They gave him a little wave as they took their place at the end of a short queue. He waved back.

'He looks wrecked,' whispered Jessica.

'I think he looks alright,' Lucy said, grinning. Jessica shook her head, pushing her bangs away from her face before ordering them two more coffees.

'Joe, how you doing?' Lucy said, as they came over with their drinks.

'Fine, fine, how are you both?'

They exchanged pleasantries as they sat down on two of the three spare chairs. They both set their handbags down on the empty seat.

'I'm sure you're tired after yesterday,' Lucy said.

'What? Sorry?'

'Having two shifts and an afternoon of filming.' She increased her voice, the café noisy with the buzzing of coffee grinders and chatter of highly-caffeinated customers.

'Oh yeah, no I'm fine.' His eyes were bloodshot, but he smiled weakly.

'Was your shift afterwards okay?' Jessica said blowing over the top of her mug.

'Yeah, yeah it was okay – nothing too eventful.'

'Good, so let's get planning out our next few dates,' she said, keen to move the conversation along.

Lucy lifted out a large diary from her bag and they began thrashing out a schedule for the next few weeks. Jessica began entering the information into her phone calendar. Then her cell began to beep.

'Sorry, I better take this… Patrick? How are you?'

She nodded an apology to them both as she listened, turning to the side.

'Oh… oh no. Crap. Is there no movement on that?'

Her face fell. She straightened out her tights absently. 'Uh huh. No, I understand. Hold on one second would you? I'm here with Lucy and Joe… one of the actors. Thanks Patrick.' She held the phone down against her left palm. 'The frigging prison is changing up our schedule. Seems they're closed to additional visitors from day after tomorrow, for at least three weeks. The Union's in a dispute about the prison guards' pay or something. There's not enough staff, some are out on strike. Hold on a sec.'

Joe and Lucy shared a look of concern. Joe took a long drink of his coffee.

'Yeah, sorry Patrick. The thing is – I could do tomorrow, Lucy too, I think,' she said, raising her eyebrows at Lucy. Lucy nodded a yes. 'Yeah, Lucy too. But we were gonna have Charlie on the second camera. It's tricky if I do it myself while interviewing. His Mom fell and he's had to fly out to her for a few days. Yeah, uhuh. I don't know – I'll have to have a think.'

Joe leaned in towards Jessica and spoke in a low voice. 'Jessica, sorry – if you want – I'm free tomorrow. I could work one of the cameras if you show me what to do.'

'Sorry – one second, Patrick... Do you think so?' She thought for a moment, weighing up their options.

'I could help him with it,' Lucy offered.

'Well... yeah thanks Joe – we could make it work.' She put the phone back to her ear. 'Patrick? Yeah, I'm sorry to leave you hanging – we can make it work. Joe can help us out – I'll sort it. Tell them yes.'

She talked on for another minute before hanging up.

'Joe, you're a lifesaver. Thank you. We'll set it all up, you'll just have to keep an eye on the frame, maybe zoom in a couple times.'

Jessica felt apprehensive, but glad that there was work around, even if it wasn't ideal. Joe's demeanour had certainly changed, now he seemed wide awake.

'No problem. I'll be glad to do it. It'll be interesting to meet the man himself,' he said.

Joe smiled at them broadly. There was something in it that made Jessica feel strangely uncomfortable.

Chapter 23

Joe strode past a cluster of ambulances and two cop cars. It was dark, but the short walk towards the hospital doors was lit by the artificial illumination from within. The rain was coming down hard, bouncing off the blacktop. Jimmy kept his head angled down as he passed through the automatic doors, weaving through smokers in dressing gowns puffing beside the "No Smoking" signs. Inside was filled with the frantic hubbub of phones ringing, visitors crammed into every seat, nurses scattered around and porters pushing patients in wheelchairs. Joe eyed the bustling reception area and strode towards it. There was a queue of ten or fifteen in front of the large desk, manned by three receptionists. He walked purposely to the third one – an oval-faced woman with glasses and a friendly face. He waited patiently as the request of the man at the front of the queue was dealt with before he ambled away.

'Yes officer, can I help you?' said the receptionist.

Joe was dressed in his complete police uniform. His holster also contained a gun, but it wasn't the dummy one he had been given.

'Yes, thank you. Sorry to jump the queue. I don't have a lot of time. Could you please tell me the location of one of your patients please? The name is Lewis Flynn.'

'Yes of course, just a moment sir.'

She clicked away at her computer. Joe smiled on, tapping the desk lightly with a finger. He kept his head low. He knew there was no chance of avoiding security cameras, but he might be able to sufficiently conceal his face, if it was needed.

'Sorry to keep you officer. The patient is on Floor 6, Wing 3, Side Room 4.'

'Much appreciated Ma'am, thank you,' he said, tipping his cap.

Joe headed off at speed towards the elevators. As he waited on one arriving beside an anxious looking couple, an NYPD cop walked towards him. He noticed him take in his own Cold Spring police uniform. Joe gave him a little nod and received one in return as the cop walked on by and down another hallway. The elevator beeped open and he stepped inside, pressing the button for six. Four other people were already inside and shuffled to the side wall as he entered and turned to face the doors. The doors shut. Three, four five.

No one spoke; all consumed by their personal troubles.

Christ.

He was so tired. What a few days it had been. But this needed to be done. It needed done *now*. No loose ends. Then maybe he could think about tomorrow. What a joy that would be. Actually interviewing the man he had framed and sent to prison. But that was later. He needed every ounce of energy and concentration now.

The door opened and Joe sighed and flexed his toes inside his black shoes. An elderly couple entered, the woman struggling with her walking stick. The doors shut again and the elevator hummed into action. Then it stopped again and the letter six flashed up on the display. Joe walked out into the hallway. There was a strong odour of bleach. It made him think of his last kill. He located the correct double doors leading to the ward. Inside was in semi-darkness, low lights only remaining switched on. Beyond was the sound of hushed whispers and the click of shoes padding back and forth on the solid floors. He hurried on, passing two bays where most of the patients appeared to be asleep. He then moved to pass a small reception area with a locked medicine cabinet on wheels in front of it.

'Can I help you?' came a voice, bringing Joe to an abrupt halt. He turned to find a thin Hispanic nurse carrying a pile of files. She set them heavily down onto the counter.

'No, I'm okay, thanks, I know where I'm going – I was here earlier,' Joe said, smiling and giving her a little wave. She nodded a flustered acceptance and turned back to her stack of files.

Joe pressed on, reading the numbers on the doors quickly as he went by. He passed by another bay, then just beyond it on the right-hand side was the door he sought. He stopped and looked through the strip of glass in the door. Inside, lit by a single dull light fixture on the wall, lay Lewis. He was lying in an electronic hospital bed, crisp white sheets pulled up to his neck. Lewis was hooked up to several monitors that were cheeping quietly, yet insistently, beside him. Joe checked over his shoulder. Nobody was paying him any attention. He pushed open the door and crept inside, the beeping noise no longer muffled. He crossed the small room and peered down on Lewis. His bruised face was grey, his eyes closed. Joe could make out the plaster from a cast on his right arm. Joe glanced back at the door. The hushed hubbub continued innocently beyond. He moved in closer. The beeping from the monitors seemed to up their pitch a notch further. He pulled a white handkerchief from his trouser pocket. He half expected Lewis to open his eyes, to glare at him, to fight him. But that only happened in the movies. Joe draped the handkerchief over his palm, then brought his hand down, covering Lewis's mouth and nose, squeezing them closed. A guttural noise came from Lewis's throat and he would have sworn that he grimaced. The numbers of the monitor beside him began to drop. As he squeezed, the numbers on the other monitor began falling too. Lewis's face reddened as Joe continued to suffocate him, pressing down tightly, but not wanting to leave any marks. He glanced anxiously back at the door as footsteps grew closer. They thundered outside the door, then walked on, disappearing down the corridor. The numbers continued to fall and now turned red. More dreadful noises escaped from somewhere inside Lewis. Now one monitor started to chirp louder, a warning. He gave one final squeeze before pulling the handkerchief away and stuffed it back into his pocket. He backed away as the second monitor flatlined and he could hear an alarm go off somewhere outside the room.

Probably the nurses' station.

He gave one final look towards Lewis, then rushed across the room, pulled the door open and hurried outside. He set off back down the hallway. The alarm could be heard buzzing further along in the other direction. As he approached the exit to the ward he glanced back as a team of nurses scurried across the hallway behind him, rushing into Lewis's room.

Chapter 24

Jessica sat eating a maple doughnut at her desk, checking her emails. She bad brought in a box of them from Tim Horton's. It was half-ten and they would have to leave soon for Sing Sing. Lucy was outside having a smoke and Bev was flicking through a copy of *The Post*.

'Going to be another Wall Street crash in our lifetime, them folks reckon,' Bev said in-between mouthfuls of a chocolate dip. 'Your lifetime at any rate,' she added, rolling her eyes.

'You're still a young woman, Bev.'

'Is that right, honey? I have bras older than you.'

Jessica guffawed; Bev had a way of cracking her up in that dry, no nonsense way she had.

'Say, doesn't that young guy Joe work over on that Havlin warehouse across town?'

'Yeah, I think so, why?'

'One of the workers fell two storeys out a loading door two nights ago. He died in hospital last night.'

'That's awful. Does it give a name?'

'No, sweetie. What a way to go.'

'Well it can't have been Joe at least – he was with us yesterday. That's terrible, though.' Jessica looked off in the middle distance towards the cluttered wall of notes and photographs. 'Funny he didn't mention anything though,' she said, more to herself.

Bev gave a little nod, continuing with her reading. Then she gave a snort. 'Ha –apparently my block is officially becoming *gentrified*. They say it's the next big area for being pulled up. Larry'll be pleased. We're moving up in the world and don't have to even step out the front door.'

Jessica smiled, but she wasn't really paying attention anymore.

After Lucy came back inside, they packed up their things and got ready to go. It took two trips to load up the van, before they said cheerio to Bev. Then they drove across town to pick up Joe as arranged.

'Sweet– nice spot,' Lucy said, raising an eyebrow at the brownstones. She slipped out her lipstick from her handbag and began reapplying it.

'Yeah, they do look nice,' Jessica said evenly, pulling up in a space between two station wagons. She was surprised that Joe could afford to live somewhere like this.

Bang!

Jessica jumped, knocking her head on the roof of the van.

'Oww!'

Joe was standing outside after banging on the glass, neither of them having seen him run up.

'Shit, Jess, you're jumpy today,' Lucy said, leaning over and pressing the central locking button.

'Sorry I scared you,' Joe said, hopping onto the back.

'Hi Joe, no worries, I was miles away. How are you?' Jessica said, starting up the engine.

Joe and Lucy started into a jovial conversation as Jessica concentrated on her driving. She tried blocking out most of the conversation, nodding along when sensing they needed her input. Her thoughts were cloudy. She clicked her tongue and tried to focus. She went through the questions in her head and how she hoped the interview would develop. The conversation became more muted all round as they grew closer, Sing Sing appearing on the horizon. Jessica watched Joe in the rearview mirror as they approached. He gazed ahead, his eyes fixed, a smile playing at the sides of his mouth. He was probably excited to be part of the actual filming. She was grateful that his being there meant the interview could go ahead. But still, she had more questions about him than answers. With Joe's help they managed to carry everything in one trip across to the main building. He walked at the back of them quietly as they were led along a hall and were briefed again by the Assistant Warden. Joe nodded and smiled a little nervously as he was informed of the rules and protocols. Jessica felt uneasy, as the warden went mechanically through everything she had already sat through before. She began questioning her decision to bring the interview forward, using Joe instead of Charlie. She couldn't afford for it to have any hitches. The first time around she had already made a misstep with David. She pushed this aside, reminding herself that all Joe had to do was point the camera and listen, keeping quiet. This time a guard marched them to a slightly larger meeting room painted a pastel yellow colour. They were left to set up and she and Lucy went about it workmanlike. Joe tried to make himself useful, passing them leads and opening up the boom stand, struggling to work the clasps.

'Well this is weird,' Joe said with a burgeoning smile.

'Right? It sure is,' Lucy said, getting onto her knees and helping him with the stand.

In fifteen minutes they were all set and Joe had been given a three minute crash course in cinematography. Jessica sat in the middle of the table with her files in front of her. Joe was to her right with a camera angled at head height, the boom further over to the right, the mike hanging over them towards the centre. Lucy sat on one of the tea-stained blue fabric chairs, a little back from the table, shooting a wider angle. Suddenly there was a click as a key card was swiped and a well-built and stocky guard entered with David Mercer close behind him.

'Hello folks,' the guard said with a friendly Texan accent.

'Hi,' said Jessica, standing. 'Hello David.'

'Hello Jessica, Lucy,' David said in his deep, warm voice. He looked much the same as last time, save for a more pronounced six o'clock shadow on his face.

'David, this is Joe,' Jessica said, turning at right angles and indicating Joe.

'Hello Joe,' said David, taking his seat. The guard took his position up by the door.

'Hello Mr Mercer,' Joe said. 'Very pleased to meet you.'

'Likewise.' David gave him a half smile, then tilted his head to the guard. 'This is Clarke. He's one of the good guys.' He shared a wry smile with the guard.

'Aww I don't know about that,' he drawled. 'There's many in here would disagree with you. I'm a good guy to those who don't give me too much bother. David here's one of those.'

'Nice to meet you, Clarke,' Jessica said. 'Thanks for your time.'

'It beats being on the deck,' he said nodding to the door. 'My pleasure Ma'am.'

Jessica asked David how he had been and they exchanged pleasantries. Lucy asked him about his appeal work and he talked for a few minutes about his slow but steady progress with his lawyer.

'It brings me on quite nicely to what I want to focus on today, if that's alright with you David,' Jessica said, feeling it was the right moment to begin in earnest. 'I want you to tell me in your own words about what you see as the main flaws in the prosecutor's case.'

'Aside from my innocence?' David said, his voice pitched a notch higher.

'Yes,' Jessica said, returning his smile. 'Other than that.'

'Alright then. Are we rolling?'

'We sure are,' said Jessica.

He shut his eyes for a moment as if selecting the correct file from a cabinet inside his brain. The lightness about him immediately faded. He blew out his cheeks.

'Okay. I think they made up their mind early on... the cops. I never stood a chance.' His eyes grew wide and deep and glistened as they stared into Jessica's. Joe swallowed hard beside her. Lucy looked down into her viewfinder.

'Because of the blood on your clothes, David? Because you found them?' Jessica asked.

'Yeah, maybe because of that too,' he said, his voice low and clear. 'But mostly 'cause I was black.'

Jessica nodded sympathetically. 'Have you any evidence of racism in the case, David?' she pressed as gently as possible.

'Have I any evidence of racism in the United States Police?' He gave a hollow chuckle, anger sparkling within his dilating pupils. 'It's like have I any evidence that the sky is blue. Any evidence that if I punch myself in the face, it's gonna damn well hurt? It ain't no secret that there's racism in the police all over. George Floyd, Freddie Gray, Amadou Diallo, Eric Garner, Michael Brown. Heck, I could list names all day.'

'But any evidence in *your* case specifically?' Jessica probed further.

He sighed. 'Yes and no. We've uncovered anecdotal evidence that some of the officers involved were racist – right wing bull on some of their Twitter accounts, one disciplined a few years ago for calling a brother a *nigger* while he had his knee in his ass. Nothing concrete about me specifically, not really. But was I treated the same as a white boy would be in the same situation? Uh-uh. Can I prove that? Nope. What I can try and prove is where police made stuff up. Misleading, lying, heck, even planting evidence.'

'They planted false evidence? You have proof that they perverted the course of justice?'

'Hell, yes. The whole system's messed up.' David turned in his seat to the guard. 'Sorry brother.'

Clarke shrugged and smiled out one side of his mouth. 'I ain't no cop.'

'Okay David,' Jessica said, trying to keep him on track. 'Tell us where you think the police haven't played fair. Tell us about this planted evidence. I assume this will be part of your appeal request?'

It was going well, already this was all great footage. She could imagine exactly how they could thread it together later with some of the other material. She knew what the claims of police corruption were, but to have it told clearly from David himself would be vital for the documentary. Hopefully later she would be able to splice it along with an interview from his attorney.

David clasped his hands together. 'Alright. First off. Why didn't they seal up the house properly? Much of my house. My garden? Crucial forensics could have been saved. That mightn't have been intentional – just could've been sloppy. But they figured it was me from the start. That's *why* many things weren't done. There was no effort to look more widely. At best there was an in-built racism that fingered me for the murders. They secured *some* evidence, spoke to neighbours. That was about the height of it. And what transpired was they mostly asked them 'bout my relationship with my daughter. And the house – we couldn't bear to sleep in it, but they failed to properly search the rest of it. After time we returned.

All kinds of people passed through our place again after that. After a few weeks it was clear I was the one in their sights. By then the other evidence couldn't be used.'

'What evidence specifically are you referring to, David?' Jessica asked evenly. She glanced at Lucy and Joe to check the cameras were rolling and still positioned correctly. David had been animated as he spoke, moving back and forth in his seat. It looked as if Joe's camera was no longer centred. Joe sat staring still at David, his eyes set and his face pale. She gave him a look and nodded at the camera. Joe bolted upright, swallowed and moved the camera a few inches on the tripod as he had been shown. He flashed her an uncertain smile.

'The blood spatter – in the hall. Once I was arrested, my attorney sought the help of various specialists. I damn near spent all our savings on it. For all the good it did. I was grieving for my only child – and on top of it all, I'm being stitched up for her death.' The pain was etched all over his face. The scars were permanent – the lines that would never leave, the lines much deeper than skin and flesh.

Jessica paused for a moment, smiling encouragingly toward David. 'Are you okay to continue?'

'Yes, yes I'm okay,' he said gruffly, waving a hand.

'Okay. Let's go back a beat if we can. Tell me about the blood spatter in the hallway.'

'We had a forensics expert examine the house, seeing as it hadn't been done properly by the cops. When he tested the walls and floors with some kind of infra-red device, he found dried blood stains on one wall. It had been wiped down, but this thing could still detect it. He found that the pattern matched the spurting that would have occurred from one of Will's fatal wounds. More than that – the blood type matched his too. But they couldn't conclusively prove it was his blood, not though DNA. And the police hadn't kept the scene secure before it was tested.'

'So what do you think happened David? Why do you think the blood was even there?'

'I think that my Ashleigh was already dead when Will got there. Somebody let him in, then killed him there in the hall. They put him upstairs with Ashleigh to make it look like they had both died up there... in her bed.'

'Why would a killer do that?' Jessica asked gently. She was in that uncomfortable spot again between being a journalist and a human being.

'To frame me, I guess.'

'And was this evidence given in court?'

'No, it was not.' David clenched and unclenched his right fist.

'Why not?'

'The evidence was *inadmissible*,' he said, almost spitting out the word. 'It was judged that the blood could have been from any time before or afterwards. The scene had long been contaminated and we couldn't get the judge to let the jury hear the evidence.'

Jessica nodded sadly, then looked down at the table, shuffling her papers. The room had become very quiet. Lucy sat rigidly, operating her camera, while Joe was now bent over awkwardly, concentrating on watching David through the viewfinder. At the door, the guard sat hunched over his knees, his expression sombre.

Jessica licked her lips, fearing how her next question would be received. 'I'd like to talk about the knife that was found, David.'

David shook his head, springing back in his chair, bolt upright. 'The knife that was *planted* there.'

'It was your knife, is that correct?' Jessica said, keeping her tone even.

'It was my knife – but it wasn't me who left it there.'

Jessica referred to her notes, though she didn't need to. She wanted to slow things down a little. 'The knife was *allegedly* discovered in your garden – in some shrubs – is that right?'

'Yeah – that's where they said they found it. Two weeks after my daughter was murdered. I mean – what kind of idiot would I be? I'd kill two people with my own knife – in my own house, then throw it my own damn garden? And leave it there for anyone to find?'

'It says in the discovery that it was buried in the garden?' Jessica said, again referring to her notes and going cautiously. 'There was also blood on it – is that right?'

David sighed again, rubbed a hand over his stubble.

Jessica set down her sheets and leaned over the table. 'I have to ask these things, David, I'm sorry – I have to go over the evidence. I'm sorry – I realise it must be so frustrating.'

He looked at Jessica, then his face eased and he blew out his cheeks again.

'No, I'm sorry – I know you have to ask these things. I don't mean to get... flustered.'

'You're doing great, David. You're doing fine. I can't begin to imagine how painful this is to talk about.' She meant it too. Though she feared she would already look too biased in his direction. It could all be edited of course. But Jessica wanted to still keep an open mind herself. But her gut screamed at her – *this man didn't do it.*

'Okay, where was I? Yeah. There was blood on it. There was blood on the knife. It was Ashleigh's blood type – different from Will's. But again they couldn't prove it was her DNA. They could have dipped it in any old sample, so long as it was her type – and they already knew what it was. Then they planted it there. It wasn't even buried. It was barely under the surface. We'd have seen it before then if it'd lay the whole time.'

'And who is the *they* you're referring to, exactly?'

'The police. The detectives on the case. They fingered me for it, built an empty case, then set me up.'

Jessica nodded.

'Why do you think they would do that to you?'

David paused. 'Because they didn't have anyone else. And because I'm black.'

Chapter 25

Joe was left in the front seat beside Jessica after they had dropped off Lucy. The two women had done most of the chatting on their way from the prison onto the highway. Joe managed to pass himself, but he did not feel right. There was too much to process. He was dazed. He had expected the interview to be a source of great satisfaction. And at the start, it had been. What he hadn't anticipated was the creeping sensation of dread as David Mercer outlined what Joe knew to be the truth about all that had happened. It was unnerving to have to sit inside a prison and have his killing exposed. It all felt suddenly *too* close. Joe began to question himself – his safety from what he had felt protected from for almost fifteen years. Too much had been going wrong recently. His murder of Lewis had left a mess and he had left himself wide open. It was reckless. And now he questioned his involvement in the documentary too. Maybe he had slipped into overconfidence and not even realised how far he had walked out onto an unstable ledge of his own creation. He had worked undetected for so long, it was too late to get sloppy now. This was his life, this was how he lived it. He detested feeling out of control from his own emotions and his failure in burying them sufficiently. He longed for the journey to be over for when he could slip off his mask and leave it at the door of his apartment, his dark cocoon.

'Thanks again for that today, Joe. You really helped us out of a spot.'

'No problem… it was really interesting. I was… glad to help.'

Jessica gave a little nod of her head as she signalled off on the intersection. 'I think we got some really good footage. I can't wait to go through it.'

'Yeah…. It went well, I think so anyway,' Joe said. He felt too hot in the car – too damn hot. Did she have to have the heating up so high? His stomach was cramped up as if in the midst of a bout of some kind of indigestion. They were only five minutes' drive now from his apartment. He picked up on a sudden stiffness in Jessica's body language.

'I heard about the terrible tragedy at your warehouse the other day, Joe,' Jessica said, angling her head towards him.

Panic drained the colour from his face. He could feel it emptying from him and he could do nothing about it. Jessica seemed to notice it too; he saw worry lines appear across her face. 'You were there that night, weren't you?' she added quietly.

It had to be a split-second decision. If he was caught out on a specific lie now it would be seen as very strange. Or he could chance it and deal with the consequences if they arose later. But he feared any more nasty shocks coming his way.

'Yeah... yeah I was. It was awful,' he said, his voice hoarse.

Jessica flashed a questioning look, then locked her eyes again on the road and didn't say anything for a few moments.

'Yes... I'm sure it was,' she said finally.

There was an uncomfortable silence before Jessica turned into the road and the conversation moved back to the usual social formalities of saying good night and agreeing when they would next see each other. As Jessica pulled away from the sidewalk, he waved meekly, then searched out his keys and traipsed up to the front door. Now he could embrace the comfort and quiet seclusion of home. But that feeling wouldn't come.

Chapter 26

Eddie purred contentedly as he lounged on Jessica's lap in her bed.

'Well that's been a weird day little man,' she said, scratching under his chin. Eddie purred deeply, slipping over onto his back.

'Did you miss Mummy, did you?' she said, smiling warmly down on him as she tickled his tummy. He soon became over stimulated and sprung up onto his legs and shook himself, before jumping down off the bed and sloping off into the living room.

'You're just like all the other men in my life, Eddie,' she said, picking up her phone and scrolling through Instagram. Nothing much there, she liked a few posts. She lifted a cup of decaf coffee off the night stand and sipped as her mind ran through the day. Another busy, challenging day, but at least the interview with David Mercer had been good. Jessica stretched out her muscles, stiff from all the lugging of equipment. Another good day of work. She was sure they had recorded good footage and she was heartened by the professional rapport growing between her and David. He had agreed to one final interview further down the line, when the prison would allow it. There was so much to process. Her mind was bubbling in particular with the theories about police corruption. She wasn't sure what to make of that angle just yet. She wished that somebody on the force would agree to be interviewed. She would love to give them a proper grilling. Early on in the planning of the documentary a junior member of the prosecution team had spoken with her, but that was it. Soon there had been built an impenetrable wall between her and the other side. At least she still had plenty of other key people booked in for interviews. She was keen to ensure that the final film would be balanced, showing all sides.

Jessica finished her coffee and set down her cup again. Her mind kept returning to Joe. What was making her feel most ill at ease with him? Again, there was something off about him during the interview. He seemed to become stranger every time she saw him. And the business about the death at the warehouse, that was plain bizarre. She had asked him the day after the fall about his shift. He had said it went fine.

Fine?

She was sure it was the same day. Yes, it was. How could he not mention it?

She closed her app and went onto Google and began to search for the news item. After a few clicks she had found it. She scanned down the article.

Yep – that was the night. A hundred percent.

She thought back to the day after. It was memorable because there had been the awkwardness the day before when he fluffed the filming in Central Park. That was the night of the accident. She had definitely asked him if his shift had been okay when she next saw him in the café. She specifically had asked him about his night! Again, how could he not mention it? Surely it was inconceivable, even if he was feeling upset about it, not to say anything. It was so weird. Maybe that's just how he was. Everyone handles things differently. She re-read the article in full. It was an overview piece from that morning.

'… Lewis Flynn had been working in the warehouse with one other member of staff. While working on the second floor, he tripped and fell to the ground below through an open hatch. The other member of staff attended to him before calling the emergency services.'

That had to be Joe. And – he had actually been the one who called 911. He was the one actually beside him when it all happened.

She read on down: '… badly injured with many broken bones and internal bleeding, he had been placed into an artificially induced coma. After initially making good progress, he sadly passed away the following night.'

Jessica sat back and rubbed a hand over her face. She didn't know what to make of it. Whatever way she looked at it, it was strange behaviour. Jessica knew she had plenty of other things she should be thinking about. Maybe she was distracting herself from the pressures of the real job in hand. She picked up her phone and ran a Google search for *Joe Ament, New York, Actor*. After the random adverts and false hits, she found the two amateur dramatic companies that Joe had put on his application form. She had already briefly visited those sites when shortlisting. But there were no others. Stranger than that was the fact of zero hits for any social media accounts. No Twitter, Instagram, not even Facebook. Most people had something – especially someone in their thirties. And the vast majority of amateur actors were very active on social media to get noticed. She went back to the two drama sites and clicked through their pages. Both were very sparsely populated, with very little recent activity.

Strange.

Her journalistic nature and her default bullshit filter both told her that something was off. She absently put the end of her cell phone in her mouth and chewed it for a second. Then took it out as she put in another Google search.

Joe Ament, New York, Criminal Convictions.

She scrolled down again through the many false hits. Then on the second search result page her search made a positive hit – '**Joe Ament**, twelve weeks community service... **conviction** for stalking.'

She suddenly felt very cold. She pulled up her duvet cover tightly around her and clicked on the link. Jessica chewed on her lip and pulled at an eyelash with her spare hand. She did that when she was nervous. An old boyfriend used to tease her that one day her eyes would be bald.

She read through the short report from a local paper – there were only a few lines. A Joe Ament had been convicted for stalking an unnamed nineteen-year-old girl, sixteen years earlier. She rubbed a clammy hand down her sheets. She felt queasy.

When she read where it happened, she almost gagged.

It was in Cold Spring.

Yes, Joe had said he was from around there originally. But he was convicted in that town for stalking? And one year before Ashleigh Mercer was murdered.

What the actual hell?

She blinked a few times, as if to make the page reload and say something different. But it didn't – it was there in black and white.

What should she make of that? She didn't know, but there was little chance of Jessica sleeping now.

Chapter 27

Joe spent the whole next day in his apartment, not stepping foot over the front door. He'd had a fitful night's sleep, not helped any by a few vodkas and lime cordial. Now he lounged about his living room in his tracksuit bottoms, t-shirt and dressing gown. It rained heavily all day – the sun never fully appearing outside. If a hot sun had been hanging high in the sky, it wouldn't have made the idea of going out much more appealing anyway. He felt displaced from his own being; uncomfortable in his own skin. It happened sometimes, but he hated it when it did. He tried to get to the root of what was bothering him, but there were too many things to unpick. He hadn't felt right for a few weeks. Now things had snowballed. He should have realised sooner that he was starting into a spiral. He had killed three people in two weeks. That alone should have told him that he was out of sync. It was way more than average. He had gotten carried away with the allure of being part of the documentary and now he had got himself into a tightly-bound twist. He felt like a jumble of a thousand electric leads, all muddled and wrapped around one another. All energy had left him and nothing seemed to make him feel any better. He tried playing some Call of Duty on his X-Box, but it didn't distract him much. He drank coffee after coffee until he felt totally wired. He sunk a few vodkas to mix it up. He sat on his sofa and flicked mindlessly through cable, finding nothing that held his attention.

Then it struck him. The thing that was his primary cause for concern. The conversation he had had with Jessica the day after pushing Lewis off the warehouse. She had asked him about his shift and he had said that it was fine.

Damn it.

He should have just told her what had happened then. Why hadn't he?

Stupid.

But would she remember? He tried to weigh it all up. She probably wouldn't match up the dates. And if she did, so what? He'd been upset, hadn't wanted to talk about it. It was too late to change it now anyway. The whole incident at the warehouse had tarnished what should have been a thrill- the interview with Mercer.

He poured himself another afternoon vodka. A large one. He didn't like drinking too much with other people, it could make him lower his guard. But he wasn't leaving the apartment today. He could do as he pleased. And maybe it would help. But he would have to keep the drinking in check. It wouldn't do to make a habit out of this. This wasn't the time to let his drinking get out of hand.

He never felt anything he would regard as *guilt* relating to his crimes. But there had been lows in his life for whatever reason. There had been one after his Auntie had died in his early twenties. When he had been finally and completely alone in the world. It had taken time for him to fully embrace that. He sat with his drink, continuing to flick through the channels, dross following dross. The vodka warmed his innards and gave him a brief headrush. But it didn't make him feel any better. He poured himself another, turned off the TV and pulled his laptop onto his knees. One thing that was always successful in distracting and comforting him: searching for a new victim. Joe knew that just like the vodka, a healthy fix for himself was not going to be found in further indulgences. He should be keeping low, dealing with all of the already pressing issues that were troubling him. He should tread cautiously. It didn't matter, he brought up Google and dived back in.

Chapter 28

Jessica woke the next day as if suffering from a hangover. What she was in fact suffering from was a terrible night's sleep. Her mind had fought against sleep. And it raged within itself to make sense of what she had discovered online. When sleep had finally come, it was restless and was only a thin veil. Nothing had been resolved. But in the cold light of day, with a coffee in her hand and Eddie on her knee, she favoured that her thinking had become all too fanciful. What was it that she even suspected? She wished she wasn't becoming fixated on Joe. She certainly didn't have time for it. She was surely seeing patterns and suspicions where it wasn't warranted. Nothing could really be proven from Joe's reactions about his colleague's accident, for a start. There was certainly nothing to suggest he had any part in it. Yes, he had been convicted of an offence, but that was the only crime she could find to link him to.

And she had looked hard.

It was sixteen years ago, he had been a very young man. People change. It wasn't as if he was likely to mention it in their first few interactions. Or ever, who would? Jessica was helming her first major project. And it was going well. It demanded her full attention. That brought its own pressure. She could make something really good. Important even. She might even play a hand in an innocent man's freedom. She wouldn't advertise it to the rest of the team. But she knew it in her heart it to be true – David Mercer was innocent.

'Charlie, so great to see you. How's your Mom?'

It was three days later, and Jessica had just picked him up in the van.

'Yeah, okay now thanks Jess,' he said, hopping in beside her, pulling the tail of his leather jacket inside before slamming the door shut. Jessica leaned over and gave him a hug. 'Gave her quite the scare, but doing fine now. Gave me a scare too. My Auntie's checkin' on her most days now. She'll be alright.'

'Good, good, great to hear. Glad to have you back.'

They caught up with each other as Jessica turned out into the traffic and along the intersection toward Brooklyn. The city seemed to have rained itself out over the last few days and the sun had returned, hanging high above the smog.

'About the interview with David...' she began, looking pained.

He raised a hand. 'Jess – don't be worrying. I understand – it was out of your hands.' He smiled warmly. Jessica was glad. Charlie could be prickly and she knew how much he wanted to be part of the interviews in Sing Sing.

'Thanks Charlie, I appreciate it. I feel really bad about it. There was really nothing I could do. But, there'll be at least one more with him and you will one hundred percent be there!' she said, smiling widely.

'Okay, okay – no problem.'

'Really though – aside from a natural disaster or act of God – we'll get you there.'

'Jesus – don't say that kind of thing in *this* town. Who knows what might happen before then.'

'That's true.'

'So, how do you reckon this'll go today?'

She blew out her cheeks. 'I don't know to be honest. I guess we'll go gently and take it from there.'

'Must have been hard on her. Really hard.'

'Yeah, the worst. I'm kinda surprised she's even meeting with us. I wanted to go easy, that's why I thought just the two of us would be best.' David's ex-wife had agreed to an interview. Jessica had originally anticipated bringing Lucy to this interview, thinking two women might be more appropriate. But she felt she owed Charlie, and wanted to keep him feeling part of the team. Besides, underneath his sometimes gruff exterior, Charlie was a softy.

Roseanne Mercer, now reverting back to her maiden name of Roseanne Simpson, had spoken a number of times on the phone with Patrick and had agreed to one short interview. She said that her daughter's story deserved to be told properly. If there was to be a documentary, then she wanted it to be done right by her daughter.

'So, she doesn't see her ex-husband at all now?'

Jessica shook her head. 'I don't think so, no.'

'And she supported him during the trial?'

'Yeah, she was by his side the whole time. Until the verdict. Maybe she had her doubts then, I don't know. I mean, she must have. The media had certainly made up their mind attend of time that it had been David.'

Charlie flicked his hair, his eyes looking thoughtful. 'She really lost everything then. God.'

'Yep. Her daughter, then her husband, even their business.'

'So, did she change sides after the verdict?'

'Well, I don't know if she changed sides exactly. I guess she just lost faith in him. Seems it was a gradual thing. Then she eventually divorced him. It's all very sad.'

Charlie nodded thoughtfully. 'You've met Mercer twice now. What do you think of him? Do you think he did it?'

Jessica checked the sat nav on her phone before signalling in and pulling up behind a yellow cab. She turned to Charlie and smiled wryly.

'I'm a journalist. I'm impartial.'

Chapter 29

It was the first time Joe had been back in the warehouse since the morning after the incident. Since his interrogation in the office downstairs. Everything was much the same, apart from there being no Lewis, and instead there was a Health and Safety officer from Head Office buzzing around the place. First thing, Lenny, the regional manager, had had a brief chat with Joe, gave him the company preamble again of how he hoped he was doing okay after the incident. The couple of other workers on the floor mumbled as much too. The manager had even offered Joe some free counselling which he politely declined. Joe tried to be cordial and gracious with them all, before positioning himself in a quiet corner to work in, then popped in his headphones.

There were a huge number of boxes of wrenches that had needed to be unboxed, relabelled, polybagged and packed back up again. It was mindless, repetitive work, but it was just what Joe needed. After his wobble, he was feeling better again. He'd just needed a few days to settle down. He could see a path through clearly where things could work out with the documentary and he was also reasonably secure that he was safe with regard to Lewis's death. Best of all, he had found a couple of good potential victims on Facebook. That had settled him right down. Very promising ones too. Joe got stuck into his work. He listened to a podcast about global warming and the rise of environmentalist anarchists. They talked about The Una Bomber and how he had claimed to be an activist and not a serial killer as such. Joe wasn't convinced that that was true. It didn't matter much to him anyway. Everyone had their reasons for killing. You could dress it up whatever way you wanted. Everyone just tells themselves what they want to hear anyway. Everyone is the narrator of their own story. Joe didn't need to make excuses for himself or his actions, he knew what he was. He wasn't a psycho like Dahmer. He wasn't driven by sexual desire or rape like Bundy. But he did appreciate Bundy's intelligence and his ability to blend into society. No, Joe was his own man. And he knew who he was and what he liked. He liked killing.

Chapter 30

'Thank you again so much for allowing us to meet with you, Mrs Simpson,' Jessica said, settling down onto the sofa.

'Please, call me Roseanne,' she said softly, easing down into the chair opposite with an almost inaudible groan. Charlie was quietly setting up the camera and boom on a stand beside Jessica, so that he could sit next to her while operating it.

'Roseanne, you've got a lovely home,' Jessica said, looking around. It was tastefully decorated, with a thick patterned floral wallpaper. The furniture was comfortable, though small, as was the room. The apartment block wasn't all that much from outside, but she had made the best of it inside. On a sideboard next to the television set there were half a dozen pictures. Two were of Ashleigh as a toddler, then a teenager. In the first she clung onto a Tigger cuddly toy. In the second she struck a faux-pose, clad in skinny jeans and a Foo Fighters T-shirt. In both the earnest smile was the same. Some other pictures were of large family gatherings, all centred around a BBQ in their garden. A few metres to the side would be where the blood-soaked knife was found, or planted. There was no sign of David in any of the photographs.

'Thank you,' Roseanne said, sweeping something imaginary away as if it didn't matter any to her if her home was lovely or wasn't. Her voice was deep, but brittle. In her early sixties, she dressed in youngish clothes over her medium build. She wore brown cords and had on a red and black checked shirt. Her long hair was held back tightly in a ponytail. There were traces of a once warm and perhaps care-free face. Now it had deep lines and there was a heaviness around her brown eyes. The whole room felt heavy.

'We won't take up much of your time today, Roseanne, we think it is really important to hear from you. To hear about Ashleigh.'

Roseanne swallowed hard and her hands fidgeted together in her lap. 'I... I wasn't sure if this was a good idea. God knows I've had enough of the media and their... stories.' She sighed wearily. 'I'm sure you've seen it all; there has been much printed about us. Terrible things about our family. Most of it untrue.'

'I understand that, I agree with you. We just want to present all points of view fairly,' Jessica said, smiling supportively. 'Just take your time and talk about whatever you feel comfortable with discussing.'

'Not much of it is *comfortable*,' she said with an irritated shudder. 'But... I'll do my best.'

'Thank you,' Jessica nodded. 'Are you ready to start?'

Roseanne nodded, closing her eyes.

'Okay Charlie?' Jessica said turning to him.

'Yes, I'm ready,' he said, then gave a little smile and thumbs up to Roseanne.

'Okay then. Mrs Simpson, Roseanne, please tell us a little about your daughter Ashleigh.'

Roseanne looked forlornly into the camera, then cast her eyes towards Jessica.

'Ashleigh is... was... she was my baby girl.' She paused, on the verge of tears already. The heaviness in the room intensified.

'As a child she was very sweet. She was a real beauty.' Three tear drops fell from her eyes and she swept them quickly away. She gave a meek smile. 'Ashleigh was the first grandchild in our family. We're both from big families. There hadn't been a baby for years. She was loved and spoiled by everyone.' Her face looked worried. 'Not *spoiled*. She was *doted on* by all of our family, but it never changed her sweet nature. She grew up right, she grew into a tremendous... young lady.' Roseanne choked on the last words and began to cry quietly, whipping out a tissue from underneath her sleeve.

'Please, take your time,' Jessica said, leaning forward. 'Can I get you anything?'

'No... thank you,' she said, waving the damp tissue and stuffing it back up her cardigan sleeve. 'I'm alright.'

'If you're sure. Roseanne... there's no rush. I really don't want to make this too much more painful for you than it has to be. I don't want to ask you about the actual deaths of Ashleigh and Will.

I can only imagine how painful that is. But I would like to ask you about something else, which I know is also very raw.'

Roseanne closed her eyes and frowned, then opened them again and met Jessica's own. 'About why I left David?'

Jessica nodded.

Roseanne sighed heavily, bent her neck, then glanced toward the camera lens. 'David and I were married for many years. We had a good relationship, I mean no couple is perfect. We had our down times. But we were a team. It was one of the hardest things I've ever had to do... I loved him. We were a partnership... in everything.'

'But you supported him initially... during the trial?' Jessica said. She felt very uncomfortable. There was nothing worse than putting victims in an uncomfortable position, prying into their most personal and painful times. People who had done nothing to invite the searing hurt and permanently resounding consequences that had befallen them. Jessica realised she was pulling at her eyelashes. She took her hand away and placed it under her other in her lap.

'Yes, I did... though God knows I had my doubts, even then. It's a terrible thing to feel so... to feel like you're... betraying someone you love... your own husband.' She looked down at the floor. 'I loved him... perhaps I still do... a little.'

Roseanne blinked wildly, then dabbed at her face again. Jessica chewed her lip, looking on sympathetically.

'What made you change your mind?' Jessica asked quietly.

'It... it wasn't any one thing.' Roseanne paused and blew out her cheeks. More lines seemed to join the others across her brow. Deep wrinkles tightened on her ebony skin around her eyelids. 'Suddenly I felt as if I was... on the wrong side? You know?' she said, staring at Jessica, almost pleadingly. 'It was like I had woken up from a dream. My primary duty is to my daughter. My child. I realised that he was to blame for her not being here anymore. I felt so stupid... so *cheated*. How could I have been so blind? Why hadn't I seen what everyone else saw? The police, the DA... the jury.'

Her eyes glistened, her face racked with hurt, guilt.

'Do you have any doubts now?'

She shook her head. 'No... not really. I mean... can we ever really be sure of anything? He had never been a violent man before. But no... I think he did it. I *believe* he did it. He lost his temper. Maybe he even lost his mind for a short while. They say that can happen, don't they? In that moment of madness, whatever it was... I lost everything.'

Jessica and Charlie were silent as they drove away from the apartment.

'Are you okay?' Charlie asked after a minute.

'Yeah I guess... you?'

'Yeah. It's terrible though. It's just horrible.'

'She's right too – in a few moments her life was basically destroyed. I really feel for her – I can't imagine what that would be like.' Jessica gripped the wheel, close to tears herself.

'I guess at first she trusted her husband, figured he was being stitched up. And the racist element – you said Mercer mentioned it. About him being black?'

'Yeah he did. I maybe should have pressed him more about it.'

'Racism in the police?' Charlie said mockingly. 'Never.'

'I know – right? But I guess just because they're racist, it doesn't make him innocent.' She felt very confused. She had become so sure of David's innocence. But now here was the person closest to him. His own wife, saying he was guilty.

As Jessica made her way through Brooklyn, she tried to not let her mind wander too far. They chatted about the footage and how it could be used alongside the other material they had in the can.

'I meant to ask, Jess – how did it go with my stand-in the other day – Joe? Do I need to start looking for another job?' Charlie said with a playful smile.

'No – you're safe,' Jessica replied, a little too forcibly.

He shot her a look, his brow furrowed. 'What – did it not go well?'

'No it's not that. Like I said, the filming was good. All he had to do was keep an eye on one of the cameras. It's well – Joe himself.'

'How do you mean?'

'Well you've met him… he's just a little *off.*'

'*Off*? I suppose he's a bit eccentric, seemed okay enough to me. He was a bit huffy that day in Central Park, I suppose.'

'There's been a few times that his behaviour has been just a little bizarre, I don't know. I wouldn't say this to anyone of course – but he gives me… well, the creeps.'

Charlie screwed up his eyes, his face hardening. 'He didn't hit on you, did he?'

'No, no – nothing like that. There's just a weird vibe with him. That and a few other things. I don't know.' She glanced at Charlie and shrugged.

'Go on,' he said, still looking concerned. 'Spill it.'

Jessica told him about Joe's omission of the incident at the warehouse and about his stalking conviction.

Charlie shrugged his shoulders this time. 'I don't know, Jess. It is all a little weird, I guess. I'm not sure he's done much wrong. He was just a kid during that stalking thing, right? Are you wanting to take him off the film?'

'No, no… I mean he hasn't really done anything, you're right. And I don't want to start trying to replace him now. We've already started filming his parts. The budget will only go so far.'

'Probably best to just keep an eye on him?'

'Yeah, I guess so,' Jessica said, gazing off beyond the traffic.

Chapter 31

Joe sat near the back of the church hall of St Anthony's on the edge of The Village. The parish had recently been renovated, but the basement had not. Bare stone, damp and clutter. It looked like a strange mixture of an old set from *The Da Vinci Code* and one from *Saved By The Bell*. It was freezing inside. Colder than outside. Joe had unzipped the jacket above his jumper, but now zipped it back up again. There were about thirty people scattered on the fold-up chairs. Some had foam cups of coffee in their hands, a few munched on slightly stale biscuits. A century's worth of church clutter lay about the room on the cold, stone floor.

'We're now going to hear a few words from John. John?' said a middle-aged bearded man at the front, indicating a younger man to his side. There was a smattering of applause as John stood, taking the centre spot at the front.

'Hello everyone. I'm John and I'm an alcoholic.'

Joe rolled his eyes internally but outwardly attempted to look interested and thoughtful. As the man described his long decline into substance abuse, Joe felt as if he had stumbled into a Matthew Scudder novel. He zoned out, leaving his face as it was, as his mind travelled elsewhere. He was there for an altogether different reason. The reason was seated three rows in front of him and was called Claire. She had been one of the most promising finds on Facebook from the last few days. A twenty-nine year old receptionist, she had been going to AA for six months after finally realising she had developed an unhealthy alcohol dependency. Claire had been very open about this online. Joe's fake profile was a member of dozens of private groups, several of them devoted to AA members. She ticked most of the boxes for a potential victim. The FBI may have had detailed profiles for serial killers. But Joe had developed a comprehensive profile for potential victims. From what Joe had already gleaned, she hit many of his desired attributes: the correct age range, unattached, emotionally vulnerable, seeking company, largely alone in a big city, living far away from her family.

By himself in the row, with nobody behind him, Joe was free to watch her as much as he did the man droning on at the front. He blocked out most of the tired stereotype of a fall into addiction, echoing around the stone walls.

Who cares?

Joe couldn't stand human weakness. This basement was full of the worst of society – the weak and helpless. It disgusted him.

Pathetic.

If you're a drunk – be a drunk.

If you're a killer – be a killer.

By contrast, Claire's body language suggested that she was fully engaged with the speaker. Sitting by herself, she nodded regularly at the appropriate cues as others around also muttered their approvals. A few even whispered *Amens*. Claire kept her blue denim jacket pulled tight around her slim frame; a tartan scarf was wrapped around her neck. She was pretty, in an unremarkable kind of way, Joe thought. That bit didn't matter much. Over the years he had had several girlfriends, even some proper relationships. But each one had become too much of a distraction from his true calling. He was never all that into them. Most people seemed to need to attach themselves to a partner. Joe didn't need to attach himself to anyone. Over the last few years there had been no more relationships and he preferred it that way. He was still attracted to some women, but he didn't particularly desire them in the traditional way. Serial killers all supposedly had out of control sex drives. Joe barely had any. Instead he fantasised about what it would be like to see their last breaths exiting their bodies. That turned him on in his own way.

After twenty minutes there was a smattering of applause and the main speaker thanked John for his testimony. He then invited everyone to help themselves to another coffee and biscuit. Joe got out of his chair and hovered around the aisle for a moment. He watched as Claire also stood, standing awkwardly by her chair, her arms folded across her chest. She glanced in his direction. He gave her a little nod and she smiled at him. Joe smiled back, then made his way out through the doors. Warmer air hit him and the smoggy night smelled better than the basement odour of damp walls, cheap coffee and stale cigarettes. This kill would take a few days, slowly, gently. The first part was complete. Joe broke into a stride, heading towards the subway. He stalked along the sidewalk like a jungle cat, smiling to himself.

Chapter 32

'Roadtrip!' Lucy shouted, hopping into the van with a little air-punch and a wink.

'You bring the beers?' joked Charlie from the back.

'Obviously!'

'No drinking on the job, you two,' Jessica said with a snort, pulling back out into the traffic.

They crossed onto the highway and headed out towards FDR Drive. It was mid- morning and would take around an hour and a half to make it to Cold Spring. On the car stereo Jessica played a Motown Best Of compilation. They were all in good spirits, looking forward to filming for the first time in the town itself. Jessica had only visited once as a child and only had vague recollections of the place. Since researching the town, memories had come back to her: a family picnic, the old world architecture, an ice cream before falling asleep on the long drive back home.

As they now approached the town, there was a familiarity, more than she had expected. The 19th Century and Victorian architecture, an "old town" of "the new world", with the mountains in the backdrop – it all came back to her. Driving through the town centre, they passed by streets lined with boutiques and bespoke stores. A family with back packs including two laden down children struggled past them, the parents looking more enthusiastic than their offspring. Jessica guessed they'd be on their way to hike up Breakneck Ridge.

Jessica parked up a side street and then they went in search of coffee. They wrapped up two interviews in the morning. The first was with Ashleigh's former headmaster. The second was with one of her classmates. Both went well. They got plenty of footage that they could use. It would be good for background and introducing The Mercer family to the viewer. Both of the interviewees spoke warmly and knowledgably about Ashleigh, and about their own personal feelings of loss over her death.

People seemed more straightforward here to Jessica. And so far Jessica had found everyone she spoke to be decent, friendly. There was a different atmosphere to this place. The smell of the fresh fall breeze was cleaner, there was an obvious change of pace too. Jessica could well imagine why city folk chose to retire here, or even to commute the substantial distance to work.

'Okay, whose was the cheese and tomato?'

'Oh, that's me – thanks Jess,' Lucy said, blowing cigarette smoke away off to the side. 'Sorry, I was gasping for one.'

They had bought sandwiches and take-out coffees, and had all sat down on the grass in Dockside Park. It was mild out and sunny. They munched on their sandwiches and talked about the day so far. Some students were taking their own lunch on the hexagonal band stand off to one side. Apart from them, the park was quiet. Before stopping for a late lunch they had also taken some stock footage of the park and the small town centre. The only other interview remaining was with a former neighbour of the Mercer family.

'Poor Bev – stuck in the office,' Charlie said, staring happily off towards the Hudson in the background.

'I know – poor Bev, we'll pick her up a Danish before we go. These sandwiches are yum by the way, Jess,' said Lucy.

Jessica smiled at them both, a little distracted by an email on her phone.

'Sorry, just a sec guys, just have to reply to a few emails.'

It was from Patrick. He had done his best to not sound alarmist, but it appeared that one of the primary funders had pulled out from the production. He had said it wasn't too much to worry about, but of course Jessica immediately did just that. Patrick said he didn't want to interrupt her day's filming, but asked if she would ring him that evening and he could fill her in properly. The email was only a paragraph long, but he did say that this may now reduce the filming schedule by a little. Jessica quickly typed back a response.

Hi Patrick,

Thanks for the email. Oh dear – sorry to hear that. That's a little worrying! I'll ring you tonight of course, no problem. Let me know if you need me to call any earlier. We've one more interview, then

we'll be hitting the road again late afternoon. If we need to reduce the schedule, I'll make it work. We're ahead of time anyway.
All the best,
Jessica.

She caught herself chewing the end of her phone, then slipped it back into her handbag. The other two paused their conversation.

'All okay, Jess?' asked Lucy.

'Yeah, yeah – just I need to link in with Patrick later on. We need to go over some of the finances. Hopefully we won't be back too late.' She forced a smile.

'He'll be checkin' the receipts for our lunch,' Charlie said.

Jessica forced a smile. 'Yeah something like that.'

They packed up the equipment back into the van. It felt heavier every time. Then they set off again, refuelled, but with Jessica now feeling that her dumbbell of anxiety had been given an extra couple of weights. They drove three miles out of town to the home of Patricia Danes. It was a smart looking street. The house was a wooden structure with a decked porch out front. The paint wasn't old, the house well maintained, as were the other houses either side.

After brief introductions, Patricia led them into her back garden to a table and chairs in a neat little patio area.

'Are ya sure I can't get you sweet young things a cup of coffee. Or something stronger?' Though in her sixties, her firm black skin displayed only a few kindly wrinkles around her eyes as she smiled.

'No, honestly Patricia, but thank you,' said Jessica, taking a seat. Charlie and Lucy had set up their cameras and were ready to go.

'Call me Pat, everyone does.' Pat sat down heavily in a garden chair, sweeping her floral summery dress down over her knees.

'Okay, thank you Pat. You were a neighbour of the Mercers. Could you start by telling us a little about the family, as you knew them.'

'Yes dear, certainly,' she said, her face taking on a more severe expression, her voice annunciating more deliberately. 'I lived two doors down from the Mercers for what must have been… oh five or six years. A lovely family, lovely people. Well – far as I knew anyway.'

She talked at length about her neighbourly relationship with the family – chatting daily with them in the street and inviting each other into their homes for occasional coffees. She knew Roseanne the best, but also spoke fondly of David and Ashleigh, describing her as "a bright young thing". After around forty minutes, the interview was coming to a natural close.

'One final question please Pat, if I can. I know it's a horrible question to be asked, but do you think that David Mercer is guilty?'

Pat pursed her lips together tightly. 'Well now, a jury of his peers says he did it. Me – I'm not so sure. If he did do it?' She paused and slapped her lips together briefly. 'If he did, well I guess it would have been a moment of madness.'

A moment of madness.

There was that phrase again. Only Jessica couldn't figure it that way. It just didn't fit for her. There certainly could have been madness there, but she didn't think it had come from David.

'It's not for me to say,' Pat continued. 'Only Jesus knows truly what's in that man's heart.' She paused and her voice seemed to return to its Southern roots for a moment. 'If he did do it and he's truly sorry, then I figure that man is sufferin' already just about as bad as a man can do. An' if he didn't do it? Well then I guess he's sufferin' all the more.'

Jessica nodded at her soberly. Lucy and Charlie peered over their cameras, sensing they had everything they needed. Jessica thanked Pat very much for her time and they began packing up the equipment.

'You're very welcome sweetie. Well, that was pretty painless,' she said with a raspy chuckle. She leaned over as Jessica slid her bundle of sheets back into her bag. 'You said you had some folk used to live 'round here working as er… extras. Can I have a peek at them? Maybe it's indulgent of me but I'd like to see if I know them… I'd be interested to see too how the folk involved are being represented.' She looked a little guilty, aware that there was no hiding her nosiness. 'Ya know – if they look much like them and that. I don't know, maybe that's silly or it'll take too much of y'all's time. You folks have a long drive back this time of day.'

Jessica didn't mind at all. She got it. Of course she would want to see that, just most people mightn't have asked. 'Yes of course... I'd be glad to. It'll just be some very rough cuts though,' Jessica said, lifting over one of the cameras and clipping it from its stand. She set it down on the table and flicked over the side screen. Jessica pressed a few buttons, then tracked through some of the footage. Pat took out a pair of thick cream-rimmed glasses, set them on, and squinted at the screen.

'Ahh there we are – that's Martha – she's playing Ashleigh,' Jessica said and turned the screen to better display it for Pat.

'Awk... look at her. Lord, it's queer how much she looks like her. Bless her, poor dear Ashleigh.'

Jessica nodded sympathetically as they watched Martha walk alongside Jed, playing the part of the young couple walking hand in hand through Central Park.

'Hold on a sec, there's some footage of a lady who lived down in the town centre here twenty years ago I think,' Jessica said, pressing a few buttons, then rewinding a little; grainy images of people walking backwards across the screen.

'Oh, who's that?' Pat said, squinting up her eyes further.

Jessica paused on a still of Joe standing in Central Park.

'Him? Oh that's Joe – he's playing the part of one of the detectives.'

'Joe?' Pat said thoughtfully. She dropped down her thick-rimmed glasses to swing on the beads around her neck. She frowned at the screen.

'I reckon I know that man. Yes – he lived in Cold Spring for a time.'

Jessica zoomed in on his pixilated face.

'Joe, you say?' Then Pat clicked her fingers suddenly. 'Joe Ament?' she said with a bright smile.

'Yes, that's right – do you know him?'

'Ock yes, of course – Joe worked at the grocery store.'

'The grocery store?' Jessica repeated slowly.

'Yeah – the store at the end of our old street.'

Charlie and Lucy both looked over as they paused bagging up their stands.

'He worked in this street?' Jessica said.

'Why yes!' Pat said, amused by something in Jessica's face.

'Oh right,' Jessica said, locking eyes for a moment with Charlie. He raised both eyebrows.

'You didn't know?' Pat asked.

'No, I didn't.'

'Nice young man he was. Moved away – must've been a couple years after the murders. Sad too. He lived with his Auntie. She done had an accident, fell down her stairs and died.'

Part 2: Pieces of a Man

Chapter 33

The basement of the church wasn't quite as cold that afternoon. Joe zoned out from the speaker again. This time it was a skinhead in his late twenties talking about his last twenty days sober from drugs and alcohol. He looked strung out to Joe.

This time Joe had positioned himself at the end of a row of chairs by himself. On the far left were two middle-aged women huddled together. Claire was seated in the row right in front by herself. There weren't more than twenty people altogether in the basement, sprinkled across the dozens of fold-up plastic chairs. Joe was feeling in a better place now that those manic few days had passed. It was as if he had been struck down with a bug. It had passed, and he was almost back to full strength again. That's what he thought anyway. He had appeared to get away with the killing of Lewis and now he had to knuckle down with the documentary and not make any more mistakes. Tomorrow he was due to film the scene of the cop discovering the bodies in Cold Spring. A small studio had been booked in Manhattan over the next two days. The satisfaction in attaching himself to the documentary had returned, along with a bubbling excitement for the next day. He was also at his most content when in the midst of a new hunt. It was his comfort blanket.

When the speaker had finally finished, Joe joined in with the smattering of applause. Again the audience members were all invited to stay for a cup of supermarket instant coffee. This time Joe stayed behind. He positioned himself at the rear of the small and largely mute queue. As he scooped up a spoonful of dusty grey coffee, Claire came up alongside him and lifted a jug of lukewarm cream.

'Shall I be mother?' she asked. Her young, uncertain expression curled into a smile.

'Sure, thanks,' Joe said. 'Can I scoop you up some of this er... *coffee*?' he said, returning the smile.

'Replace one poison for another? Sure, why not.' She held out her cup.

They chatted off to the side together for a few minutes as others also split into little groups of twos and threes. Claire emitted a youthful shyness, but she also chatted openly about her family and her recent struggles with drinking too much. Joe listened intently, repeating things back to her to show he was listening. He claimed to have developed a heavy vodka dependency, which he had recently tried to put a stop to. He echoed her own feelings as he spoke of how sometimes the temptation had been too much when he had tried to stop. That he had given in. That sometimes he had really wanted to stop, but couldn't. She was easy to talk to and it wasn't difficult to manipulate the conversation to what he wanted it to be. They ended up sitting back down again, this time on seats away from everybody else. The conversation flowed easily back and forth. Joe almost forgot why he was talking to her in the first place.

Then something strange happened.

As she shared more about her own troubles, Joe spoke about his own addiction. His *real* addiction. He just replaced the word *killing* with *alcohol*.

'Look, I'm half-starved – do you fancy grabbing a burger?' she asked, fiddling with a piece of hair, before tucking it behind her ear.

'Sounds good – I could eat, for sure.'

They walked a block and found a McDonalds. It was only the middle of the afternoon and it was half-empty. They each got Big Mac meals and took a table upstairs at the window.

'My, I was ready for this,' Claire said, tucking hungrily into her burger.

'Me too.'

'God, I love the McD's curry sauces,' she said, eagerly pulling off the top of a sachet.

'McDonalds curry?' Joe said, making a face.

'Aww yeah dude, have you never tried them?'

'No.'

'You have to try it – go on – have a dip.'

110

Joe dubiously dipped a fry in the cold, yellowy sauce. He put a bit on his tongue.

'Well?'

Joe pulled a face. 'It's alright, I guess.'

'Gah, it's wasted on you then,' she said playfully, pulling back the sauce and drenching her fries in it.

They worked through their meals quickly, slurping their Cokes dry at the end. The conversation was easy. There was no further talk of addiction, only the apparent understanding that it was something that they shared together.

'I guess we were hungry,' Joe said.

'I guess so.'

They both sat back, dabbing their mouths with napkins. Claire pulled out her phone and checked the screen.

'Jeez, I better be getting back. Hey, that was really fun,' she said standing. Her smile was warm and full.

'It was, it was good chatting with you.' Joe moved to stand up.

'No, don't get up,' she said gently, placing a hand over his. 'Will I see you tomorrow?' Her face reddened in a way that was endearing to Joe. 'I mean, are you going to a meeting?'

'Yeah, I think I'll be at the evening one.'

'Great, probably see you there then,' she said, walking away and giving Joe a little wave.

'See you.'

Joe watched her as she left. He watched the little bounce she had in her walk and the way she held onto her handbag strap across her chest.

Once she was out the door, he allowed his face to drop.

Chapter 34

'That seemed like a good day's work. What do you two reckon?' Charlie said, pulling one leg awkwardly over the other in the back seat of the van.

'Yep,' said Lucy, 'The interviews were great, it was real good just being in the town. Think it'll give us a grounding in the place.'

Jessica glanced at her, gave a brief shake of her head. She couldn't help but bring it up. It was her overriding thought. Jessica couldn't focus on the rest of the day. How could they just chat as if nothing was wrong?

'Did you two not think that was pretty weird about Joe?'

'What?' Lucy said briskly.

Jessica gave her a look. 'About him working in the freakin' shop at the end of their street and not thinking to mention it to us.'

'Jess, he told us he was from the town,' Lucy said defensively.

'He never told us he knew the family.'

'We don't know that he did,' Lucy said with a sigh. 'I don't get the problem.'

'It's weird is what it is. It's a pretty relevant thing to bring up. Heck – we made a point of looking for people who knew the town – he purposely didn't tell us.'

The atmosphere had grown tense. She looked back at Charlie in the back, looking awkward. Jessica cracked a window.

'I think you're making a big deal outta nothing. You're a journalist Jess – you know you can't second guess why Joe never said about it. What does it really matter?' Lucy gave a strangled laugh.

'It matters because he *chose* not to tell us. Of course he should have said something. And that's not the only thing he failed to mention.'

'What do you mean?' Lucy said quizzically.

Charlie continued to stay quiet in the back, moving his leg back from over the other and leaning forwards.

'The day after that guy died in the warehouse, I asked Joe how his shift was. He said it was fine. Then it turns out he was on shift when the guy fell.'

'How do you know he was there?'

''Cause he was the only one on shift. Then I asked him about it again the other afternoon.'

'And what did he say?'

'He said he *was* there.'

'Jeez, what's the problem then?' Lucy said with a tight smile. 'I don't know what you're getting at.'

Jessica took a hand off the wheel, gesturing irritably. 'It's that he keeps keeping things from us. I don't know why he would do that. People keep things hidden that they don't want other people to know about.'

'Seriously Jess? I don't get why you're so down on him. You're, I don't know... cold towards him.'

Jessica couldn't believe how things were escalating. She knew she should wind it down, but couldn't, or wouldn't. And she didn't like how Lucy was reacting.

'I haven't been *cold* to him, Lucy. I know how to do my job. But yes, I'm wary of him, there's something odd about that guy.' She shot an exasperated look to Charlie in the rear mirror. 'Help me out here. What do you think?'

Charlie cleared his throat, then squirmed a little on his leather seat. 'Well... I uh – I admit it is a little strange.'

'Aww come on,' said Lucy, swivelling around.

'It *is* strange, Lucy, I don't know that it means very much. But I will say that. And yeah – I think there's something off about him.'

Lucy shook her head. She turned back around, then stared out her window at the bumper-to-bumper traffic.

'And there's something else,' Jessica said, clenching and unclenching her grip on the wheel. She was struggling to keep herself in check. She'd never felt close to falling out with Lucy before, but it looked like she was now. 'Joe was convicted of stalking before.'

'He what?' Lucy snapped.

'Yeah – here in Cold Spring. A year before the murders.'

'Jesus – how do you know this?' Lucy said.

Jessica shrugged. 'I was Googling him.

Lucy snorted. 'Do you *Google* all of us? I mean, fuck.'

'What? Lucy, it's not *my* fault if he's not on the level, don't shoot the messenger,' Jessica said, failing to hide the frustration in her voice.

'Come on girls, let's not argue about it. We've had a good day,' Charlie offered.

Lucy glared back at him.

'So he was caught for stalking. When he was what – twenty? What does it matter? What is it you're actually suggesting about him? You've got this weird downer on him, Jess.'

Jessica blew out heavily. She wasn't getting anywhere and it wasn't the time to verbalise what exactly it was she did think. More than that – she didn't even know herself.

'I guess we'll agree to disagree. But I'm not happy with him on board. It's too late now anyway, so let's just make the best of it we can.'

There was virtual silence for the rest of the drive back to the city. Everyone was uncomfortable; nothing was resolved before they each went their separate ways.

'Hi Patrick, I hope it's a good time?'

Jessica had wolfed down a pre-bought salad and was now seated at her small living room table. It was a little after seven. She was exhausted. She was frustrated. And now she was worried again about the money situation.

'Hi Jess, yes it's fine, just a second.' His voice trailed off as it sounded like he was sitting down. She thought she heard a grunt. He sounded *older*. In many ways, Jessica often thought of him as almost ageless. 'Sorry,' he said catching his breath. 'How did you get on today, Jess?'

Jessica made a face, ran a hand through her bangs. 'It went well, Patrick. We got the interviews and footage we wanted. It was good getting a feel for the place, ya know?'

'Good, good. Jess, I can hear you sound worried, so I'll cut to the chase. Evan – you know from "Bertrund-Chase"? He rang me first thing. He was quite frank really. It's nothing to do with the film, they would have loved to continue to back us, but they simply cannot.'

'Okay, right…' Jessica said hesitantly.

'They crunched their quarter-year figures and things aren't looking very good for them. They're not quite calling in the administrators yet, but things are not rosy either. The bottom line is they can't afford to put up the remaining money.'

'They're not pulling out altogether?'

'No, it's complicated. They are already tied in for a certain number of points on the film that they're already all paid up for. We have a contract rolling from month to month, with the option and up til now *expectation*, of buying in again for the following month. Unfortunately, the situation is such that they can't afford to put anything else into the film for the foreseeable.'

Jessica's heart was hammering. She got up and crossed into the kitchen in search of wine. 'So, what does that mean in practice?'

'Well… it means tightening our belts. Quite considerably.'

'What are we talking here?'

'Well, I know we can't really afford to take anyone off of pay roll.'

'God, I hope not. We're small enough as it is. We're not even paying the extras.'

'I appreciate that. No, that shouldn't be necessary. But in terms of the cost of pay roll for the next few months, and any other large costs, we need to make major cuts. Really tighten our belts. In terms of filming time, to be candid – we'll need to cut it in half.'

'Oh, God, right.' Jessica sat back down and poured herself a glass.

'But you're ahead of schedule already, isn't that right?'

'Yeah, we are. I guess we won't have the luxury of re-shoots and extra editing time.'

'I'd advise you to try and get everything else filmed in the next ten to fourteen.'

'Oh right, okay.' She breathed out heavily, working the schedule through in her head. Pragmatically, she could half-visualise a route forward. 'We can do that Patrick. We've got into a good stride.

The team's working well together.' She thought of Lucy and her stomach did a little flip.

'Good, that's good, Jess. Another thing though. I was looking through the budget. The other biggest cost outside of salaries is these three days of filming at the studio. I'm sorry, but we're gonna need to cut it to one.'

'Crap, really? We start in the morning. We have to do it all in the one day, you're sure?'

'I'm afraid so. Max – the studio rep, owed me a favour. I took the liberty of contacting them. They've squared it that we'll only use it tomorrow and they won't charge us a late fee on the other two days. Alright?'

'Oh. You did?' She took another sip of cool but sharp Australian Chardonnay.

'I'm sorry – I don't mean to interfere – you know it's not my usual style. We really have no choice. Can you make it work?'

'Yeah, yeah I know Patrick, it's not your fault. It is what it is.' Jessica set down her glass and pulled out her laptop and flicked it on. 'I'll make it work.'

After the call, Jessica made herself a coffee and started work on her computer. There was a text message waiting from her ex on her phone. He had been texting her a few times since they ran into each other. She was happy to remain friends, but these texts were becoming too regular. She hadn't time to think about *them* or if they might be worth another shot. She opened up a spreadsheet, then put through a call to Charlie. It was twelve hours until they needed to begin filming three days of footage into one. They had a lot to discuss. It would be a late one, she had much to consider and organise. The issues with Joe would have to wait. Tomorrow she needed him.

Chapter 35

Joe was stood outside the studio at nine thirty am. He had driven this morning and parked it in the private bay. It was partly to avoid the subway rush hour and partly to give the car a run out. He tried to do that every couple weeks. Sometime he might need to get some place in a hurry and he couldn't afford for it to cut out on him. The whitewashed exterior of the small building at the end of the block had a small information plaque and a buzzer. Joe found the number on it for reception and pressed the button. A bubbly front-of-house girl welcomed him in and pointed him in the direction of the elevator, telling him the team were on the third floor. He strode across the thick carpet of the long hallway, the walls lined with autographed photographs of actors and directors.

'Hiya Joe, welcome to the madhouse,' Lucy said, struggling past with a rug under her arm.

He stepped out of the elevator, smoothed down the lapels of his cop jacket. 'Thanks. You have the right to remain insane.' They shared a quick smile.

'C'mon through,' she said.

'Lemme help you with that,' Joe said, taking an end of the rug.

They walked through an empty reception area and into another area with two separate rooms. He could see right into the actual studio – a mock-up of a bedroom, with cameras positioned and leads trailing out through the doorway. Beside it was a narrow control room with three monitors on desks with accompanying swivel chairs.

'This is the real deal, huh?' said Lucy, pulling the rug back under her arm.

'Yeah, looks that way.'

She led him first into the studio, setting down the rug in the corner.

'Hi Joe,' said Charlie from down on his knees, fiddling with wires behind one of the cameras.

'Alright, Charlie?'

'Hi, sorry, don't mind us.'

Joe's face fell as he was face to face with a black couple dripping in blood, blocking his way. Martha grinned as she squeezed past, Jed following, giving Joe a wink.

'They look good, right?' said Lucy, giving Joe a little shove. 'You look like you've seen a ghost.'

'God, yeah – good make up job.'

This topped all of the unworldliness of the other parts of the filming so far, even meeting Mercer. It was like the biggest trip of all time. Joe looked into the set. Then his eyes *surveyed* the room. He couldn't believe it. They had dressed the room closely to the way Ashleigh's room had been. Really close. That room was one image that had never faded. He could barely believe it. Memories of the real room flooded through his mind.

'It's just like it, isn't it?' Charlie said, moving towards him.

'What?'

'Just like the photos of her room.'

'Oh yeah – yeah it is.' Joe swallowed, 'Is Jessica here?'

'Yeah she's about,' Lucy said flatly.

'Have a look around – we're gonna go grab a coffee before making a start,' said Charlie. 'We've been at it already for an hour and a half. D'ya want anything?'

'No, no I'm alright thanks.'

'See you in a minute,' Lucy said, plucking a cigarette from her deck.

They left him alone in the dimly-lit room.

Joe took in a deep breath, rubbed his eyes. It was some job. It really was. He took in the wrinkled Bob Marley poster hanging on the pink walls. The old hi-fi, the stacks of books and desk with assorted make up, pens and framed pictures. Joe crept across to the bed. The sheets were pulled back, soaked in blood, *or corn-syrup*, or whatever substitute had been chosen. He tensed his body as one overwhelming memory pushed into his mind.

Stabbing thrusts, down, down. Her screams.

He recalled the intense thrill it had been. He put a hand to his heart hammering in his chest, as if to quell it.

But not everything was quite as it should be. There were little things. He ran a hand fondly over the sheets. Then he pulled up the bottom fitted sheet to display the bare mattress, as it had been. He fixed the pillows. The Beyonce poster was wrong too. He knelt on the bed and cast a glance back to the door, remembering himself. Then he leaned across and pulled it off the wall, careful to bring the tac with it. He moved it a few feet further along the wall, on the other side of the bed. He smoothed it down, running the back of his hand tenderly across the sheen of the paper.

Chapter 36

Jessica froze.

She felt sick.

'Someone's just walked over my grave', isn't that what people say?

Jessica stared open mouthed at the screen.

What the heck is he doing?

Suddenly, naturally, and as if it had been staring her in the face all along, she knew.

What do I know?

Go on, say it.

'He killed them,' she whispered to herself. Fear swelled somewhere in the pit of her stomach, all but making her retch.

When she had returned from the ladies' room, Charlie and the extras were gone. But Joe had apparently arrived, now on screen. It all felt too surreal. She inched closer to the monitor. What was he doing? He was rearranging the murder scene, that's what. Because he *really* knew how it was meant to be. He had been there.

It was him. He did it.

No, that's madness.

She watched him fix the poster back onto the wall, then step away staring at it. Abruptly she ripped herself from the chair, running her hands frantically through her hair, walking over to the window. She needed fresh air. She pulled at the handle, desperate to force it open, but it wouldn't budge. She gave the handle a frustrated punch. Jessica stared outside, watching commuters hurry along, cars whizz past. Nothing was running faster than her mind. People getting on with their lives. Jessica was frightened, terrified. Had she invited a monster into their lives?

'Hi Jessica.'

She spun around.

'Joe.' Her mouth was dry. She was afraid, there was no hiding it.

His brow furrowed. 'Are you okay?'

'Yeah, fine. You... you just gave me a start.' She glanced at the monitor. He followed her gaze. Then he looked back at her, his lips apart.

Fuck.

She stepped to the side, blocking the monitor.

'The... uh room looks good, doesn't it?' she said quietly.

He just stared at her. The mask had slipped. It had fallen away. The layers of pretence had evaporated, and she was staring back at a stranger. A stranger who might be everything that she feared. Everything that any sensible human being feared.

Footsteps and chatter approached along the hall.

And just like that, the mask was back in place. 'Yeah, yeah it looks really well,' he said, averting his eyes. He acted as if he had been put on pause for a moment.

'Hi guys,' he said, smiling and greeting Lucy and Charlie as they came through the door.

'That's me all caffeinated and nicotined,' Lucy said, returning his smile. Charlie shot Jessica a questioning look. She smiled weakly back at him. She was dizzy, nauseous.

Joe continued to smile at everyone, but his eyes were almost black.

'We should get started in a few minutes,' Jessica announced, brushing past them all. She needed a minute. She went out into the hall gasping for air. She was relieved to hear the three of them continue to talk casually inside the room. It was hard to hide it all. She just needed a few seconds. It was all too confusing, it was all too much. She would need time and space to process, to think things through. At the same time she couldn't let everyone down. That couldn't be done right now. They only had this one day of filming. There was nothing for her to do right now. She needed to get this done, then she could think about Joe, think it all over properly.

Then she had an idea.

She shouldn't do it. It was the last thing she should do right now.

Jessica strode back into the room. 'Joe, I'm just locking up all of the other guy's things in the locker. Mobiles, keys. It'll keep everyone's things safe and it means no phones will be going off or anything, too.' She impressed herself with the casualness of her voice.

He paused for a moment, holding her gaze. 'Yeah, sure, thanks,' he said pulling out his keys and cell phone.

'Great,' she said breezily, locking eyes again. 'If you guys talk Joe through the shots, I'll just be a minute. Oh hi guys,' she said as the two blood-soaked extras returned too.

Could this day get any more mental?

Jessica's heart pulsed a painful beat in her chest as she hurried off down the hall. She passed through the empty reception and stopped at the grey metal lockers at the end before the fire exit. She looked down at the I-phone. It was locked and she wasn't even considering trying anything with it. She pulled out her locker key and opened the door. She placed Joe's cell in carefully with the other ones. She closed it again. Then she looked down at her sweaty hand holding Joe's bunch of keys. There was a plain black keyring with one metal band. On it was a car key fob alongside two ordinary keys. She assumed the other two were for his apartment and the building front door. She hoped they were.

Jessica stuffed his keys into her handbag and zipped it shut. Then she headed back up the hallway. As she approached she heard nervous chatter from within. She stood in the doorway, composing herself. Her mouth was dry and she felt a queasiness inside her stomach. But at least now she had a plan. More importantly than that, she had moved from a stifling flux. She had suspected something of Joe. But now if not one hundred percent certain of anything, she at least could be satisfied that she had joined a side. There was some comfort in that. Just like when she had come to the realisation that she didn't think David was responsible for the murders. Now she came to the realisation that it had been Joe.

Chapter 37

Lucy talked animatedly about the set-up for the day's filming. Joe smiled and nodded, but little was seeping into his brain. He was filtering it out. There wasn't room for anything else. Survival instinct. He needed to block out this stupid girl and think.

Jessica had watched him rearranging the room.

Stupid.

Damn stupid.

Chapter 38

Jessica avoided looking directly at Joe as she discussed the next scene with the group. She directed where the fallen lovers would lie and how Joe would enter the room and what he would say. Inside the set, she waved her hands about, telling everyone what she wanted. She actually felt a certain freedom. It wasn't her most pressing priority anymore and it was liberating to just say specifically what she wanted everyone to do. Jessica also reminded Lucy and Charlie of the background shots she wanted them to get. They'd work for a few more hours, break for lunch, then mop up any other shots they had missed. When she was finished speaking, Jessica gave Lucy a look and a friendly nod of the head to join her outside. They went into the hall, Lucy's face darkening.

'Listen Luce, we never talked about yesterday. I'm sorry if I... came on too strong.'

Lucy's face instantly softened and she placed a hand on Jessica's arm. 'I'm sorry too, Jess, we were probably both tired, ya know?' She tilted her head toward the room. 'And really – I honestly think there's nothing to worry about there.'

Jessica forced her best possible smile and nodded. 'Okay Luce, we'll see.'

Jessica went on into the control room and sat down at the monitor. She bowed her head and ran her hands through her thick scarlet hair. It needed a good brush, but she didn't care. She set her handbag up on the desk beside the monitor. She looked on at the screen as Lucy moved back from the two extras and spoke to Charlie and Joe off to one side.

There was a small microphone on a desk stand to the left with a button below it. Jessica pressed it and her voice echoed through the speakers in the studio next door.

'Okay guys, will we try a take?'

Charlie turned to the other camera and gave a thumbs up. The two on the bed lay rigid as Lucy and Charlie took up positions at their cameras. Jessica watched anxiously as Joe moved out of the room, ready to make his first walk on. This was meant to be as if it was the first time discovering the dreadful scene. He emerged into the hallway between the two rooms. Jessica looked at him and he turned to look in at her, the door lying open between them. He smiled. But it was barely that.

'Good luck Joe,' she called out to him.

He made his way back into the room as planned, one camera tracking him closely, the other with a wide lens.

Jessica watched the screen as Joe repeated this a few times, directed by Lucy in the room. After the fourth or fifth time, Jessica pressed the button down again.

'Okay guys, that was really great. Good stuff everyone. Joe, let's try a little of your dialogue. Okay, so you've spoken to a frantic David downstairs and now you're entering the scene for the first time. You're describing into your dictaphone what you're seeing. Go ahead.'

She watched Joe first cock his head, then stare into the camera. She enjoyed seeing him look uncomfortable, unsure. He looked into the lens and gave the briefest of nods.

Jessica let them go through this three or four times, with Lucy directing Joe. Joe actually did a fair job, with at least one decent take.

'Okay, great,' Jessica said speaking into the mike again. 'If you guys do some more general stuff with Joe inspecting the room, getting a few different angles etcetera. I've gotta step out for a moment to take a call from Patrick.'

'Okay Jess,' Lucy shouted toward the door, giving a thumbs up to the camera.

'Thanks guys.'

Jessica took off quickly down the hallway and over to the elevator. As she rode it down, she shuffled nervously from heel to heel. She rushed out into the street. It was cool but dry. The street was busy and she seemed to be pushing against the flow as she worked her way up the sidewalk. She had noticed a hardware store near the end of the block earlier on. But would they cut keys? She pressed on, in five minutes she was out the front of the store. 'Samson's Goods', the sign declared. She pushed open the door and it gave a little ring from a metal bell hung above inside. She passed rows of buckets, brushes and door mats as she navigated her way to the counter. A thin elderly man was behind it, talking with an elderly woman. There were tins of paint stacked up on the counter. Jessica checked her phone. She'd already been nearly ten minutes. No texts or calls anyway. She gripped the strap of her handbag slung on her shoulder tightly as she waited.

'That'll be seventy two fifty,' the man said finally. 'Call it an even seventy.'

The woman thanked him, passing him fresh crisp notes.

'I'll be right with you,' the man called across to Jessica.

'No problem, thank you.'

He packed the tins carefully into tall paper bags. Jessica stood behind nervously, desperately trying to be patient. When really she just wanted to shove the woman out of the way and get her damn key cut. Her bladder felt suddenly full as well.

Terrific.

'Is your car outside? Lemme give you a hand with those.'

'Oh thank you. You're very kind.'

Come on, seriously?

The elderly man struggled with the bags badly enough himself. The woman hurried ahead of him, opening the door.

Tring a ling.

Come on.

It had been fifteen minutes now.

Jessica watched them loading up the trunk through the glass, trying to mentally make him hurry up. Finally he heaved the woman's trunk shut and came back through the door again. The bell rang a third time, the shrill timbre grating on Jessica skin.

'Now, ma'am, what can I do you for?'

'Yes, thank you,' Jessica started breathily. 'I'd like to get some keys cut, do you do that?'

He frowned. 'Oh, no ma'am, I'm afraid we don't.'

'Shit...sorry, oh dear. Do you know anywhere close by that does?'

He looked momentarily disapproving, then looked out of the window, scratching his balding head.

'Lemme see now. Em... Ahhh yes. I think Joe Sherman does keys. He's a boot heeler – half way along the block at the corner there,' he said, casting his hand, pointing further down the road.

'Just over there at the corner?' Jessica said, stepping back toward the door, pointing.

'Yes, on the left-hand side, you can't miss it.'

'Okay, thank you, thanks very much.'

Jessica rushed out the door and along the sidewalk. 'Crap,' she muttered under her breath. She had to go for it now. She felt sick. She wanted to find a public toilet too, but that would have to wait. She pressed on. Rounding the corner, she weaved between yellow cabs, crossing the street.

Joe Sherman's Heel Bar.

And there it was. Like the promised land.

This time there was no queue. There was another oldish man behind the counter inside. In just a few minutes he had cut both the keys and was slipping them into a small brown paper bag. Jessica thanked him repeatedly, told him to keep the change, and hit the sidewalk.

She ran – off and on, as much as she could manage.

Christ – what am I doing?

Twenty-seven minutes.

Jessica rounded the corner, crossed the road, breaking into a half jog, then settling into a fast walk. She hooked out her cell phone as she went. A missed call from Lucy.

Damn.

She was out of breath and sweating all over when she finally made it to the building. She heaved open the door and rushed in, almost colliding into Joe.

'Joe!'

'Whooah.'

'Oh sorry. I... er saw I'd a missed call from Lucy, you guys getting on okay?' She struggled to catch a breath.

'Yeah fine, I think. But were you not on a call?'

She couldn't read his face.

'Yeah, I was... then I went to grab a coffee.'

Does he know I know?

127

His eyes met hers. 'Where is it?' He half smiled.

'What? Oh, I drank it already.'

'Speaking of which, Lucy said for us to go grab a quick coffee if we wanted. Can I grab my cell phone first?'

'Yeah, 'course. If you wait here, I'll nip up and grab your stuff.'

'Sure I'll come with you, save you coming back down.'

'It's no trouble, I can come back down.'

'No, I insist,' he said, holding the door for her.

'Oh... okay, thanks.'

They waited on the elevator, then Joe gestured for her to go in again first. She felt a cold chill as she brushed past him. They silently went up as the elevator ground into life. In those few seconds, locked in with him, she had never felt more frightened. When the doors opened again with a ping, he gestured for her to ahead again.

'It's just along here,' she said, moving off at a brisk pace. As she did so, she zipped open her bag, grabbed his keys, and hid them inside her closed palm.

'No rush,' she heard him say, the pace of his footsteps increasing behind her.

Finally she made it to the lockers. She balanced her handbag over her arm and fished out the locker key in one movement. Joe appeared at her side and she fumbled the key and it fell back into her bag.

'Sorry, just a sec.' She used her free hand to awkwardly retrieve it from the jumble of cosmetics, perfume and pens.

'Here we are. Watch out there, sorry Joe,' she said pushing gently into him, blocking his view of the locker with her back. Jessica pushed both hands inside, dropping in Joe's keys as she did so. Then she rifled around for his phone before bringing it out and stepping away to the side.

'There you go, do you... uh want your keys?'

'My keys? No that's okay.'

She flashed a smile towards him, before closing the door and locking it shut. Jessica pulled her bag off her shoulder to pocket the locker key. The brown bag with the new keys wrapped in cellophane inside had been bobbing at the top of her handbag.

Now the bag fell to the ground with a thud. Jessica gave a tiny gasp.

Joe bent down and picked it up, holding it aloft.

'Thanks Joe… my lunch,' she said, taking it from him.

'You wouldn't want to lose that.'

'No. I wouldn't.'

Chapter 39

Joe stood leaning against the outside wall of a drug store. He was on the corner of the block opposite the church. He had been standing there for over half an hour, watching as people struggling with various degrees of addictions ambled through the doors. Joe had a pounding headache. His good mood and optimism had been short lived. He had reverted back to a state of high agitation. Anger, frustration, fear; it was all wrapped up somewhere underneath his skin. He wanted it out and he didn't know how.

Hell.

The day had begun with high hopes for the recording. Then he was going to meet Claire and he would take her. He would take her life. It would be beautiful. He was even going to recreate Ashleigh's death as closely as possible – making it all the sweeter. Minus the boyfriend this time, of course. It would be a special kill. But now everything was going to hell. And the appetite for it had vanished. He didn't even know why he had still gone there. After the filming was finished, he had decided he wouldn't go through with it. Maybe he would never do *it* again.

Kill

He didn't have to.

Yes, there was something about that thought that pleased him. It would be hard, but maybe he would enjoy the challenge. He could change. He could be anything he wanted to be. Joe was still relatively young. Why not? Maybe he could even be... better? He knew that was a stretch too far. That wasn't it, he knew that. But something was pushing him to make a change. Was it just the fear of being caught? It didn't please him, but he accepted that was probably the simple root of it.

He had never really considered *not* killing. He went for spells when the desire was in a lull, but he had never stopped. Even when he still lived at home with his Aunt he had killed regularly. The spaces between were wider, but still constant. That was one reason why she had to go. That and getting full access to all of the inheritance. An old lady falls down the stairs and breaks her neck.

Her nephew is very upset by it, then moves on. Nobody bats an eyelid.

But now things were such a mess. He had made one mistake too many. If Jessica hadn't seen anything within him before, she surely had now. There was no hiding it this time. And she knew he knew. Somehow she knew it all – but how could she really? So what now?

'Joe?'

He jolted away from the wall, as if ripped from a deep slumber. 'Claire... hi.'

'You look frozen,' she said, patting his arm.

It was already ten minutes after the start of the meeting and he had assumed she was inside already. A light drizzle had started to fall. Joe pulled up his collar. Lucy pulled her hair away from her face and slipped up the hood on her purple zip-up fleece.

'I'm alright.'

'Are you not going in?' she said, a little out of breath.

'I uhhh, I wasn't sure.'

'You not feeling like it tonight?' she asked, titling her head.

'No, I guess not.'

'I was running late. I wasn't even sure I was gonna go in either... I hate walking in late at things, everyone looking at you... Listen to me, I'm babbling on. You weren't uhm... you weren't thinking of drinking, were you?'

Joe met her gaze, then his eyes darted away. 'Yeah, I guess I was. A little. But I decided against it.'

'Well that's something, and you haven't yet?'

'No, not yet.'

'Well don't. Please don't. How 'bout grabbing a cup of coffee with me some place anyway? We could *skip school*?' She smiled widely, pulling a comical face.

Joe couldn't think straight. His mind had never felt more overloaded or conflicted.

'Yeah sure, that sounds nice.'

'My apartment's just 'round the corner – we could get out of this rain – what d'ya think?'

'Your apartment?'

'Yeah...' she giggled playfully. 'Just coffee, I'm not gonna jump your bones.'

Joe tried a laugh. 'No, of course, sounds great.'

Within ten minutes they were seated in Lucy's small apartment. They both sat on one end of her stubby sofa. The only other furniture was a single dining chair and a small wooden table with an old LED television set on it.

'Excuse the mess –I've only just moved in,' she said, unzipping her hoody. 'Well I suppose that's a lie – it's been like a month and a half,' she said with a little laugh, stretching to lift the few empty glasses and a stack of magazines out of the way.

'You've a nice place, I've seen plenty worse. You should see mine,' he said, forcing another smile.

She gave a little shrug and got to her feet. 'So, a drink. Well – a coffee, anyway?'

'Yeah, please.'

Joe's stomach was twisted up, his head pounded and his brain was fried. He just needed to stop it all. Stop everything! It was all too much.

Claire stepped away through to the little kitchen annex. She busied herself with cups and jars, her back turned. Joe stood silently and padded to the door, watching her closely from behind.

'Do you take sugar?'

'No thanks,' he said. His voice was rough, with a serrated edge.

'Shit.' Her shoulders tensed at the closeness of his voice and she released a small, nervous giggle.

'Just a little cream?' she asked, pouring boiled water into a French press.

He watched the delicate muscles in her back work, shoulder blades arching out from her slender body.

'Yes, please,' Joe whispered.

Two steps and his feet were planted behind her own. She gasped and dropped the coffee jug. The glass smashed against the sink and black, sludgy water splashed all around the inside of the bowl.

His hands gripped around her neck. He squeezed her pale skin tight against her bones and she wheezed. He arched his own back, forcing her head lower, almost touching the sink. He wanted it to be over with quickly. And he couldn't allow her to turn her face around. He couldn't bear it. Joe squeezed with all his strength.

But this wasn't what he wanted. He had wanted to stop.

She was weak. There was no question of the outcome. She may have well as been a twig that a small child could snap between their fingers. He gave a final adrenaline-pumped squeeze, then snapped her head devastatingly to one side.

He released her body and it fell limply down to the ground.

He slumped down beside it, crying violently, his body racked by the sobs.

Chapter 40

Lucy poured herself a large glass of red wine. It was a little before four when she got home, but hell it was five o'clock somewhere, if it mattered any. She leaned back against her sofa, pulling her stockinged legs under herself. Eddie jumped onto her lap from somewhere.

'Fuck!' she said with a jolt. He froze, giving her a questioning look.

'Sorry little pal, Mummy's just a little jumpy tonight.' She stroked him with her free hand.

'What the heck is going on... ay Eddie?' she asked, tickling underneath his chin. He began purring, tilting back his head.

She took a long sip of her wine and stared out of the window at the rain, now heavy. She shook her head.

Joe. Is it him? What – a killer?

She shook her head again and took another drink. It was already pleasantly warming her stomach.

Am I just going nuts?

I stole his frigging keys.

Jesus.

She set her empty glass down and set about giving Eddie a thorough tickle.

Jessica tried ordering all of the details better in her brain. Her suspicions.

His weird reactions.

Not telling us about the warehouse death.

The stalking charge.

Working in the street of The Mercers.

A dead Auntie?

And today – whatever that was.

She tried to make better sense of it all, but everything was too cloudy and mixed up. She really needed to talk it through with someone. But who? She poured another large glass of South African Merlot. Not Lucy. In the last year, she had become something of a good friend. This was different. She couldn't talk

134

to her anymore about this. What about her other friends? Her *best friends* as she thought of them, who she had known since college. But recently she had been too busy; she could barely remember the last time she had messaged any of them, never mind seen them. Her Mom? No, she couldn't burden her with this. She'd enough to worry about, what with her Dad's heart attack two years ago. She hardly ever let him out of her sight now.

God.

She needed to phone her Mum though – she had been a bad daughter recently.

But not now.

Jessica cast it aside for the minute and flicked through her phone. There were a few work emails that could wait and unimportant updates in her Facebook groups. The news stories couldn't even distract her.

She'd never replied to Paul. Could she text him now? Would that be unfair? Just to talk. She had almost told him more about Joe the last time they had met.

One text surely wouldn't hurt.

'Hi Paul, sorry 'bout the late reply. Things have been pretty hectic. Hope you're good. Be nice to get another coffee and a catch up soon. Give me a shout, I'm pretty free the next few evenings. *Thumbs up emoji.*'

After a few minutes, a reply came through.

'Hi Jess. No probs, I know how things get. I'm working mostly days this week. I'm free tomo. Or even tonite if it's not too much short notice. *Smiley face.*'

She poured another glass of wine, thinking.

Why not?

'I'm free now, having a glass of vino. I could actually do with a chat. Chinese? x.'

She wasn't sure about the x. She sent it anyway. Jessica didn't want to lead him on, but wanted to be friendly. It did worry her. She was pleased to have the company. God knows she had to talk with somebody.

They exchanged a few more texts and he said he'd pick up the food on the way. Half an hour later Jessica reluctantly left the half-bottle of wine where it was and dragged herself up off the sofa. She flattened down her dress and picked up her phone and put on the reverse camera.

'Yuck,' she said, sticking out her tongue and throwing the phone onto her sofa. She pulled her hair back into a tight ponytail, then took out her make up bag. She set to work, just a touch up. Jessica was in the side kitchen pulling out plates and cutlery when the front door buzzer rang. She ran a fleeting hand through her hair again and crossed the room to the intercom.

'Hello?'

'Your delivery Ma'am.'

'Haha, hi Paul.'

She buzzed him up and a few minutes later there was a knock at the door. She pulled off the chain and let him in.

'Hi Jess,' he said smiling, holding up two paper bags. 'We won't go hungry.'

'Oh yum, thanks for picking it up, I'll get my purse.'

'Don't be daft.'

'Well, thank you,' she said, and leaned in and gave him a brief hug and a peck on the cheek.

He went by her with the bags toward the kitchen. She thought she saw his cheeks redden.

'It's great that we can still meet up,' she said awkwardly, before closing the door.

Maybe this was a bad idea.

They pulled out the cartons, chatting as they did so. Then they stripped off the lids and set them in a row on the coffee table in the living room. Jessica sat back down on the sofa and Paul on the chair beside her.

'Jeez, we're gonna be pigs.' she said. 'Looks yum.'

'Well, we all need a treat now and again.'

'Ain't that the truth,' Jessica said, spooning out some rice onto her plate. Paul thumbed the cap off his bottle of beer and took a swig.

'It's nice and toasty in here, it's horrible out,' he said, taking off his opened shirt, leaving a tight-fitting blue polo shirt underneath.

Jessica picked up the T.V remote and flicked on VH1 Classic on quietly in the background.

'So how's work?' she asked, hitching up her legs on the sofa and balancing her plate on her knees.

'Yeah, it's okay. I'm pretty beat. Been a couple of long eight-hour shifts. Jesus – there was this kid today. Must've only been four or five. He couldn't swim yet, but jumped in at the deep end after taking off his arm bands. His mom was way at the other side with a baby on her shoulder.'

'God– what happened?'

'The little kid sank like a stone. The mom screamed. I jumped down off my platform and dived in. It was fine, I had him straight out. He was just a bit panicked, is all. The mom too.'

'I'm sure she was. God. New York's own David Hasselhoff,' she said with a grin.

'That's me,' he said, crunching on a prawn cracker. 'So, how about you – how's work?'

She frowned, then reached for her newly-topped-up wine glass. 'That's a question.'

'The filming not going well?'

'The filming's okay. It's not that.'

'Is it the guy you were saying about – wasn't really working out, was he?'

Jessica blew out her cheeks. 'You're gonna regret asking,' she said, and took a large gulp of her wine.

Jessica told him about what had started off as a bad feeling about Joe. Then she explained about the death at the warehouse and lastly about Joe's conviction for stalking. Paul listened attentively as they finished their meals and Paul started in on another beer. Jessica's bottle of wine was nearly empty by the time they rinsed their plates and loaded them into the dishwasher. Jessica sat back down on the sofa and this time Paul sat on the edge beside her. Jessica moved on from Joe to tell him about the money issues and calls with Patrick. She'd probably already said too much. She didn't want to sound like a crazy person.

'Well, you sure have been through the ringer recently,' Paul said, and placed his hand on hers.

She looked down, trying to not exactly grimace, lightly pulling her hand away again. 'Thanks, it sure has been a weird few weeks, I don't know.'

'And then there was you and me too,' he said, locking eyes with her.

'Yeah, all of that too,' she said, looking away.

Paul moved closer. 'Let's not talk anymore about this fella Joe, he sounds like an ass. I wouldn't worry about him.'

Jessica's face hardened. 'I haven't even told you it all yet...'

'Jess...' he said, looking at her intently and placing a hand to her face.

She pulled away again. 'Paul.... don't, please...'

'C'mon Jess, we're good together,' he said, suddenly leaning in, placing his other hand firmly on her face and kissing her.

She backed off and stood up abruptly, knocking over her empty wine glass. The stem broke away from the rest. 'Jesus, Paul, I said *don't.*'

'Fucksake Jessica,' he said with a wan smile, his face like a chastised child.

'I thought you wanted to listen to me,' she said, bending down to carefully pick up the shards and placing them on the table. It made her feel lightheaded and her face already felt flushed.

'You're giving me all these mixed messages,' he said, getting up now too.

'I don't know what to tell you,' she said.

They both stood there, arms hanging at their sides.

'I better get going,' he said sullenly, walking over to pluck his coat from the back of a chair.

'You don't have to,' she said calmly, giving a shrug.

'I'm gonna go,' he said, and headed towards the door.

She followed him silently.

He pulled the door open, then turned and said, 'See you.'

'Bye Paul,' she said, and closed the door.

She turned and leaned back against the door.

'Shit!'

Chapter 41

Joe reluctantly entered in the new addition to his journal and returned it to its place on the shelf. He realised that he had been crying again and wiped a sleeve across his face.

What's the matter with me?

It was still only early evening. He had no desire to eat. He'd love to just go to sleep, but knew he wouldn't be able to. He traipsed into his living room and fixed himself a vodka. A large, straight one. He swigged half of it back. It burnt his throat. That was good. He threw the rest back and poured another. He had never felt like this after a kill before.

Really. What the hell's the matter with me?

He had felt no pleasure in the killing, but still he felt the need to go through with it. His emptions were a tangled mess. He couldn't separate them out – that still tighter jumble of cables twisted round one another. He sat down on his sofa, bringing the bottle and his glass with him. And there was something new in the mix. Something that he didn't remember feeling before.

Guilt?

Perhaps.

Yes, it must be that, how strange.

Remorse, regret?

Yes, he felt that too. But he knew given the chance, he would have done it all again. He would still have taken her life. There had some kind of realisation that killing was now in some way hurting *him*. But it hadn't been enough to make him not do it. Perhaps not so much a want to stop killing, but a fear of what may happen if he continued. He poured a smaller measure of clear vodka and threw it back quickly. Joe wasn't stupid, he realised that a desire to kill people again and again was not a normal desire to have. He had told himself before that he was in some way above the norm, a super-human perhaps. He was elevated above the norm. But he also recognised that there must be a reason why he did what he did. Joe considered himself someone very much in control over his own destiny. But to some extent he recognised that his genes and environment played a part in his shaping too. He had read enough books about serial killers to know the various theories. And there was a dark kaleidoscope of theories and types of killers. He never really believed any of them applied to him. He never even chose to fully internalise them and try to apply them to himself. Who did analyse themselves fully? Who pushed into every corner of their being objectively to view themselves? He supposed that that was why some chose to go to therapy. But that was weakness, that wasn't for him. Joe was unique. He would choose his own path, make his own choices. And more than just that, Joe knew he would kill: again, and over again. That's just how it was. He must have been kidding himself – thinking that he might stop. Had he even believed that to be possible? It had been the fear of getting caught. Well that was no reason to stop. He just had to up his game, work smarter.

After several further drinks, Joe took himself off to bed and to his surprise, tiredness took him in its grip and he drifted off to sleep. It had been deep. The resolve to embrace again fully who he was had surely something to do with it. Another sign that he should never try and stop.

He had a shift in the warehouse the next morning from nine until two. Two pints of water, a coffee and a bowl of cereal had roused him enough in the morning to force him out of his apartment. Still tired, he had considered ringing in sick. No, he didn't want to do that. He had pushed through the shift, head down, earphones in, a painful headache finally subsiding. He was due at the documentary office for recording a few overdubs at three p.m. When he got there, he was feeling a little brighter, at least well enough to cover himself. He chatted to Bev on his arrival. She even made him a large cup of coffee, which he gratefully received. Soon enough Lucy brought him into the second room, where a microphone was waiting, already hooked up.

'We should be done in about an hour or so.'

'Yes, no probs. I'm in no big rush,' he said, trying to appear keen. In a way he was. He had started this thing and he would see it all through, whatever that meant.

'You were working this morning, right? I'm sure you're tired.'

'Yeah I was, no it's fine. I'm all set.' He forced a smile.

'Okay, awesome. Here's the lines, just roughly try following them. They don't need to be exact,' she said, pushing across a typed sheet of paper. We've the whole doc roughly storyboarded out. We just need to hit some of these notes. You'll find the lines don't really connect to each other, but hopefully we know where they'll go later,' she said, and gave a taut little laugh. 'Right then, let's make a start.'

'Is Jessica not in today?'

'No, she had something she had to do.'

Chapter 42

Jessica held her cell phone to her ear, listening to the rings until she was put through to voicemail. She hung up, keeping the phone in her hand. She ran a hand through her hair. The light wind was blowing through it. She was standing on the corner of the block dressed in a purple hoody. She hovered awkwardly on the spot, then slotted the phone in her pocket, before pulling up her hood. She felt the cell begin to vibrate inside the pocket of the hoody.

Good.

'Hello, Lucy?'

'Hi Jess. Sorry – we were just recording there.'

'Oh right, sorry. Is it going okay?'

'Yes, all good. I'm just with Joe now.'

'I won't hold you up then. Just to say I won't be back in the office the rest of the day.'

'Okay Jess, no probs.'

'Alright then – I'll maybe buzz you later,' she said shortly. 'All the best, Luce.'

'No probs. See you Jess.'

Jessica dropped the phone into her handbag and rifled inside for the keys. She grasped the bunch and squeezed them tightly within her palm. She looked across at Joe's building and took in a sharp intake of breath. She crossed the road carefully between traffic. She stood at the kerb, waiting for a mother pushing a pram to pass by. There was a glare from the sun and Jessica cupped a hand above her eyes as she looked dead ahead at the building. She blinked, gripped the strap of the handbag over her shoulder and strode to the front door. As she fumbled with the keys, her heart hammered inside her chest. A drop of sweat rolled down her back beneath the hoody. Jessica did a quick check behind. She turned the key, pulled the handle and hurried into the hallway.

It worked, thank God.

Her footsteps echoed in the empty hallway and she clip-clopped slowly along. Jessica searched the walls for a floor plan but there wasn't one. She took off down the hall, looking at the door numbers as she went. She knew the apartment number was seven, but had no idea which floor it was on. She got to the end of the hall and it wasn't there. She doubled back to the foot of the stairs. It was dark beyond. It was musty and uninviting. She began to climb the staircase and a light clicked on above as it detected her movement. She felt queasy, her mouth was dry. She pressed on. At the top of the first flight, there were three directions to go. She clocked apartment six and took off along that corridor. Sure enough the next one along was Joe's. There was still nobody about. Jessica shut her eyes.

It's not too late. You could just slip back outside again, no harm done.

No, not gonna happen.

She slotted the key home into the lock, pulled the door open, stepped inside and shut the door.

Now you've crossed a line, girl.

Jessica had to force herself to catch her breath. She perched on the edge of the nearest sofa, feeling faint. Her throat felt like somebody had served her broken glass in her food.

Calm down. You're okay.

She pulled off her hood and looked around the room for the first time. A normal looking apartment. Not Buffalo Bill's basement or Ed Gein's shack; she was glad about that. Or would she had preferred if it had been more like that? Then at least she would know for sure.

Jessica stood up slowly and began to walk tentatively around the room, careful not to touch anything. It was tidy – especially for a single man. She went over to the laptop sitting on the coffee table. She picked it up and sat down on the sofa. She chewed at a rag nail then pressed the standby button on. As it booted up she asked herself what she hoped to find. A file titled "*I'm a murderer and I like it*"? The computer cheeped into life and a log-in screen popped up.

'Crap.'

What did I expect?

Who doesn't have a password?

Jessica thought carefully for a moment, hovering over the box with the cursor. This wasn't the movies and she had no idea where she would even start with a password. It had been the same with the phone. She held down the stand-by button again until the screen went black. She closed the screen over and set it back onto the table. As she did so she knocked over a stack of magazines. A T.V guide, film magazines and a New York directory all tumbled across the floor.

'Damn it'

Jessica got straight down on her knees, stacking the magazines back into a pile, trying to keep them in the correct order.

Fuck.

Jessica thought of *Misery* and the knocked-over penguin ornament that James Caan's writer placed back the wrong way around. Jessica arranged the magazines back as best she could, interrogating the way they looked. She tried to keep the panic at bay. She stood and ran a hand through her hair. Jessica gave them a final look, then blew out her cheeks. She checked her watch then headed into the kitchen. It was clean and tidy too; a single clean empty glass stood upturned on the draining board. A half-empty bottle of vodka rested on the counter beside it. There was nothing else much of obvious interest.

Was there?

She stepped gingerly over to the fridge and opened the door.

No severed heads. Thanks Christ.

She shut it closed and headed over to the bedroom door. She pushed it open and stepped inside. There was a fusty odour – the room crying out to be aired. But again it was well kept, and nothing out of the ordinary. It was sparsely furnished, with a small bed and little other furniture. She went over to the bookshelf, crooked her neck, and examined its contents. The titles were certainly on the dark side – gritty graphic novels, pulp fiction and several true crime books. At the end of the row was some kind of journal. She glanced nervously back at the door, then reached the book down. She opened at a random page. Her eyebrows knitted together. She flicked through a few more pages.

Weird. What is this?

Then she flicked through chunks of it, stopping to leaf through random pages. Page after page of seemingly random letters and numbers.

What is it? Some kind of code? Dates?

She set the book down on the bed and pulled her cell phone from her bag. Yet another boundary she was crossing. And she had a sudden piercing urge to get out of there before she was caught. At moments she almost forgot what she was doing, conflicted. She quickly began taking pictures of random pages. Then she set her phone on the bed and carefully replaced the book on the shelf. She'd go through the pictures properly later. Jessica picked up her phone again. She'd like to do another sweep through the apartment, but nervousness was getting the better of her. She decided she'd ring the office first and see how the recording was going. See what time she had left.

'Good afternoon, Bev speaking.'

'Bev, how you doing? It's Jess.' She gave a cough, rattled by the strangeness of her own voice.

'Oh hiya dear, how you doing?'

'Yes good, thanks,' Jess said quickly. 'How's things there?'

'Yeah good, I was gonna close up soon, it's pretty quiet.'

'Oh – so are Lucy and Joe finishing up soon too?' Jessica said, trying to hide her anxiety.

'Oh yeah – it went very quickly, they finished ages ago. I think Lucy was on the phone with you as they were leaving.'

'As they were leaving?' Jessica said, her voice ragged, a coldness spreading through her bones.

'Yeah – that's right... are you alright, dear?'

'Yes, yes I'm fine. Okay thanks Bev, I better shoot on here.'

'Okay, bye love.'

Jessica hung up the call, stuffing the phone back in her bag.

'Damn!' she hissed.

She felt sick. That was it, it had all gone to hell.

What I was thinking?

Jessica cast an anxious eye over the room, then rushed through the bedroom doorway, closing it behind her. She ran across to the living room front window.

Jesus.

She couldn't believe it. There was Joe crossing the road in front of the building. And Lucy was with him.

What the hell is she doing with him?

She ran through the apartment towards the door. She looked back at it. There was no time for a final check. Jessica opened the door, slipped through it, and shut it quietly behind her. She felt faint again. Her guts ached.

What now?

She wouldn't have time to get down and out before they came inside. She was almost overcome with sheer panic. The hallway was quiet. Could she wait down one of the other hallways. No – what if someone came? The stairs – she'd hide on the staircase. She ran across and jogged quietly down the first few steps. But what if they took the stairs? If she heard them coming she would have to sprint up again and try and make it to the lift.

Damn.

She knelt down in one of the wide corners, half a floor down and waited. She strained her ears. She felt very lightheaded.

Don't pass out.

Then there was a distant click and the sound of the front door opening. It was followed immediately by the easy two and fro of a casual conversation. Steps moved across the hall.

Are they going towards the stairs?

Jessica tensed.

She felt elated at the whizz of the elevator coming to life as it returned back downstairs. She waited until it stopped with a thud before the doors clicked open. She heard Joe and Lucy's voices more clearly now – it was definitely them.

But it wasn't over yet.

Jessica still needed to get out of the building. She couldn't afford for them to happen to spot her through the window once they made it to his apartment, either.

The doors of the elevator shut with a crunch and it spurted into life once again.

That was her cue. Jessica jumped to her feet and raced down the remaining stairs. She visualised Joe and Lucy rising in the other direction.

What is Lucy doing here? She might be in danger.

Jessica sprinted across the hallway. Out of breath, she threw herself at the front door, fumbling with the lock then all but ripping the door from its hinges, swinging it open.

Fresh air.

She bolted out into the fading sunlight and down the steps. She didn't stop running or chance looking back until she made it all the way to her car round the bend. She clicked the key fob, launched herself inside and locked the doors.

'Damn it!' she said, and hammered the steering wheel.

She looked back up the street. Nothing out of the ordinary. She gunned the engine and sped away off down the block.

Chapter 43

'It's a nice building Joe. Much nicer than mine at any rate,' Lucy said lightly.

Joe smiled at her as he slotted his key into the lock.

Lucy continued to chat to him as they walked into the living room. He did his best to answer and nod, but he was distracted.

What's that smell? Perfume?

The vague scent of perfume seemed to be in the air. Was it just Lucy? They had driven over together, surely he'd have smelled it before now.

'Thanks for having me in for a coffee,' Lucy continued.

'Of course, it's the least I could do,' he said, trying to focus. 'Giving me a lift home and all. How do you take it?'

'Just a little cream, if you have it.'

'No problem,' he said absently.

Joe walked on into the kitchen as Lucy's phone began ringing behind him. He strained to listen in over the sound of the boiling kettle.

'It went great, we were done pretty quickly, think we got it all…Yeah I'll say hello to him for you. Joe?' Lucy shouted.

Joe appeared in the room, staring at her.

'Joe, Jess says hi.'

'Oh. Say hello from me.' He forced a smile and turned and went back into the kitchen.

He scooped two tablespoons of coffee into the pot, still straining to listen to the conversation beyond. One cup would do the irritating bitch. At least *she* didn't appear to suspect him of anything, but he did find her annoying. He also got the impression Lucy might quite like him. He could do without that. He'd enough on his mind.

On his return, Lucy had finished her call and was seated on the single chair. He passed himself with bland conversation, but remained cool enough that she wouldn't feel invited to stay long. He was preoccupied – he wanted to check the news reports again about Claire's murder. The morning's articles were brief and she hadn't been named yet. She hadn't been found for a whole day. He had stolen some money and jewellery from her apartment, making it look obvious. He had dumped them on his way home. He had found some bleach under the sink and thrown it around. It was worth it to destroy any DNA, but he didn't want to establish a pattern either. It wasn't long since he had killed the old lady and made it look like a robbery. It wouldn't do for his murders to be linked.

There was that smell again.

The conversation began to naturally dry up after half an hour. His eyes fell on the pile of magazines. There was something odd. That wasn't how he'd left them. He'd been reading a film magazine the day before and now it was in the middle of the pile.

What the hell?

And the perfume.

...Surely not.

Joe thanked Lucy again at the door and she left, with a small degree of obvious reluctance.

Right.

Now he cast a critical eye over the room. His eyes fell down on the magazines again. He crossed the room and opened his bedroom door.

Again – perfume? Stronger in here.

He circled the small room, then absently ran a hand over the bed, straightening the sheets. Joe stared at the bookshelf – it looked okay. He returned to the living room, he could hear his own pulse in his ears. He felt hot. Sitting down again on the sofa he pulled up his laptop and switched it on. His mind wanted to swirl in all directions, but he did his best to stop it. One step at a time. He waited impatiently as the computer booted up. His leg jiggled. He thought of a pouring himself a drink. No, not yet. Finally it started up, he put in his password and his home screen appeared. He ran a hand through his hair. His chest felt tight.

He clicked on the app.

Circles.

Another few seconds and it started to run. He clicked through, until he found what he wanted. Suddenly the laptop screen was filled with a live feed of the living room. There he was in real time, on his laptop, the picture taken from above, off to the side. His home surveillance system was situated in the corner – the tiny camera attached to the side of his smoke detector.

He clicked on the rewind icon. The screen tracked backwards, Joe moving about the apartment. Then Lucy walking backwards into the room as Joe held the door open. He clicked on the faster tracking. They sped up – like a Charlie Chaplin movie. Lucy and Joe sitting, then walking back and forth. The Joe in the recording backed out and left and the apartment was still again, empty.

The screen went black. And then it wasn't.

An earlier recording began, triggered by movement.

Oh God.

He pressed pause.

Jessica stood just in front of the camera, her anxious face looking towards the door.

His heart hammered and a chill ran through him.

What the hell? How?

He was nothing but a tight ball of emotion now – anger, fear, hate. One wrapped around another like a ball of coiled elastic bands.

Suddenly he lunged to the side and vomited over the floor, traces of the burning bile splashing against the stack of magazines.

Joe wiped the back of his hand across his chin. There was at least some physical relief from expelling the contents of his stomach. He fixed his eyes on the grainy, quivering image of Jessica.

Joe knew instantly what needed to be done.

Part 3: New York is Killing Me

Chapter 44

'Thanks Charlie, it's kinda important.'

Jessica was back in her own apartment, pacing up and down, her cell to her ear. The door was double locked and there was a large glass of wine in her hand. She hung up and continued to pace the room.

It hadn't gone well with ringing her ex, that was for sure. Lucy was out. Her mom?

God, I'm such a bad daughter.

Jessica texted her mom every few days, rang her most weeks – but it was mostly a kind of "how are you, how's dad?" type thing. They weren't the closest of families, but there were no rifts as such either. Life just got busy and the more she went down the rabbit hole about Joe, the less she found herself being in touch. Maybe it was to protect her mom, or to protect herself, she wasn't sure.

Charlie said he'd come right round. She didn't know who else to call. She'd no idea what to do next, but couldn't face this thing alone. All she knew was that she was filled with fear and an impending sense of dread.

Half an hour and a half bottle of Shiraz later, Charlie was at the front door. The sharp ring of the buzzer coursed through her veins with a jolt. Her voice was breathy and fearful as she made sure first that it was indeed Charlie and that he was alone. She checked the peep hole and waited to make sure he was definitely alone, before opening the door on the chain. Make sure Joe wasn't waiting behind him with a knife or something. She scolded herself, acting like she was in a nineties horror movie.

'Hi Jess,' he said quizzically.

'You're by yourself?' she said, trying to sound casual.

'Yeah, it's just me.'

She undid the chain, opened the door and hurried him inside, then locked it behind them, panting.

'Jess, what's wrong?' he said, his face open and worried.

She threw her arms around him, clinging to him. She started to sob.

'Hey, it's okay, what's wrong?'

She didn't want to give any other man wrong signals this week, but she was beyond the worry of that or anything else right now. There was a relief in being with somebody. About to share the burden with someone. Maybe she would even feel safe again *sometime*. Right now that seemed unlikely.

'I'm sorry, I'm sorry,' she said, muffled against him. 'Just give me a second.'

She pulled away again and took a step back. She dabbed at her eyes, running a finger over her lids to mop up any stray mascara. 'I'm sorry, come in – I've basically just accosted you... lemme get you a drink.'

'It's alright, take your time.'

'I could use one anyway.'

Jessica poured them both a glass before they sat down together on the sofa.

There was a charged silence as they both sipped their drinks.

'Is this anything to do with Joe?' Charlie asked softly.

Jessica nodded, then took a gulp of her wine.

'Okay, just hear me out... please.' She took a deep breath, then went over her initial concerns about Joe again as coherently as she could, in her current state. Charlie nodded along. Then Jessica described the look on Joe's face at the studio, the look of a face where the mask had slipped. The weird things he was doing in there. She reminded him of the stalking conviction and the interview with the neighbour. Then she stopped abruptly and looked away, taking another sip of her drink. She felt overwhelmed.

'I'm guessing there's more to come?' he said, sitting back, cradling his own glass.

'Yeah. But you agree there's enough there to be concerned about already? That we oughtta' do something.'

'Yes...' he said slowly, 'there is... I guess... but what's wrong? What have you done?'

Jessica shot him a startled look, something like guilt crept up inside her, then she rubbed a hand across her face.

'It's okay Jess, I'm not gonna judge you, I just wanna help.'

'Alright.' She clasped her hands together. 'I... uh.' She closed her eyes and breathed out steadily. Her stomach felt like there was nothing in it but acid and wine.

'It's okay,' he said again, gingerly putting his hand on her arm briefly.

'Thanks Charlie. Okay... just hear me out. I know I've maybe frigged up here. God. Okay.' She bolted upright, determined. 'So, his reaction in the studio. It was all seriously messed up, right? Moving the poster, then when he knew he was caught out. His face. Horrible.' She shuddered, more tears pricked behind her eyelids. 'I just *knew* then. So I got an idea and I suppose... it was a little rash.'

Her eyes met Charlie's. He raised an eyebrow, giving a half smirk. It helped crack the double-glazed tension.

'Okay, well I sort of *borrowed* his keys.'

'His keys?' Charlie repeated. '*Borrowed*?'

'Yeah, I may have made a copy.'

'Jesus, Jess.'

They both gave a nervous laugh.

'Yeah,' she said wincing. She lifted her glass and took a quick swig. 'And that's not all. I went to his place this afternoon.'

'Fuck me, Jess, are you crazy?'

'Please don't, Charlie,' she said, her voice quivering with panic.

'I'm sorry,' he said, his lips tight. 'It might be dangerous. I'm just worried about you getting into trouble too. You didn't get caught?' he said, looking fearful.

'No. Well I don't think so. I nearly did. He came back as I was leaving. And Lucy was with him.'

'Lucy was?'

'Yeah. That panicked me all the more. I rang her straight after. I was just so frightened. About getting caught... but for her too. I don't know what he's capable of.'

'What did she say?'

'She said she'd given him a lift and was having a coffee. I made it clear he knew that I knew she was there. I thought that might

153

keep her safe. I don't know anymore, maybe I was being stupid. But not overall.' She stopped and searched his face, her eyes pleading for him to believe her, even just a little. 'He's a killer Charlie. I just know it.'

'Did you find anything?'

'I don't really know. There wasn't a smoking gun or anything. I did find this.'

She grabbed up her cell phone and scrolled through the pictures. She explained about the journal and showed Charlie the photos.

'I don't get it,' he said, squinting at the screen.

'Neither do I. There were just pages and pages of this. I snapped a few random pages. Some sort of code I guess. But who even *does* that? If they haven't anything to hide.'

'I don't know,' Charlie said, shaking his head, looking thoughtful. 'It's weird.'

'It is, right?' Jessica said, feeling encouraged. 'And look at this one.' She pulled the phone up closer to her face and flicked through the pictures. 'Here, this one,' she said zooming in, before pointing the chipped nail of her baby finger towards it and holding the phone out. 'If this last bit here is a date – it would be last week. And the one before it, if it was a date too… I checked it – it would be the night of the fall at the warehouse.'

'Shit.'

'Yeah.'

Charlie frowned. 'So, what are you saying? That these… entries… are dates of… murders?' He struggled to get the words out.

'Yeah… maybe.'

Charlie exhaled heavily, then leaned back against the cushions.

'I think you'd better speak to Luce again. Just to make sure she got home safe.'

'You do? So you believe me?'

Charlie chewed his lip, met her look.

'Yeah, I suppose I do.'

'Thank you Charlie,' she said, leaning in and kissing him on the top of his head. His face instantly flushed.

'Alright, alright. I still think you're mental for nicking his key and going in there though.'

Jessica shrugged, a smile playing at her lips.

'Okay, I'm just gonna do it. I'll ring her now.' She stood up and chewed her finger nail, looking blank. Then she picked up her phone and began to pace. 'Okay, here goes.'

Charlie took another sip of his wine as he watched Jessica walk back and forth in front of him with the phone to her ear.

'It's ringing,' she said urgently.

'Hi Jess. Sorry just a sec.' There was a rustling noise as Jess clutched the cell nervously against her cheek.

'No probs.'

'Sorry, that's me sorted – was just carrying my plate there. That's me now.'

'Hi Luce, sorry… are you getting your dinner?'

'It's okay, just a micro. I'm all comfy on the sofa now, what's up, chick?'

Jessica felt nauseous. Hearing Lucy sound so *normal* and in the dark about everything, she could hardly face shattering that.

'Are you sure? I can ring back,' Jessica said weakly.

Charlie shook his head at her, his eyes saying to keep on.

'No, it's fine – I can munch and chat.' Lucy gave a little laugh. 'What's up?'

'Okay… it's… difficult.'

'Oh?' Lucy paused, her tone changing. 'Please tell me this isn't about Joe.'

'It is.'

'Come on Jess, we've been over this.'

'Wait, just hear me out.'

'God, Jess.' There was a deep sigh. 'Go on then,' she said in a clipped tone.

Jessica felt wrong-footed already and was regretting the wine. 'Okay, well… I already told you about the weird stuff about the warehouse.'

'Not that weird, but continue.'

'And the fact he didn't tell us about that, didn't tell us about knowing the Mercers either,' Jessica said, pressing on.

'We don't know he *knew* them as such.'

'Then there was the conviction for stalking, and... some of his weird reactions.' She struggled to piece it together into a proper argument.

'Get to the point will ya Jess?'

Charlie looked at her with a worried and powerless expression. Jessica continued on, her own voice now sharper, frustrated. 'The other day in the studio there was something else. He didn't know I was watching him on the monitor. You and Charlie were outside...'

'So you're spying on him now too?'

'No! Lucy, let me finish, please,' she said firmly.

'Alright,' Lucy said irritably.

'He started moving things about the set – posters and things... it was like he knew the place. Knew how things were meant to be.'

'Like he *knew* it? What are you saying Jess – he's a killer now?'

'Then he came in and saw me staring at the screen. He knew that I knew.'

'He knew that you knew? Seriously Jess – I think the pressure's getting to you or something. This is crazy.'

'You should have seen his face, Lucy. It was horrible – such a darkness.'

'Jessica. This is seriously all pie in the sky. I can't believe you're getting so caught up in this all, your mind's playing tricks on you, you're not making *The Jinx*. Fine if you think that Mercer didn't do it, but don't go looking for a killer in the freakin' cast now.'

'Charlie sees it too. He believes me.'

Jessica looked pleadingly at Charlie, mouthing "sorry" to him. He waved a dismissing hand back to say that it was alright.

'Well he would do,' said Lucy pointedly.

'What's that supposed to mean?'

'It means Charlie would agree with anything that *you* said.'

'No he wouldn't, why are you saying it like that?'

Charlie stared at her, his face looking even more concerned. Jessica turned her back and began to pace in the other direction.

'That's BS, of course he doesn't,' she said, lowering her voice.

'Sure he does. We all see it – me and Bev have talked about it before. It's obvious. He's had a crush on you, for like, forever.'

'That's not true,' Jessica said, her voice increasing again. Her head felt woozy. This was not going any kind of well.

'Look Jess, I don't wanna get in a big row with you. I'm gonna get my dinner here. I'll see you.'

The phone went dead and Jessica let her arm drop down with it at her side.

She turned and met Charlie's gaze.

'Sounds like it went well then,' he said.

Chapter 45

Joe dragged the box-cutter knife slowly and purposely across the middle join of the box. He'd spent most of the morning slicing through a big pile of boxes. At least it was mindless work that didn't occupy his thoughts. There was already too much going on in there. He had his earphones in, but he wasn't listening to anything. It was just a deterrent to any of the other workers around him striking up a conversation. He was tired. Barely any sleep had come the night before. He'd finished the bottle of Smirnoff. That had helped get him a few snatches.

His body ached from constant bending and slicing, folding and stacking.

Bending and slicing, folding and stacking.

He was weary. Weary of it all. Yes, weary from the killing. Perhaps he could have made a go of stopping the murders. On his own terms, not because he was *stopped*. That wasn't possible now. Maybe it was already too late. He had come to that fact for the most part already. No, he was still in control enough. He could overcome all that had conspired against him. Jessica didn't know that he was onto her snooping. Not about his apartment at any rate. Yes, there would need to be more killings. But he would have to be careful. He couldn't afford for any loose ends. But he also couldn't afford any more heat on him. He'd been lucky at times recently, he knew that. Discretion and consideration was what was needed now. It would all need to be thought through. But he knew he didn't have much time either.

Then out of nowhere, the answer hit.

The germ was there.

He carried on with the slashing of cardboard, the piles of stacked, broken-down boxes growing around him. First the idea, then the path to and away from it, arrived in his head. It was perfect. He'd have to be cautious, exact. But it could work, he knew it.

Chapter 46

Jessica stared into her own face. The pocket mirror reflected tired, red eyes. Jessica barely recognised them. She hadn't slept much, so she had got up, made a cup of coffee, fed Eddie and taken her time over applying her makeup. There was something calming about these familiar routine and rituals. She needed to be in the office for after nine. David Mercer's defence attorney was meeting her there at ten. Lucy was due off for a few days and it was just her and Charlie filming with the attorney. It was an important interview and she couldn't afford to mess it up. The downturn in funding had made everything more urgent. If she wanted to make a documentary of the quality she wanted and *demanded* of herself, there was no room for error.

They'd agreed there had been nothing more they could do the night before. There was much still to be talked about. They would need a proper plan about how to look into everything to do with Joe. They certainly couldn't go to the cops yet, never mind admitting to breaking and entering. Jessica had told Charlie about Lucy's reaction, leaving out the part about him having a thing for her. They would talk again after the day's filming. But not about that. Jessica dragged herself through breakfast and shower and at eight thirty was on the subway. There were no seats, but she found a bar to hold onto which wasn't too crushed by bodies, away from sweaty armpits and noisy school kids. She slipped in her headphones. She hadn't felt much like listening to music recently. She wasn't in the mood now either. More than anything, she just needed to dampen down the outside world. She chose *Innervisions* by Stevie Wonder, an old favourite. The organic and soulful rhythms always took her back to her childhood, dancing around the kitchen with her Mom. It didn't quite manage to do that for her now, as she sat in a trance. Jessica shut her eyes. She couldn't even focus properly on the encompassing issue of Joe. Her mind was too worn out. It was so very strange to feel certain about Joe, but with little actual evidence to back it up. Her other worries swirled around and each took a turn to come to the fore. The money issues with the documentary, heck, even focusing on the documentary itself. The next interview. She wasn't giving it the concentration that was needed. And what Lucy had said about Charlie.

What the hell was that?

Surely that wasn't right.

Was it?

Half the time she felt Charlie was cool towards her, terse almost at times. But he had been good about everything to do with Joe. He had supported her, comforted her. Had he been hiding feelings for her all along? She had no idea how she would feel about that if he did. And now wasn't the time. Pragmatism was what was called for and she knew she needed Charlie right now as a friend, a confidant. She didn't have anybody else she could trust.

The journey went quickly and she had been glad to get up the steps and into the fresh air. Jessica put on her best game face as she chatted with Bev and Charlie in the office. When she and Charlie went to set up in the other room, they were able to chat briefly. Charlie was concerned about her, though he was anxious about everything too, saying how he had barely slept either.

Spot on time, the attorney, Fiona Lynch, arrived and Bev made her a cup of coffee and seated her in the little waiting area by the back wall. Jessica took a deep breath and showed her into the adjoining room. Fiona was in her late forties, with an open but controlled demeanour. She had dirty blonde hair, tied back in a tight ponytail. She sported a fashionable navy trouser suit with a white blouse underneath. Jessica considered that she would make quite the imposing impression in court. As Jessica explained about the recording and thanked her for coming, she also reflected that Fiona had the all-important *likeability* that a public defender required.

'Okay, so as I said, the camera's rolling. We'll be chopping this all up into little bite- sized chunks, so don't worry if you stumble over anything, we can just start any part over.'

'Thanks Jessica, I'm sure I'll be fine,' she said confidently.

'Okay great. We'll make a start then. Alright Charlie?'

Jessica took a sip of her coffee. The sleepless nights were catching up with her; she felt exhausted. Charlie gave a thumbs up.

'Alright then. So Fiona, please tell us how you first became involved in defending David Mercer.'

'Thank you. My name is Fiona Lynch and I am pleased to act as the defence attorney for David Mercer. I was first instructed by him a little over a year and a half ago. At that time he had already dismissed his previous counsel and was without representation. I believe him to be innocent of all the alleged crimes that he has been charged with. Furthermore, I believe him to be a man of considerable honour who has been unfairly imprisoned, after already suffering the worst tragedy a parent could endure.'

Yes, she would be quite the force in a court room.

'Okay, tell us a little bit about what stage Mr Mercer's appeal is at now, please.'

'Certainly.' Fiona pursed her lips for a moment, then flashed a smile at the camera. 'David has consistently declared his innocence, since first being wrongly accused. His testimony has always been the same and he has never wavered from this.' She paused. 'That is because I believe it to be the truth. At this time, we have already sought an appeal hearing for David's wrongful conviction. We have amassed substantial new evidence and the preliminary hearing is scheduled for early December.'

'And what exactly is the evidence that you have unearthed?'

Fiona winced slightly, then broke into a half smile, her jaw protruding out on one side. 'I must be careful not to offer any evidence pre-dating the trial that could influence its integrity. We must protect the jury, though there is of course a mass of information about the case in the public domain. However, I can outline to you now that there are two crucial areas of new evidence. Firstly, the knife found in the garden.' She gave a mirthless chuckle. 'I have many concerns regarding this. The blood sample itself, the supposed lateness of finding it, and why it would even be there. I have many concerns over that. Secondly, the blood spatter evidence in the hallway. This was not entered into the original trial. It is a crucial piece of evidence. It is key to helping us try and work out who actually carried out these dreadful crimes.'

Jessica nodded, pleased with the clear and concise responses. It would come across great on film. She was, to a certain degree, able to be in the moment and felt the interview was going very well already. 'In terms of the knife and the problems you have surrounding it. What is the overall strategy of the defence regarding it? Can you tell me if one theory is that there was police corruption in this case?'

Fiona shot her eyes for a moment, then nodded and looked directly into the camera. 'Yes, I believe there is ample evidence to prove that the police department did not always operate in a transparent and proper manner.'

Jessica nodded, looked over to Charlie, then back towards Fiona. 'Ms Lynch, if David Mercer is innocent. If police even had a hand in a wrongful conviction.' Jessica paused and chewed on the end of her pen. 'That means there is a killer still out there. Who do you believe that is?'

Fiona bit down on her bottom lip, then released it, her eyes sharp and face set. 'Yes, there is still a killer out there. Who that is I can't be sure. But I would wager whoever it is, they've done it again since. Perhaps many times. It is another important reason why David Mercer must be freed, and a proper investigation is carried out, albeit severely belated. My job is to ensure justice for David Mercer, it is someone else's job to find the real killer. We merely have to prove beyond reasonable doubt that my client did not commit these crimes. There is no question of that in my eyes.'

It was seeming more and more that this responsibility did lie with someone else. And that person was Jessica.

Chapter 47

The glare of the afternoon sun was making Joe squint. He slipped on a pair of shades. He fell into a faster pace, working out the minor aches from the morning work in the warehouse. Sometimes the incessant noise and overpowering mixture of smells of New York was welcome. The white noise helped to dull his senses. He could just pass through the city – a mind, a brain, disconnected. A brain that was bent to the darker side of life. One that was presently very overloaded and under pressure. He could have taken the subway, but he needed to walk out some of the stress. Shake loose some of the pressure. Even if only ridding himself of a few drops of tension, it was worth it. He stopped at the corner. Skyscrapers towered all around him. Sometimes the city reminded him how small he was. But not insignificant. His life played a big part in many people's lives, and deaths. Across the street was a little bar called Auntie Annie's with tables out on the sidewalk. There were a few free. Joe headed inside, ordering a large vodka and orange. He took it outside, replaced his sunglasses, and took a small table to himself. He laid back in the metal chair, sipping his drink and watching the bustle of New Yorkers passing by. It was soothing. He had nowhere to rush to himself. He breathed out heavily. He watched them as they passed. So many people, so many different types, so many different lives. But they would all end up the same way. Eventually. In ten years' time, several would be dead. One or two may even be the victims of a violent death. Joe could figure which ones. He knew which ones *he* would choose to snuff out. He could almost tell just by looking these days. Like an equestrian sizing up a buck or a butcher picking out the prime cuts. Joe was an expert in his own way. And wouldn't it be a sin to waste one's own talents?

Chapter 48

Jessica and Charlie returned to the larger room after showing Fiona out. They chatted to Bev briefly and Jessica first made them all a cup of coffee.

'Well I sure as heck wouldn't fancy going up against her,' Charlie said, easing back into one of the chairs.

'I know, right? It was a good interview.'

'Yep. We got some good material I think. Interesting in the wider context too,' he said, raising an eyebrow.

'It was. Aside from anything else, I really don't believe David had anything to do with it. Not one bit.'

'I don't either. Obviously a million things could happen at the appeal or even at a re-trial, but I reckon he has a good chance. She sure knows her stuff, she's his best shot.'

'I hope so too. You're right – she'll nail all the angles if anyone can.' Jessica gazed into the middle distance and took a sip of the steaming coffee. 'Somebody else did those murders, Charlie. And I really think I know who it was. As insane as that might still sound to other people, it's what I think.'

Charlie closed his eyes thoughtfully for a moment. 'I'm pretty much there myself. Like I said the other night. The question is, what do we do next?'

'The million dollar question, ay?' Jessica said with a wry smile. 'I don't know either. I guess for a start, we keep digging. I've a few ideas where to start.'

There was a quick tap on the door and Bev popped her head around the corner.

'Hey Jess, Charlie, have you guys got a few minutes?'

'Yeah of course, Bev,' Jessica said.

'It's just Joe's called in there, he wants to have a quick chat.'

'J... Joe wants to see me?' Jessica said, her voice betraying her instant sickening feeling.

'He's here now?' Charlie asked, trying to cover his own faltering voice.

'Yeah,' Bev said smiling uncertainly, 'He's just outside, okay if

I bring him in?'

Jessica felt like she was having a palpitation. The room drew smaller. 'Sure thing, of course.' She glanced at Charlie, offering him a half-hearted smile. 'Bring him on in.'

'Will do dear,' said Bev, disappearing out again and shutting the door.

'Christ,' Jessica muttered, running a hand over her head, fixing her hair.

'Don't worry, it'll be fine. Just play it cool,' Charlie said urgently, rising to his feet.

There was another tap on the door, before Joe appeared in the doorway.

'I hope I'm not interrupting anything,' he said, casually half leaning against the door jamb.

'No, not at all,' Jessica said, getting up suddenly. 'Come in, grab a seat.'

Jessica set a hand on the table, steadying herself. She moved around to the other side of the table and her and Charlie sat down. Joe closed the door behind him and sat himself opposite them. The camera pointed at him from the side, the light blinking on standby.

Joe's stare lingered, moving between Jessica and Charlie.

'What can we do you for?' Jessica said, as brightly as she could muster.

Charlie leaned forward, keeping his expression neutral.

'I was just passing by, you know?' Joe said, 'Thought I'd see how things are going.'

'Oh,' Jessica said, squirming in her chair, looking from Joe to Charlie and back again. 'Yeah, it's going well. We're on the home straight now really,' she said, and forced a curt laugh. 'That was one of the last interviews there, this afternoon.'

'That's good,' Joe said looking at them both with a straight smile. There was something of a serpent in it, Jessica thought. 'I thought I'd call in and check if you need me for anything else.'

'I think we've got everything we need, really,' said Charlie squarely. 'Haven't we Jess?'

'Yeah, I think so,' Jess said too eagerly. 'We just need to piece things together now. We'll be in touch with all the actors when we've a rough cut pulled together. That'll take a little time.'

'Uh huh,' said Joe, crossing his legs, looking very comfortable. 'Great. That sounds terrific,' he said quietly. 'Well, I guess I'll mosey on then,' he said, slapping his leg and getting to his feet. Jessica and Charlie followed suit. A grain of relief began releasing itself through her body.

'You two take care now.'

'And you,' Jessica said, trying another smile. She walked past him, leaving a wide space and pulling the door open for him.

'That's a nice perfume.'

'Sorry?'

'Your perfume. It's nice.'

'Oh... thanks,' Jessica said slowly.

Joe put his hand on the door handle, then turned to her again. 'It was nice to have Lucy around to my apartment the other day.'

Jessica met his eyes. There was a metallic taste in her mouth. She swallowed hard, didn't say anything, couldn't.

'You should come over sometime. You too, Charlie,' he said with a wide, thin smile.

'Cheers,' said Charlie, before clearing his throat.

Jessica nodded. Joe's eyes bore into her own.

They twinkled.

And then he was gone.

Jessica closed the door carefully, her grip on the handle making her knuckles turn white. She swivelled around and leaned back against it, her face scarlet. She breathed out. Charlie stepped towards her.

'He knows,' Charlie said softly.

Jessica swayed against the door, her head down, then she gave the briefest of nods.

Chapter 49

Now Joe knew exactly what to do. There was no doubt that Charlie was suspicious of him now too.

They would all have to go.

Joe had taken the subway across to The Forty Two. There was something about the grime and filth of *The Deuce* that he found very appealing. Almost soothing. He wished he had been of an age to see it in its depraved heyday of the Seventies and Eighties. There was still enough of the atmosphere, with its dilapidated old theatres, grindhouse movie houses and porn shops, to offer a taste of that still. He knew where the most close-to-the-bone and barely legal movies were still shown. He bought his ticket and slipped into a worn chair near the back. The fabric of the seat was torn and what remained was stained with a disgusting array of liquids. The ancient theatre was barely a quarter full. The lights that still worked dimmed down.

Joe ran the plan through his mind.

It ventured down the various avenues, testing out where things might lead. It would be a true thrill to pull it off; committing a murder, framing the father, joining the documentary about the murder, then killing the documentary makers.

Incredible.

Joe would dedicate himself to finishing this thing. Maybe after that his head would feel clearer again. He had looked into news reports for his most recent victims. There didn't seem to be anything to worry about. Even Claire's murder looked like it had gone cold. This plan was all that mattered now.

With just a few tweaks, it could work just fine. All of the parts were there. Planning a murder was almost the sweetest part sometimes.

Almost.

The old sound system crackled and wheezed into life. Then a grainy, monotone image rolled across the screen with brash, red lettering. Joe took a sip of his soda and eased back into the seat.

Chapter 50

The next day Jessica, Charlie and Bev were all working quietly on their screens in the office. It was doing Jessica some good, throwing herself into her work. It had to be done anyhow. She might as well use it as a distraction too. There were plenty of emails to reply to and invoices and payments slips to organise. Patrick had sent through a heap of financial end-of-month reports to go over too. It was one area that Jessica hated. But it needed doing and at least it offered some respite from her other thoughts.

'Jess, honey, there's a call for you here. Guy says you might wanna interview him.'

Jessica looked up. She thought Bev had been looking at her funny all day. She was perceptive, she knew when something was up with her.

'Oh, okay thanks Bev. Patch them through, would you?'

Jessica picked up her desk phone and waited for it to connect up.

'Hello?'

'Hello, is that Jessica?'

'Yes, hi, how can I help you?'

'My name is Clarke. I'll get straight to the point. I was with the Cold Spring PD and later the NYPD. I was part of the Mercer case.'

'Oh, right okay, and are you still with the NYPD?'

'No, I'm retired. Look, I think the real truth needs to be told. I'm willing to go on camera. One time. I'll tell my story.'

Jessica chewed on the end of her pen excitedly. There was something familiar in the voice. It was deep, but faint. And did it have a mid-western twang to it?

'Well... we would love to hear it what you have to say... er Clarke.'

'I'm moving away in a few weeks; to Canada. That's why it's a good time for me to do this. It needs to be done.'

'Can you come down to us here sometime? We have a studio next to our office out in Broughton Road.'

'I could come tonight.'

Charlie caught a whiff of the conversation and stopped what he was doing and looked over questioningly.

'Tonight? Well er... I could maybe get the team together later I guess...' She peered over at Charlie and he nodded.

'I would appreciate that. Strike when the iron is hot – you know? I'd like to get it over with. Just a one-time thing – could that work?'

'Yeah, I could get at least get one of the crew along, I'm sure.'

There was a pause.

'I'd feel better if it was definitely all recorded. No glitches. I'm still a little hesitant.'

'Well, sometimes we would only have one camera. It would honestly be okay.'

'How about if you speak with your team and I ring you back later on?'

'Well, you could do that I suppose...'

'I'll ring you back in an hour then,' he said, and the line went dead.

'Weird,' Jessica said holding the phone aloft, shaking her head. 'The guy says he was a cop involved with the case.'

'And he wants to film tonight?'

'Yeah. Sounds nervy. I dunno. Says he wants the whole team.'

'You think he might pull out if we don't? I mean – I'm happy to come back or just pull a late one.'

'Thanks Charlie. Yeah, I think he might. I suppose I'll ring Lucy and see if she's free.' She wouldn't look forward to placing that call.

Jessica rang Lucy as Charlie paced about the room, fiddling with a rag nail. The conversation was easy enough, Jessica focusing on the issue in hand, putting their disagreements to one side. Lucy agreed to come around for the evening and Jessica said she would text her once a time was set.

Sure enough, an hour later almost to the minute, the man called again. He was brief and they agreed to meet at the office at half past seven. Jessica and Charlie chatted for a few minutes excitably, then went next door to fill Bev in on what was happening.

'I'm gonna go feed the cat, maybe even have a small glass of red. Then I'll see you later Charlie. See you tomorrow, Bev.'

Then they all went their separate ways.

Chapter 51

Joe flicked though the pages of his journal slowly. It was propped in front of him as he lay face down on his bed like a teenager with their secret diary. He closed his eyes and let the memories come back. Some were harder to pull out and were ultimately more vague than others, but he could remember something of every one of them. He ran a finger across the entries. These were his precious memories. Other people had old photographs and mementos, Joe had this.

Some entries were considerably old. Was he a different person then? Joe didn't really think so. He didn't feel he had altered much since his late teens. Not that it was something he dwelled on. He didn't envy what others had. He knew who he was, what he was. What would his Aunt have thought of his life? He didn't care much. What might have his parents have thought? He never really knew them. Anyway, children hid their addictions, their infidelities, even their crimes. How was he any different? He had felt his Aunt had suspected there was darkness within him. She may even have had an idea of what he was capable of. That was why she had needed to be dealt with.

Joe flicked over the pages and cast his memory back to some of his favourites. The woman he had met in a McDonalds. That one was eight years ago and hadn't even been planned. It had been one of the finest. Everything had fallen into place and he had improvised.

Then there was the teenage girl he had groomed online. It was the first time he had tried that. Five years ago now. That had taken several months. But the end result. There had been none sweeter.

Suddenly he thought of Jessica. That bitch had been here – among his things, snooping. She had been here in his bedroom, touching his precious book, he was sure of it. Her fingers fingering these pages maybe. Her foul perfume infecting his home.

How dare she!

Joe clenched his fist and punched the wall. His knuckles reddened.

How dare she try and unmask him.

Joe punched the wall again. And again. His fist began to bleed. He punched it again.

She would pay.

They all would.

Chapter 52

The office block was empty. Jessica had rarely been there at this time of night. It was strange. All the other office workers had left, security had left too. The hall light clicked on. It felt different. It was somewhere changed, somewhere unknown. Jessica rode the elevator up alone. She felt nervous. She couldn't place the root of it, but she couldn't remember the last time she hadn't felt nervous and anxious. She unlocked their office and switched on the lights in both rooms. That helped a little. They had set up all of the equipment earlier. They could just focus on the interview now. Jessica jolted slightly when Lucy let herself in to the office. She jolted again a little less when Charlie came in a few minutes after that. The three of them had a stilted conversation, then Jessica went into the little kitchenette to make them all a pot of coffee. It wasn't the time to try and repair the rift between her and Lucy. They just needed to get through this interview. Even so, it upset her that things weren't right between them. She had become one of her best friends. And Jessica wasn't used to falling out with people.

'Give you a hand?' Lucy said, abruptly coming in behind her.

'Sure, thanks,' said Jessica, turning around.

Lucy looked questioningly at her. Jessica sighed, made a face.

'Hug?' Jessica said.

Lucy smiled and wrapped her arms around her. They squeezed each other. It felt good. Jessica could have stayed like that all night. She pulled back.

'I'm sorry Luce about… well you know. I don't want things to be all weird.'

'I know, me too,' said Lucy, cutting the path of the conversation off gently. She broke away and began lifting mugs from the cupboard. They chatted more easily together, then brought the coffees through to where Charlie was seated in the second room. He looked relieved that they appeared on better terms.

'Thanks,' he said as Lucy passed him a cup. 'I was runnin' low on caffeine levels.'

'It's decaf,' she said, making a mocking worried face.

'Better not be,' he said.

'I know better than that,' she said, giving him a wink.

'Decaf, what's the point, right?' Jessica said, dropping down into a chair beside them. She checked her watch. Not long to go now.

Jessica made an involuntary little gasp as the door buzzer sounded from the outer office.

'Easy on, Jess,' Lucy said with a half-smile, half-frown.

'I'm just a little jumpy tonight,' she said, getting to her feet. She locked eyes with Charlie as she made her way to the doorway.

'We're on then,' said Charlie getting up and rubbing his hands nervously together.

The buzzer sounded again and Jessica scurried across to the intercom.

'Hello?'

'H…m…. … …erview.' The intercom was making a crackling noise and the voice was muffled. It was either broken or someone was speaking too close to the receiver.

'Hi… uh… I can't really hear you.'

There was another unrecognisable mumble.

'Em… sure I'll just buzz you up,' she said. 'We're on the third floor, the elevator is right ahead of you.'

She pressed the entry button and her stomach gave a little flip.

It seemed to take an age for anything else to happen. They spoke very little. Then the distant hum of the elevator could be heard beyond and the noise of the door opening.

Chapter 53

Joe strode along the hallway and stopped in the open doorway. He stared impassively into the room. He allowed a half smirk to form on his lips as the three looked towards him with a range of expressions going from surprise to terror.

'Joe?' Jessica said, standing up, 'We uh… weren't expecting you.'

'Well, then I've given you a nice surprise. Just thought I'd call in,' he said, keeping his voice even, friendly. He shut the door behind him, then pulled his backpack off and set it down on the floor beside him.

Charlie got to his feet too, eyeing him suspiciously.

'Yeah, nice to see you Joe,' said Lucy, a little unsure, walking towards him. 'What can we do for you?'

'Oh nothing,' he said, the confidence now streaming through his veins, invigorating him. He kept his back to the door, but paced a little on the spot, a ball of energy. He noticed Jessica looking at his gloved hands. 'I don't need an excuse to see my *friends,* do I?' He set his eyes on Jessica as he said this, an ugliness emanating from somewhere deep behind his pupils. She looked away.

'Good to see you, Joe,' she said, still looking away. 'But we kind of have an interview booked in so we can't be too long I'm afraid.'

Joe continued to stare at her. She turned her head to stare back. He looked almost trance-like now. His smile had all but fallen away. A nervous atmosphere enveloped the room. Joe could feel himself feeding from it.

'Sure, you could interview me,' he said, and forced an empty laugh.

'Well, I think we've finished all of your filming now,' said Charlie, moving closer.

Joe set his eyes on Charlie's now, allowing his own to begin to burn, like sparking kindling. 'I don't mean playing a part. Why don't you interview *me*?'

'C'mon Joe, you been drinking or something, buddy?' Lucy said breezily, but with a nervousness. 'Sure come outside with me and

I'll have a smoke. We can chat.'

'No thanks,' he said with another mirthless smile. He stared at each of them in turn. The realisation of others that something was very wrong was always one of his favourite stages. He dared them to make a move. The power of pure intimidation while doing very little was intoxicating.

Jessica continued to stare back, then her eyes hardened.

'What is it you want?' Jessica asked coldly.

'What do *I* want? Is that the question? What did *you* want when you went snooping through my apartment?'

'What?' Jessica said indignantly.

Charlie's face fell. Lucy looked questioningly at Jessica. 'Jess?'

'I don't know what he's talking about. C'mon, I think it's time you were going, Joe,' Jessica said, taking another step closer to him.

'You weren't in my apartment? You didn't go through my things?' Joe asked quietly, swaying on the spot, like a hyper child.

'No, what are you talking about?'

'I have a camera set up in my living room.' He paused, looking pleased with himself and feeling it too. 'You didn't spot that, did you? I've footage of you letting yourself in and going through my stuff. I guess you stole my key at the studio?'

Flustered, Jessica swept her bangs away from her face. Lucy looked frightened now and looked nervously again at Jessica.

'C'mon, we'll talk another time, you're not yourself,' said Jessica, putting her hand on his arm. Abruptly, he pulled his arm away, as if it had glanced a hot flame. His eyes bore into Jessica's.

'I'm very much myself,' he said loudly.

'Right that's enough of this shit,' said Charlie, walking straight up to Joe and placing a hand firmly on his arm. 'We've got an interview to do. Let's get going.'

Joe swung sharply around, whipping his arm back before landing a punch to Charlie's face. Charlie's head snapped back, his face red from the punch.

Jessica and Lucy both gasped. Lucy put her hands on her cheeks, her face in shock.

'I *am* your interview, you dumb fuck,' Joe spat. Then he punched him again.

Charlie stumbled backwards, a hand going to his bloodied nose.

'Leave him alone!' shouted Jessica, stepping backwards. She riffled in her jeans pockets for her phone.

'Don't you touch that,' ordered Joe, looming over her.

'Joe, what's come over you?' Lucy said gesturing wildly with her arms near his face, her voice raw.

He swept a backhanded slap across her face. She shrieked as her face reddened, almost falling to the ground. Jessica pulled out her phone, backing away quickly.

'I said don't you touch that!' Joe snarled. The pleasure had dissipated from him and irritation was taking over.

Enough playing, it was time to get this done.

He pulled out a Glock 10mm pistol from his jacket pocket and clicked the ammo clip. 'Throw the cell phone down. Do it!'

Jessica looked helplessly towards him, then reluctantly did as she was told.

'What do you want?' she screamed.

'Isn't it obvious? I want you all dead.'

Chapter 54

Jessica's wrists burned. They were tied behind her with two taut cable ties. Lucy was beside her and Charlie seated on the floor at the end of the row. Each were bound the same. Their backs were against the left-hand wall of the second room. Joe had forced them in at gun point. Charlie had given off and had received a punch to the guts. He didn't look so good, blood clotting on his two head wounds. Lucy's face was still red with a purple tinge accompanying it. She was breathing heavily, her face filled with terror. Joe was pacing about the room, looking up at the ceiling, checking out the window, knocking on walls with his fist every so often.

'It's okay Luce, take it easy. Breathe,' Jessica said quietly. 'Just breathe normally. I know it's hard.' She was saying it to herself as much to Lucy.

Lucy nodded weakly. Then her breathing slowed, concentration flashing across her eyes. Jessica was already focused on her own breathing. How it had suddenly come to this? Jessica knew it wasn't the time for any one of them to hyperventilate. She was frightened, yes, but she also felt a strange calmness. Something had kicked in, some survival default.

'Charlie... Charlie how you doing over there?' she asked, trying to strain forwards to look over at him.

'I'm okay, Jess,' he said inbetween coughs. 'Are you okay?'

'Yeah, I'm the only one not to have got hit.'

'We can easily remedy that,' Joe said cutting in, crossing the room to stand in front of them. 'Jesus, what a sorry sight,' he said smiling cruelly, shaking his head.

'It's not too late, Joe,' Jessica said, looking up at him with all of the strength she could muster. 'You could still get away. This isn't going to help you.'

'Oh, I think it will do just that. I didn't have any worries before I got involved with you people.'

'But you were still a killer,' Jessica said firmly.

He guffawed. 'Got it all worked out, haven't you? You don't

know shit about me.'

Jessica figured she may as well keep on. 'I know you framed David Mercer. You killed those kids. Killed the guy in the warehouse too. Probably a load more as well.'

He shook his head, jutted out his lower lip. 'You've no proof of any of that and neither does anyone else.'

'Then let us go,' Lucy wheezed inbetween laboured breaths.

'I think it's a little late for that, don't you?' he said glibly, gesturing around the room. 'Besides, you people were digging around too much.'

'At least let the girls go,' Charlie said, his voice hoarse. 'You're not gonna get away with this, whatever happens. You'll still have to run.'

'It's a little late to play the hero Charles. It hasn't worked out so well for you so far. Besides, I *will* be getting away with it all. Once I've dealt with you three.'

'Other people know about you,' Jessica blurted out. The thought had come to her a second before. And no other plays had presented themselves. So why not?

'What?' Joe said sourly, taking a step towards her. He kicked her leg absently with his left foot. 'What d'ya mean? That's not true.'

'Yes it is. Other people know it all. You do this and there'll be no doubt.'

Joe very slowly and deliberately got down onto his knees. He held his face a few inches away from Jessica's. He brought up the gun and pressed the barrel lightly against her forehead. He licked his lips.

Jessica closed her eyes. Her stomach was flooded with acid. She could smell Joe's stale breath on her face.

He kicked her again, harder.

'Leave her alone,' said Charlie.

'Shut the hell up!' Joe shouted, turning towards Charlie.

'It's not true, is it Jessica?' Joe squinted, searching her face. 'C'mon now.'

Jessica swallowed hard. Jessica had never handled a gun before, never mind had one thrust threateningly in her face. The odour of oil and cordite almost made her gag. She could feel the bile in her stomach wanting to wash upwards. She was sweating all over, she ached all over too from the way she was bound. She opened her eyes and set them on Joe.

'It *is* true. Several people know – I told them everything. And it's all on my laptop as well. There's emails too.'

Joe's lips pursed, his eyes narrowed. Anger flared across his face. Suddenly he pulled away and stood up. He bent down again and grabbed Charlie by his collar with one hand, shoving the Glock in his face with the other hand.

'I'm gonna work some on your friends 'till you tell me the truth. The *whole* truth.' He swung back the gun, swivelled it, then cracked Charlie hard across his face.

Jessica screamed. 'Don't! Please!'

Lucy looked on, stunned. Charlie made a guttural sound and his head flopped forwards, now only half-conscious. Blood flowed freely again from his nose.

'Is it true?' Joe demanded in an icy voice, eyeballing Jessica.

'Yes,' she whispered.

'Right, well, don't say I never warned you,' he said, turning to Lucy.

Lucy looked back at him, like a terrified deer with a transit van rushing towards it.

Joe stared purposely down at her breasts, then flashed a smile at Jessica. Then he stuffed the gun down the front of his pants. Joe settled down onto both knees, in front of Lucy. Then he raised his fists in a mock boxing stance, grinning. Lucy tried to strain her head away, beginning to wail. He made a few pretend jabs, then gave a wink to Jessica. Suddenly he released a right-hand jab into Lucy's face. She cried out as the fist hit her around her left eye.

'Don't, please… Joe… don't,' Jessica begged.

He shrugged, then launched another jab into Lucy's face. She screamed, then began to cry with long, heaving racks.

'Okay, okay – you win!' Jessica shouted. 'I didn't tell anyone, I swear.'

'Is this the truth?' he said, shuffling closer to her.

'Yes.'

'And there's nothing on your computer? Truth now.'

He searched her face.

Jessica looked back, wide-eyed.

'No.'

'Good,' he said, before releasing a closed fist into Jessica's face.

Chapter 55

Joe stood back up again, and shook out his legs and stretched his spine. He checked his watch.

It was time to speed things along.

He lifted up his back-pack and carried it over onto the table. He unzipped it, pulling out the contents and lining them up in front of him: a bottle of cheap whiskey, another of vodka, matches, an ashtray, kindling sticks, and today's New York Post. He grabbed clumps of other paper from the stacks on the table and began making three small piles underneath the table. He ripped up the newspaper and stacked the rough strands on top of it. Then he placed a few pieces of kindling onto each pile. He stood up, rubbing his hands together.

Jessica looked on in fear. Lucy and Charlie both still appeared dazed, but also were aware of what Joe was doing. They each stared at the stacks of kindling in terror.

Joe got up and went over to Lucy.

'Hey, hey,' he said, gently slapping her cheek to get her attention. 'Where's your bag at – your cigarettes?'

She looked dully at him, then nodded her head to the right. Joe searched around the far side of the desk, first picking up Jessica's bag, then finding Lucy's with her cigarettes near the top.

He began whistling. A tuneless, meandering noise.

It was all coming along nicely. Joe walked back to the ashtray, picking it up and setting on top of the table. He lit four cigarettes, one after another and placed each one into the grooves in the ashtray, letting them begin to burn.

He turned to the terrified trio. 'Don't worry – there ain't no sprinklers in here. And I've already taken care of the smoke alarms.' As an afterthought he crossed to the table, plucked out one more cigarette and lit it. He walked over to Lucy and rammed it in her mouth.

'You might as well have one too.'

'Joe… please… you don't have to do this,' Jessica said again.

'But I want to.' He paused, carefully lighting Lucy's cigarette.

'God, I think we've been over this already. Just accept it. This is life and it's shit sometimes. It has to end anyhow. Just that it's gonna end very fucking soon for you.' His face contorted into an even crueller shape.

Lucy's half-smoked cigarette fell from her mouth, but she barely seemed to register it. In the background, the other cigarettes were still smouldering in the ash tray, a light mist trailing through the room.

'You won't get away with it. You've… gone too far,' Jessica tried weakly. 'What – kill us – make it look like an accidental fire? Nobody'll buy it. We're tied up for a start. The police will work it all out. You'll be in a better position if you just let us go.'

Joe tutted, shaking his head. 'Jess, Jess, Jess. This isn't my first time,' he said with a manic laugh. 'As you well know. I'm quite proficient at this. Hence I've never been caught.' He turned to the scene behind, pointing. 'So, the three of you are having a drink… a lot of drinks in fact. You let Lucy smoke in here too. Something catches fire and the place goes up – the booze and paper accelerating it. The trick is to not do something stupid like splashing a heap of gas about or something. An amateur might make that mistake. If it looks like an accident, that's just what it is. Cops don't want no extra work.'

'It'll be obvious that we've been held here… against our will.'

'No, it won't. I'll have taken off the cable ties before then.'

He let that hang in the air, enjoying watching Jessica try and work it out.

'It'll look better if it at least one or two of you die of smoke inhalation. Nobody's gonna worry about your injuries so far. There won't be much of ya'll left after the fire,' he said in an exaggerated drawl, enjoying himself.

Lucy vomited down her top, some chunks dripping onto the floor. Charlie had come round some and glared at Joe. Jessica gazed off to one side.

'In a fire, folk often get hit with falling-in ceilings and the like. Knocks them out. It's just got to all look plenty reasonable. That's why it was so easy to frame Mercer. The cops don't want any extra work. Helped the cops left some fake evidence of their own, too.

182

That sure was a sunny day.' He paused, licked his lips, then looked directly at Jessica. 'But you're right. I can't have you all still tied up and I can't have you getting away either. You see, I'm gonna beat each one of you until you're unconscious.'

Chapter 56

Jessica's head swam. She was all out of ideas. This was it – there'd be no second take. A kind of sense of resolution fought to creep in, but she pushed it away. She wasn't going out like this.

Joe looked over the scene. The cigarettes had all burned down now, leaving a strong musty odour throughout the room. He clicked his fingers. 'Glasses.' He strode out of the room towards the kitchenette, as casual as if he was hosting a drinks party.

'How you guys holding up?' Jessica said softly, looking fearfully at her two friends. The three of them were a sorry sight, bloodied and all but beaten.

Charlie tilted his head, vacant, no words coming to his lips.

'Jess, I'm sorry…' Lucy started, before coughing hoarsely. 'I'm sorry I didn't believe you.'

'Shush, shush. You weren't to know. None of us really knew *I'm* sorry. I'm so sorry… I brought him into this.'

'What're you lot whispering about?' Joe said, striding past them back into the room. 'It's rude to whisper y'know?'

He set three glass tumblers down onto the table. He poured vodka into two and whiskey into the third. Then he splashed some from both bottles onto the carpet next to the piles of paper and kindling. He took a swig of the vodka.

'Terrible to waste it.' Then he set the two bottles on the floor with their caps off.

'Right, now,' he said eagerly. 'We're almost there,' he added rubbing his gloved hands together. Joe picked the Glock up off the table and turned to the others. 'I guess we'd better get started.'

Jessica's stomach did a little flip. She forced her mind to think of something.

Anything.

She begged it to.

Joe swiped the box of matches and got down on his knees again He struck a match, cupped a hand around it, then lit the first pile of kindling. It took a few seconds before the paper started to crackle and catch alight. He moved onto the second pile, doing th same. He stood, watching for a few moments, making sure they didn't go out. Both piles of paper and wood began to burn slowly, sending smoke wafting away through the room.

Joe crossed to stand in front of the three friends. He swivelled the gun in his hand so that he was holding the gun by the barrel. He loomed tall above them.

'Please Joe, don't,' said Jessica. Terror encapsulated her once again.

She twisted her wrists awkwardly, frantically behind her. Her skin burned and there was no give in her bonds.

'Leave... leave them alone,' Charlie said feebly, his voice sounding strange to Jessica. It unnerved her further. This was it.

'Shut up!' Joe said firmly.

Lucy closed her eyes, mumbling a prayer under her breath.

Joe smiled thinly, swinging the gun in his hand intimidatingly. 'Let's do eeny meeny miny moe. That'll be fun, ay?' He gave Jessica another little kick. He pointed at each of them as he recited the rhyme.

'Eeny... meeny... miny... moe. Catch a NIGGER,' he said accentuating the word, grinning, 'by the toe. If he screams... let David go.' He gave a cruel chuckle.

Then slower and quieter, he carried on, more menacing with every syllable.

Behind them, the two smouldering piles began to swell, the flames growing and smoke rising in thick black plumes.

'Eeny... meeny... miny... moe!'

He crashed the barrel of the gun down, with a sickening thud.

Lucy fell to one side from the blow. Her eyes rolled in her head.

'No!' shouted Jessica.

'Stop!' Charlie cried.

They both scrambled harder to pull themselves to their feet, squirming against the wall.

Joe swung the gun again, down onto the side of Lucy's head. Her blonde hair was now streaked with blood.

Jessica felt as if her heart was going to give out, but continued to wrestle herself upwards. Finally, just as Joe was turning towards her, she managed to get to her feet, bunny-hopping with her hands still wrapped behind her. She launched herself at Joe. She fell on top of him, the gun falling away. Charlie was now on his back again, panting, failing to get to his feet. Desperately he tried to kick out at Joe, landing a couple of blows to his mid-section.

Pure survival instinct kindled the flames of survival inside Jessica as she tried to shoulder and knee at Joe, any part of her body that would move. Stunned, Joe managed to writhe away from the two sources of the blows. He swiftly re-grouped, feinted to the side, before flipping Jessica over and crawling on top of her.

I can't breathe.

All of Jessica's breath seemed to evacuate at once as Joe placed his large gloved hands around her throat. She writhed. She could feel her eyes almost popping out of their sockets. He bore down at her, the face of a sweating demon. She could smell a mixture of putrid smoke and copper. But the air wasn't making it down into her lungs.

Charlie was now out of reach, still frantically trying to kick out at Joe to no avail.

Blackness entered the sides of Jessica's vision.

Blackness streaked with blood.

She had never been more helpless.

I'm sorry.

The last drops of life were being squeezed from her.

A noise.

All at once the pressure around her throat ceased. She realised that her eyes were shut. They shot open as she hungrily took in a lungful of smoky air. Then she burst into a fit of coughs, writhing on the floor. It was getting hard to see, the smoke stung her eyes.

Jessica squinted upwards.

'Bev?' she croaked.

Bev stood above them, with a bloodied metal hole-puncher in her hands. Smoke swirled around her and out the open doorway.

Jessica looked to the side. Joe was crumpled on the floor beside her, groaning.

'Sweet Jesus,' Bev said, her mouth open, surveying the scene.

'Scissors,' Jessica said urgently. 'On my desk, quick... please.'

186

Bev looked vacant for a moment, then her eyes came alive again. She ducked out of the room, then came back in again quickly. Bev got down behind Jessica and began snipping at the cable ties.

'Dear God.'

'Bev, you've saved us all. Thank you. Thank you,' Jessica said, awkwardly turning her head, straining to hold back the tears. With her limbs free, a fresh surge of adrenaline coursed through her body.

'Lordy, I really whacked him,' Bev said, throwing the ties to the ground.

Jessica grabbed the scissors and ran over to Charlie, working on his bonds. She eyed the growing fires as she did so. Charlie was lying on the floor – conscious but disorientated. Lucy lay on the ground, still slumped over. Joe was bleeding heavily from the side of his head, but still trying to work his way onto his knees.

'He was going to kill us all,' Jessica said to Bev, cutting through the last cable tie. 'You saved us.'

'Is he... the killer?'

'Yeah... he framed Mercer and killed God knows how many others.'

'Lord.'

'How come you're here?' Jessica said, getting to her feet, massaging her wrists. She felt breathless and there was a rattle in her chest.

'Forgot my phone again. And thought I'd have a nosey at the interview.'

'Thank God you did,' Charlie said thankfully, rubbing at his wrists, managing to get onto his knees.

'You bitch,' Joe said suddenly, now fully conscious and trying to stand as well. He eyed the gun, lying off to one side. He looked terrifying, blood dripping down his face, his eyes smouldering with pure hate.

All at once, Bev stepped forwards and struck out again, cracking the hole puncher off the top of his head, opening a second gash.

'Christ Bev, I'll make sure I never get on the wrong side of you,' Charlie said, struggling finally to his feet.

Joe wheezed on the floor, on the verge of unconsciousness again. Behind him the flames grew taller, one table leg catching fire and more of the carpet around the piles now alight.

Jessica rushed over to Lucy and helped her upright, gently patting her cheek. 'Luce, Luce... come on, everything's going to be okay.' She turned to the others. 'Bev, bring the scissors, set Lucy free. Charlie, will you grab the fire extinguisher?'

They both nodded and went to start on their tasks.

To all of their horror, Joe got to his knees once again, mumbling gibberish to himself, his head bleeding heavily from both lacerations. Jessica bounded away from Lucy and scrambled towards the gun. She scooped it off the carpet, just as Joe got up onto his feet.

He gaped at her – a wild animal, a beast.

She pointed the gun at him, her hand shaking. She searched for the safety, clicked it off.

Joe continued to stare, then turned and fled through the door.

Chapter 57

Joe couldn't tell if he was awake or not.

He didn't know if this was real.

His whole body felt on fire.

Perhaps he *was* on fire.

Maybe he was unconscious still, with the flames licking his body. But he did appear to be moving. There was a dull sensation. He was aware of pain. And he seemed to be moving.

Yes, it's real.

This isn't a dream.

He was in motion. Running, staggering through the hallway, pressing the button on the elevator, then jumping inside. He was fully aware again, the memory of the last ten minutes flooded back. The elevator car seemed to take a lifetime to descend. As it did, pain suddenly flooded through him as well. He was very much awake, and in pain. He wiped his hand over his head and regarded the thick blood on his fingers.

It's all gone to hell.

He didn't know how it had gone so badly wrong. This had never happened before.

The elevator door pinged open and he staggered out.

Bang!

He ducked as a shot rang out in the hallway. Plaster exploded out of the wall next to him. He turned to see Jessica running down the staircase, gun in hand. *His* gun.

They both stopped. Their eyes met.

Then Jessica raised the gun again and aimed.

Joe skidded away, weaving through the hall, desperate to reach the external doors. He didn't look back.

Just a few more steps.

He made it to the door. Clumsily, he pulled at it, then fumbled with the lock.

Then another bang resounded and the left pane of glass in the door shattered, raining glass down on him. Finally, he worked the lock free and threw the door open. He lunged through it, scrambling out onto the path. He ran along it, out to the empty sidewalk.

Joe chanced a look back.

Jessica had made it through the doors too.

She was half aiming the gun towards him. Two cars passed behind him, unaware of the drama unfolding so close. Jessica stared at him, then lowered the gun. Joe turned and sprinted off into the darkness beyond.

Chapter 58

'I couldn't catch him,' Jessica said breathily as she hurried back into the smoke-filled office. The flames had been put out, Charlie was swaying beside the burned-up patch of carpet, a fire extinguisher dangling down at his side.

'I fired off a few shots, but I missed,' Jessica continued excitedly. 'Did someone call the cops?'

'Yes darlin', they're on their way,' Bev said quietly. She was kneeling, with Lucy's head in her arms.

Jessica was suddenly aware that both Bev and Charlie were crying.

'How is she?' Jessica said urgently.

Bev looked away.

Jessica moved closer, her eyes pleading and filling with tears also.

'How is she?' she asked again, her voice just a whisper.

'I'm sorry Jessica, I'm sorry sweetheart. Lucy's dead.'

Chapter 59

10 Months Later.

It had been the biggest story in New York consistently, week in, week out. One of the biggest in the whole country. It had been a fairly big story all over the world. If *Serial, Making a Murderer, The Jinx* had been big deals, cultural landmarks, this was something else again.

This story was massive.

"The story of the decade."

Everything about it was sensationalist. It had everything that stoked the imaginations of the true-crime-loving public. Everything in one dark and troubling bundle. The fact that the documentary that had uncovered the truth played a deadly part in the twists and turns only whet the appetite of the public all the more.

At first the team had shunned the publicity, retreating together to deal with their own traumas and grief. They all had spent time in hospital, but their rehabilitation, particularly mentally, would take much longer. Those wounds would not heal quickly, if at all. They had cried together, had meltdowns together, held each other. Slowly, they had begun to face the events that had unfolded and tried to piece their fractured lives back together in some form. Patrick had been the first to embrace the incredible potential of the events. Jessica had wanted to scrap the whole documentary at first. Patrick was supportive, but gently and consistently argued that they could not do that. It would not benefit anyone if they did that, particularly the victims. They were victims as well. Eventually Jessica had seen that what she could do was to tell the story, tell the truth. She owed that to Lucy, to David Mercer. She owed it to all of Joe's victims.

After about six months, life had not slipped back to anything appearing normal. But Jessica had somewhat accepted that life had very much changed for good. They were all in the spotlight and there was nothing that would change that. What she wanted more than anything was to do something good, something positive. They set to work on proving David's innocence. They dug deep into the police corruption. Then with a new and much increased team, they looked into other deaths and possible links with Joe. Jessica led her team with passion and commitment. The NYPD announced that Joe was not only wanted for Lucy's murder, but the suspected murder of four other historical homicides, as well as Lewis's death. Jessica now knew for certain that it was only the very tip of the iceberg. Joe was a full-blown serial killer. Patrick had secured a seven-figure deal to support the rest of the production with a lucrative streaming service deal and even a theatrical release. Gradually those involved, particularly Jessica, began to speak publicly about what had happened. There was no major newspaper or TV network that didn't cover the story and few that they did not give specific interviews to.

While Joe had gone on the run, there were ruined lives left behind in his wake. He had disappeared, but the results of his actions never would. Lucy's life was grieved by all who loved her, and those connected with the production were all left in utter shock. A manhunt had ensued, the likes of which never seen before in The United States.

But he did get away.

Joe had planned for this.

Planned it for a very long time.

Joe sipped his coffee, then placed the cup carefully in its saucer. He closed the newspaper, another feature speculating on his current whereabouts, and stretched out his legs towards the sidewalk. He let the midday sun shine down on his face. The first day on the run, he had shaved off his hair and dressed only in smart suits – ones he had previously bought but purposely never worn. He added thin-rimmed glasses to his appearance and wore green contact lenses to change his eye colour. Within two weeks he had grown a substantial beard which he dyed grey and continued to grow out into a finely-trimmed goatee. A decade earlier he had sold the small holiday house in Georgia he had inherited from his dead parents. He had bought a similar sized little house under an alias, furnished and situated by a lake on the outskirts of New York County. He had made a point of never once visiting it before now. A local realtor organised the general upkeep every year for a nominal fee. They would visit the property once a month, send him a few emails and bill him once a month too. That was the extent of his connections with the place. It was where he had gone as soon as everything went sour. He wasn't hiding somewhere still in the city, fled to Europe or migrated to somewhere in South America, like many of the speculators claimed. One sighting carried in many newspapers had him placed him in a Tunisian beach resort.

No, he had just slotted into the plan he had ready set in place.

Joe had money hidden away for just such an eventuality, not much, but enough. He had mostly kept himself to himself so far. Eventually he would need to find some kind of work, perhaps cash in hand for a while. Just to keep his reserves high. Or he could slowly build up a new identity. That wouldn't be cheap to get started, but he knew how to access the dark web and its many opportunities. It would have to be done sooner or later.

Joe plucked out a cigarette from the deck in his jacket pocket. He hadn't smoked in years, but this was another addition to his new persona. He lit up and breathed in deeply. It felt good. As he casually watched a passer-by, it almost felt like a lazy afternoon on holiday. Yes, Joe had fitted quite easily into his new life. If nothing else, he knew how to adapt. He always had done. And there was also the pleasure of hiding in plain sight. He had no real connections he needed to take risks in contacting. That was no issue for him. He wasn't trying to cross any borders or use any of his old bank accounts. He felt really quite safe.

That wasn't to say he wasn't angry.

He was very angry.

He was used to forging his own paths, leading the direction of his life.

His life.

They still would have to pay.

But it would all be on his own terms. He had to play with the cards he had been dealt, but now that he had successfully followed his contingency plan, he was back in control once more.

Joe flicked ash into the little plastic tray and took another sip of his still-steaming coffee.

He felt calm, he felt good.

One thing that he hadn't done now for almost a year, was to take a life.

But that would also change very soon.

Chapter 60

'Coffee?'

'Yeah, please,' Charlie said, rolling across the bed sheets, rubbing at his eyes.

'I may even manage to rustle up a few eggs,' Jessica said. Wearing only pyjama bottoms, she pulled on a vest over her naked upper half.

Charlie's mouth curled into a playful half smile. 'Might be safer just sticking with the coffee.'

She gave him a playful punch in the arm before getting out of bed and heading for the door.

'I don't mind you cooking naked.'

'Typical man,' she said with mock indignation, allowing herself a smile.

Jessica and Charlie had comforted one another through their grief, their shared trauma. Things had naturally progressed until one day they both realised they were much closer than friends. And it had been going great. It was good for both of them. They just worked. It had been staring her in the face longer than she had known. And Lucy had been right – Charlie had carried a torch for her for a long time before Jessica's feelings had aligned.

Jessica listened to the hiss of the kettle as she sat on the toilet, flicking through her cell phone. She yawned, pushed her bangs out of her eyes. It felt right to wake up with Charlie most mornings. She could already hardly imagine life without him. Yes, the previous year had been the hardest of her life. A more difficult year she could never have thought up. But now, she saw light again. She wasn't quite *happy* yet. But now she knew that she could be again.

Twenty minutes later and they were seated at Jessica's small wooden kitchen table. They were both tucking into coffee and some over easy eggs with toast. CNN was on low in the background and they both checked through messages on their phones. Jessica saw a frown creep onto Charlie's face.

'What's up?'

'Oh… it's just another text from Lucy's mum.'

Jessica's face fell. 'How is she?'

'Doing okay. Just checking in.'

'Yeah, I was texting her yesterday too. She's a very strong lady.'

'A hell of a woman,' said Charlie.

'Should I be jealous?' Jessica said, standing and kissing him on the forehead.

Charlie stared up at her, softly, into her eyes. 'There's nobody you should be jealous of.'

'You're sweet,' she said ruffling his hair before stacking her dishes in the sink with the pan. 'I need to go shower. Frig – I'm meeting David in an hour and a half.'

'Okay, see you in there,' he said with a goofy smile, before forking up some more of his breakfast.

Jessica tutted before leaving the room. She felt a glow in her stomach – she liked that he found her attractive.

It was the first that Jessica had been back in Sing Sing since everything had happened with Joe. Since their lives had become public discussion. This time she came alone, no company, no cameras. She drifted through the drive there, then the security, the same talk –but from the warden himself this time. There was an intangible shift in the way she was treated by everyone, something closer to friendly. Once she was seated in the room with the same security guard as the last time by the door, and David Mercer in front of her, Jessica's nervous energy faded. It was replaced with something altogether more positive, some kind of excitement, hopeful; something purely *human*. She had spoken to David a few days recently on the phone. But it felt more like as if she hadn't seen or spoken to him for years. Like a close old friend she had been out of touch with for a long time. He looked well – years had fallen off him. His face was less drawn, some sense of hope was wrapped inside his expression too.

'Jessica, it's wonderful to see you. It really is,' he said, reaching forward and gripping her hand fondly.

'You too David. You too,' she said, suddenly choked, tears playing at her eyelids. 'How are you doing?'

He pulled back, smiling broadly. 'Better now… thanks to you.'

Jessica gave a shake of her head. 'I didn't do very much.' Then she paused and said quieter, 'And I could have done things much better. Maybe… maybe it would have… made a difference.'

David nodded sadly, gazing into her now-glistening eyes, 'There's nothing you could have done. I'm damn sorry 'bout what happened to Lucy. Seemed like a lovely girl. That bastard….' he said, giving the table a thump with his large fist, 'that bastard will pay for what he's done.'

Jessica nodded, attempted a smile, then wiped away her tears. She gave a cough, got a hold of herself. 'I'm thrilled with how your appeal went.'

'Me too,' he said, and they shared a deeply-connected smile.

'I don't know if it means much, but you know I already believed you? I mean before everything with… him.' She hated even saying his name.

'I know. I hoped so. And yes, it does mean something. It means a lot.'

'So what's next? What happens now?'

'Well, that's the sixty four million dollar question,' he said with a chuckle, glancing back at the guard. The guard smiled back and shrugged jovially.

'I think my favourite inmate is about to be an out-mate,' the guard interjected in his deep drawl.

'I hope so too,' Jessica said. 'Three police officers suspended so far I believe, as well. That'll help things.'

'Yeah, it sure will,' agreed David. 'And your testimony and Charlie's. The fact that you gave an affidavit of a confession for the crimes from a wanted murderer goes a long way too, Jessica.'

'Good, I sure hope so. You think they might acquit? I mean, not even go through with a new trial?'

David blew out his cheeks. 'I'm trying not to hope for too much, but… well yeah it might go that way.'

Jessica nodded.

'My attorney's pretty hopeful.'

'Well – she's a real firecracker that one. Great person to have in your corner.'

'I've always been blessed with strong, good-hearted women in my life,' he said, catching her eye. He looked away toward the barred window. 'I still can't believe he had the nerve to sit here, in front of me like that,' David said, his voice hardening suddenly, 'It takes some kind of a psycho to do that.'

'You're right. The worst kind of person in every way.' Jessica sighed, 'That's exactly who he is.'

David nodded, closed his eyes. When he opened them again his expression had softened. 'Roseanne came to see me,' he said quietly.

'She did?' Jessica said hopefully.

'Yes. A few times now. Every week recently.'

'That's great David. Is it... going okay?'

He sighed heavily. 'It's hard... for both of us. We'll see.'

Chapter 61

Three Months Later

Joe flicked onto another news item on his phone. The story wasn't new, but the interview was. It was an online newspaper interview with David Mercer. He began reading. Joe felt irritated and got up and went into the little kitchen. He lifted up his bottle of Smirnoff off the counter and poured a small measure. It was still morning, but what did that matter? As long as he evened out the same amount over the day, it was fine. Things had felt different recently. The last few months had been hard. A degree of cabin fever had set in. He had no job anymore, no acquaintances, no routine, no responsibilities. At first that had been just fine. Joe had realised over the last few months that those had been things that had actually sustained him. That was a surprise. Not in the usual way that it was for most people. He had manipulated these people and things and made them spin around him like moons to his planet. Now they were all just memories and he was alone. There was nobody to torture left, other than himself.

On his way back into the living room, he stumbled into his overflowing bin. Chinese food cartons and an empty liquor bottle spilled onto the floor. The place was becoming a state. There was nobody to see it but him. Joe made a mental note that he needed to make at least an effort to tidy up in the house. He had remained in a strange and artificial mode like being on holiday or inbetween house moves. He guessed that probably wasn't very healthy. But then Joe wasn't exactly a role model for a healthy lifestyle. He sat back down and lit up a cigarette, before reading the article again from the beginning.

To the right of the text was a picture of David seated on a bench in Central Park. He was smiling, dressed in a smart brown suit – the weather balmy. Joe took a long sip of his drink. In the interview David spoke of how it felt to be set free. He talked of his experiences in prison. And of course, he talked about Joe. Three weeks earlier, David had been released without prejudice. The

200

prosecutor had chosen to dismiss the case due to a lack of evidence. Aside from the overwhelming public opinion and the practical impossibility of there being a "fair trial" due to the evidence in the public domain, it was generally held that their case had entirely crumbled. Along with that was the evidence of police corruption. The interviewer pressed David on this.

'Why do you think the prosecution finally dropped the re-trial and let you go? Was it to salvage some credibility?'

'Well, yeah, I think you're right. It's true, they were in a very different position to where they were when I was first put on trial. I mean – even then I should never have been on trial anyhow. There was no evidence – no *real* evidence. But now, I mean – they've got the detectives from the case suspended for police corruption. We had the new blood spatter evidence and everything. Then we have a confession. A confession from a murderer, a wholly unstable, violent, sick and depraved individual. I mean, my attorney said they would have got pummelled in court.'

Joe chewed on his lip, then swiped the story away and set the phone down onto a pile of newspapers next to him. He downed the rest his drink, then returned to the kitchen for the bottle.

He checked his watch. Then he poured another three fingers of vodka.

He still had a little time.

Chapter 62

Jessica had never tasted food like it. Salmon had never tasted like this before. She had never tasted salad leaves that could be utterly transformed by a drizzle of sauce.

'Patrick, this is something else,' she gushed.

He laughed heartily, his large form quivering beneath his shirt and trousers. The jacket from his tux hung discarded on the back of his chair.

'It's good, right?'

The whole production team and selected backers and plus-ones were seated at a trilogy of long tables in a grand reception room inside the Waldorf Astoria. It oozed old world charm that had not been allowed to fade. Jessica had felt such a burst of excitement when she had first entered the grand Art Deco entrance hall. Everyone had stayed there from Charlie Chaplin to Muhammad Ali. Some had even made it their home like President Eisenhower, Marilyn Monroe, and even Mafia boss Frank Costello. All of the team had been booked in for the night, Jessica in a stunning double suite with Charlie. He sat on her right, also looking like a nervous child feeling out of place at a lavish wedding or bar mitzvah. An hour earlier, they had inspected their room in giddy excitement, whooping with delight at the décor, the plushness of the bathroom, the complimentary dressing gowns and slippers. It was one of nearly one and a half thousand elegant rooms in the hotel. Then they had plucked a drink each from the well-stocked mini bar before falling onto the bed and making brief, passionate love. Then they had showered together before dressing in their finery; Charlie in a tux and Jessica in a long, flowing and classic black gown.

'No, not for me, thanks,' Jessica said to the waitress urgently, covering the mouth of her glass. She had already drunk plenty.

'Oh yeah, I'll take some, and hers,' Charlie said to the waitress cheerfully, grinning.

It was early to be dining in a fine restaurant such at this – only five o'clock. There were around fifty guests in all. They had to be at the cinema for seven, to greet the audience before the documentary premier began at eight. The "World Premier" of their completed documentary; *Killer Casting*. None of this seemed real. Jessica had been overwhelmed many times over the last year, but this was something she could enjoy and want to never forget.

Patrick dabbed at his mouth with a while linen serviette before getting to his feet.

'Ladies and gentlemen, I will only keep you for a few moments,' he began in his deep baritone. 'I will give a more formal speech before the film is shown this evening. There are many people I wish to recognise and thank.' He smiled warmly down at Jessica. 'But for now, a simple toast.' He reached down and lifted up his champagne flute, raising the glass aloft. A little choked, he declared, 'To Lucy.'

Jessica's stomach gave a little flip. Then she held her own glass up, tears in her eyes and repeated with everyone else, 'To Lucy.'

Patrick sat back down then locked eyes with David Mercer across the table, seated beside his former wife. Patrick gave him a little nod. David nervously brushed a hand down his own black tuxedo before getting to his feet.

'Ladies and Gentlemen, I have been permitted to say just a few words too. I declined to speak at the premier tonight, but I'd like to say something just now. Just a few words, so please indulge me.' He cleared his throat nervously.

The guests all fell silent, all eyes on David.

'I am a lucky man.' Again louder, he stated, 'I *am* a lucky man. That may be a strange thing to say on this day of all days. But I am. I have known pain. Pain like no other,' he said, glancing towards Roseanne. 'But I have been blessed. Amongst other things, I was tremendously fortunate to be blessed with a beautiful and wonderful daughter. I have grown to hold onto that.'

Even the waiting staff had stopped moving about the room. It was deathly quiet. Jessica gripped Charlie's hand tightly beneath the table. He moved closer to her, protectively, his eyes flitting between her and David. David gave a little cough, appearing a little overcome, but he carried on. 'I have had many, many blessings. What I want to say tonight, and I did say I would be brief,' he said giving a nervous half smile, 'what I want to say tonight, publicly, is thank you.' He paused, the champagne flute in his hand shaking. 'The words cannot carry the weight of all that that means.' Then he looked directly at Jessica. She felt her already flushed cheeks redden, her hands clammy within Charlie's comforting grip. 'Jessica, thank you. It has been said that no one individual can truly save another. But Jessica, you surely have saved me. You've believed in me, you went the extra mile for me, and here I am, here with you all tonight.'

An impulse gripped Jessica and she got up on her feet suddenly. She hurried around the edge of the table, looking down, avoiding all of the staring faces. The short journey seemed to take an age. She rushed up to David and flung her arms around him, tears flowing freely. He wrapped her in his strong arms, now crying too. And they stood there, in an embrace of pure, platonic love. Warm, soothing tears ran from both of them. Then, slow and steady, an applause rose from the group surrounding them. Then, one by one, every person got to their feet, applauding as one.

Chapter 63

Joe had made an extra effort with his appearance. He was as close to unrecognisable as could be. He had trimmed his beard neatly and put on his best suit. Along with his shaved head and glasses, the overall change in appearance was effective. He had left his car near to Washington Square Park and walked west along Waverly. It was the first time that Joe had been back in the city. It was odd. Despite his disguised appearance, he felt exposed. He hadn't counted on that. He thought he had it all straight in his head. It didn't feel good. Joe needed something to take the edge off. He was okay for time and stopped into an Irish pub on the way. He had two shots of vodka. It warmed his insides nicely. He went outside again and felt a little better. The evening sun was fading, but it was a mild, pleasant night. He lit a cigarette and smoked as he headed closer towards The IFC Centre. The former *Waverly* came into view; the huge arched billboard protruding outward with *Killer Casting* displayed in neon lights. There was already quite a crowd outside – maybe two hundred people. There was a lot of press too. As he joined the end of the queue, a white limo whooshed past him and pulled up at the front steps. Security guards pulled red ropes taught, forming a canal leading to the doors. A dozen photographers and videographers squeezed up, forming a gauntlet away from the limo. The door popped open and flashes began going off from all sides. Joe felt a rush as he watched some familiar faces climb out from inside: Bev, Charlie... Jessica. Instinctively he stroked the outside of his jacket, checking for the bulge of his compact Sauer P365 nine-millimetre handgun. Joe continued to stare. An older man – probably the producer – Patrick, touched Jessica on the shoulder, smiling broadly and waving to the crowd with his free hand. Jessica turned, looking uncomfortable, and gave a little wave to the queuing audience. Joe craned his neck to continue to watch her. Jessica paused awkwardly, posing for a flurry of flashes going off. He felt a fury burn in the pit of his stomach. He wanted another drink, another cigarette. He looked on, simmering, as Jessica was led over to a camera crew and began to give an interview off to one side.

The doors opened and the queue began inching forwards. Joe pushed his feelings back down deep inside and planted a half smile on his face.

Not long now.

Chapter 64

'Jeez, that was something else,' Jessica said, out of breath, as they gathered themselves inside a long hallway lined with film posters.

'Piece of cake,' Patrick said with a wink. 'You're a natural.'

'Don't know about that,' she said.

The small group all shuffled about together, gazing up at the film posters, listening to the excited hubbub from the arriving guests outside.

Charlie leaned in, smiling proudly, and kissed Jessica on the cheek, 'He's right, you *are* a natural.'

'How's the make-up doing?' she said with mock concern.

'D'yall think I'll make the cover of Vogue?' Bev said, striking her own pose, with a deep chuckle.

'I'll have a word with them,' said Patrick with a wink.

Jessica put her arms around Bev, cuddling into her. 'I love this woman. Bev – it's because of you that Charlie and me are here… at all.'

'Oh, shoosh pet, shoosh,' she said, batting her arm.

'It's true – before any of this you were already one in a million,' Jessica said, giving her a kiss on the cheek.

They had fifteen minutes left before they needed to take their seats. Jessica went to the ladies, then met Charlie back in the hallway.

'You holding up okay Jess?' he said, taking her hand in his.

'Yeah I think so, you?'

'Yeah, I'm enjoying it. Weird – like.'

'Very.'

They shared a nervous giggle together.

Gill Scott-Heron's muffled voice could be heard emanating from the auditorium beyond. Jessica had arranged for his last album to be played as background while the audience took their seats. On a largely spoken work track, his distinctive, whisky-oiled voice could be heard singing about "running".

'Charlie…' she said looking hesitant, 'I know it's probably dumb… but… you don't think he's here, do you?'

Charlie lowered his eyes, took her other hand in his too. 'No, I don't, love. I really don't. That piece of shit is somewhere far away. Somewhere very far away.'

Chapter 65

Joe finally filed into the cinema behind a rowdy group of businessmen. There was an excited buzz in the auditorium. In the background Gill Scott-Heron howled that New York was killing him. Joe stopped, allowing the group in front to shuffle into their seats. Two cops in uniform stood in the middle of each aisle ahead. Joe fixed his half smile back on and looked off into the middle distance. He passed by them casually and a green uniformed usher took Joe to his seat, about a third of the way from the front on the ground floor. Joe settled into his chair, rubbing his sweaty hands together. A smartly-dressed young couple were seated on his right. On his left were a group of possibly Korean-extraction journalists. He absently ran the back of his hand down over the slight bulge in his jacket pocket again. The feeling of the gun comforted him. It was very humid, but he couldn't risk to open out his jacket. Maybe just one button. He let out the top one and the top button on his shirt. He was glad to have decided not to wear a tie. Half of the lights lowered to a dim glow, the music faded out and the screen widened and turned black. Joe watched as Jessica and the rest of the team entered from a side door and took their seats over the first two rows. Then the whole auditorium went black.

It was a strange experience. There was no way around it. It was literally his life on the screen before him.

What could be weirder?

He hadn't really known what to expect. Yet there wasn't only one emotion he felt as the film played out in front of him. There was certainly fear too. He discreetly flitted his eyes around the semi-darkness constantly, feeling vulnerable, fearing a tap on his shoulder at any moment. Images of him appeared at various points across the screen and of course there were interviews with Jessica and NYPD detectives about the hunt for him. That was quite pleasing to watch. The two main strands of the film were the overturned conviction of David Mercer and the piecing together of the crimes of a serial killer.

Me.

He reflected on what a different kind of film it might have been if things had gone otherwise. He could have been seated in front with the rest, still revelling in his anonymity. But Joe was essentially a pragmatist. There was much that angered him about the film and deeper still of how he had been unmasked. But there was pleasure to be felt too. Flattery even. He had evaded capture and had done now for a considerable time. He was being spoken of in terms of as a Manson, a Dalmer, even a Bundy. Maybe something even bigger, grander. And here he was, seated among them. That was its own joy.

Idiots.

Then it came; the tap on the shoulder.

His blood turned to ice and his head shot up to look at the figure behind.

'Excuse me sir,' whispered an usher leaning over from the edge of the row behind. 'We have a late arrival who thinks you're in his seat. Could I see your ticket please?'

Joe felt a buzzing in his ears as he first reached into the pocket with his pistol, then quickly to the other side as he pulled out his ticket.

'Yes of course,' he whispered, his voice cracking. He passed the ticket over.

A dim torch turned on behind him. Joe watched as the usher read it carefully. Then he nodded briefly and returned the ticket to Joe's outstretched hand.

'Sorry to disturb you sir, you're in the correct seat, my apologies,' he said, and began filing back out of the row behind.

'No problem,' Joe whispered mechanically, returning the ticket to his pocket and looking back towards the screen. Joe stared through the screen, the film now only a blur and white noise. He focused on controlling his breathing, calming his mind. The danger had passed.

It's okay.

Sweat dripped out from every pore. His sight and hearing focused out again, away from the threat as he watched as David Mercer was seen leaving the prison gates, greeted with hugs from his former wife and from Jessica. It angered him to watch it. He only half paid attention to the final quarter of the film. It hadn't been the experience he had wanted. Nervousness returned as the house lights came up again and there was a rapturous round of applause from the audience, half of them getting to their feet. Joe joined in, absently. The crew in the first rows got to their feet, turned and linked arms, giving a little bow. Then a smartly suited and booted compere came onto the stage, with an usher setting up two microphones on stands beside him. Joe's mind wandered off to the appealing notion of wanting a drink and a cigarette as the compere commented on how wonderful the film was before introducing the primary producer onto the stage. There was a ripple of applause before this *Patrick* gave an almost ten-minute speech. Joe zoned all of it out, only aware of an occasional communal chuckle from the audience. Then Patrick introduced Jessica onto the stage.

Joe shifted uncomfortably in his chair, watching Jessica begin to address the audience, looking nervous, but admittedly both professional and radiant.

How he loathed her.

Her voice cut through him like glass. His disgust turned to the audience as they laughed encouragingly along with her weak jokes. He could also make out Charlie in the front row, gazing up at her like a teenager with a crush. Joe reached into his pocket and allowed his fingers to stretch around the gun.

He could do it right now.

End her.

But not yet. He had no intention of being caught.

Soon.

Chapter 66

Jessica hiccupped, covering her mouth with a giggle. She was back in the limo, drinking champagne, along with Charlie and Bev, seated either side of her.

'Well, what y'all think?' said Bev, topping up each of their glasses.

Jessica felt the alcohol hit her and decided to leave another glass for now. She swore that the bubbles got her more drunk.

'I'd already seen it. We kind of make it, Bev,' Charlie said, giving Bev a playful elbow.

'Well duh. I mean the event – the atmosphere. Cheeky boy.'

Charlie laughed loudly, then said, 'It was great. I'm literally stunned. The whole thing was nuts. And seriously –the film Jess – you got to be so proud.'

'I *am* proud. Proud of my amazing team!' she said, and swung her arms around their shoulders for a clumsy group hug. 'It's not *my* film, it's everybody's.'

Jessica felt elated.

Such an experience. It was all more than she had ever dreamed of before starting the film. The positive reception from the audience was the icing, the validation.

Thoughts of Lucy kept swirling around her head too. The part in the film about Lucy's death had made her cry, as it had done many times before. But there was no need to dwell on it now. They had been respectful to her memory; it had been a tragedy. But today was a day for celebration, even for healing.

They spilled out of the limo as David, Patrick and the rest had just emerged from the other vehicle. They greeted each other as three or four photographers snapped them on the way through the doors of The Waldorf. They had been quick. Or maybe they had stood posted in waiting the whole time. It was dark now outside, a stark contrast to the neon lights inside the limousine. It took her eyes a moment to adjust. A light drizzle of rain began to fall. Hotel security prevented the paparazzi from going any further as they fired off a handful more flashes before the doors closed. Jessica and co filed in through the doors.

Inside the vast reception area, there was a pleasant buzz of excited chatter. Groups from the premier huddled in animated groups of five and six.

'Bravo Jessica, bravo,' Patrick said walking over and giving a little clap. A smattering of applause echoed back from the surrounding groups.

'Couldn't have done it without you, Patrick,' Jessica said, leaning in and giving him a kiss on the cheek.

'Steady on,' said Charlie, winking at Patrick.

'No fear Charles, I'm too old for that type of thing,' Patrick boomed. 'David, will you join us for a few libations,' he said, with an amicable slap on the back.

David stepped across from the group he had been mingling with. 'Yeah, sure. I might just pop to my room for a minute.' Then turning to Jessica he said, 'Jessica, terrific, really terrific,' He patted her arm for a moment.

'Thanks David, you're very kind. You're on our floor aren't you? I need to powder my nose for a minute too, don't know about you, Charlie?' she said, raising an eyebrow.

He made a show of touching his face. 'No I think I'm good. Will I get the drinks in?'

'Sounds like a plan.'

'See you in a minute, love,' he said, going over to Roseanne and kissing her on the cheek. 'Madam,' David said with a little theatrical bow, offering Jessica his arm.

'Why thank you,' she said dramatically, 'See you guys in a minute.'

They took the elevator up, chatting easily as it quietly rose up to their floor. David stopped two doors down from Jessica's room, pulling out his key-card.

''Bout ten minutes or so suit you, we could head back down together?'

'Yeah, sure, I'll give you a rap,' she said and inserted her own key-card.

It made a short, sharp click.

Chapter 67

Joe stiffened at the noise from the door lock. It had been pitch black inside the wardrobe. Now there were streams of light coming in the through the edges of the door. Inside reeked of the two vodkas he had downed in the hotel bar before using his skeleton key card. Joe hoped the smell hadn't escaped into the room.

This time I've let myself into your room.

He loosened his left arm as it hung at his side, the pistol facing down, with a makeshift silencer on the end. He listened intently as the door to the suite closed shut. Then there were steps crossing in front of the wardrobe.

One set?

Yes, one set and no talking.

High heels – she's by herself.

Joe had envisioned killing them both. But he didn't care much either way about Charlie. Should he rush it now? Would it be an anti-climax? It didn't really matter. Charlie would suffer either way. He had come this far. He just wanted her dead. *Needed* her dead.

He heard the bathroom light click on and steps shuffling inside. Minutes passed by. Then there was the flush of the toilet. He strained his ears. Nothing. He visualised the plan of the room. The wardrobe was a few metres from the door, almost opposite the little en-suite. Then there was the double bed, a table, and the windows with the curtains drawn.

Footsteps.

Then nothing.

Had they come across towards him? He tightened his grip on the gun.

What is she doing?

Then he heard a faint brushing sound.

Of course, she must be combing her hair in front of the large mirror on the outside of the wardrobe.

If he was going to act, now was the time. But he wasn't sure. He doubted himself. Something that he was doing more and more recently.

Do it, do it now.

Slowly, he pushed the door outwards, pointing his gun with his other hand.

Chapter 68

Jessica's mind was miles away as she dreamily pulled the brush through her hair. She felt good, excited. She couldn't wait to return to Charlie and the rest of the group. Now she could just relax and enjoy the evening, have a few drinks and reflect on the events of the day. It was time to celebrate.

Her reflection began moving.

What's that?

Jessica's hand froze mid-air, not sure what was happening at first.

The door's moving?

Then her reflection was gone and instead Joe's face was staring back at her, a gun outstretched in his hand.

'Jesus,' she said, dropping the brush and backing away as if suddenly receiving a static shock. She faltered backwards across the room.

'Oh, God.'

Joe smiled at her, his eyes wild. He stumbled out from the wardrobe as terror held Jessica in its grip.

'Hello Jessica,' he said quietly.

She continued to back away into the room, speechless, her heart hammering audibly in her chest. She could hear it echoing in her ears too, as if on a latent delay. Jessica took in his appearance fully. He looked so different. Yet, she had known instantly it was him. His eyes.

'I enjoyed your little film,' he said, with a sourness in his voice, edging out towards her.

'You... you were there?' Jessica mumbled.

'Of course. You didn't think I'd miss it, did you?'

This was worse than any of the nightmares she had suffered since that terrible night.

This can't be happening.

She swallowed hard, her eyes darting about for something to use as a weapon, or some way of escape. 'What... what do you want?'

He smiled cruelly. 'I think you know what I want.'

An ice cube ran over her perspiring back. Perhaps someone had just stepped over her grave.

Joe moved closer still, as she continued backing away, feeling her way around the rear of the bed.

Joe was so close now, the outstretched gun almost touching her. His arm was quivering. She could smell a reek of alcohol on his breath and sweat from his body.

Then all at once, Jessica ducked down, pulling her hair grip from the back of her head and lunging at Joe with it. He was caught off guard, tripping backwards. He cried out in pain. She clawed at his face with it, digging gouges out of his skin. His glasses fell away and smashed under their feet.

'Help! Somebody help!' Jessica screamed.

Joe corrected his footing and begin to angle the gun back towards her. Jessica dropped the hair grip and made a fist. She bounded across and hit him with everything she had. The punch landed perfectly on his face. His cheek immediately burst into a deep scarlet hue. He was stunned for a moment before spinning back around and pointing the gun again at her. Jessica dived away across the floor. Joe squeezed off a shot, it making a loud pffft sound. The bullet went wide, smashing loudly into a painting above the bed of the New York skyline. Jessica jumped to her feet, heaved her suitcase off the ground, turned on her heel, launching it at Joe. It flew into his torso, making him spill the gun away across the room.

'Help, somebody help!' she yelled again, scrambling after the gun. Jessica began crawling on her hands and knees, inches from the gun. Joe hurled himself at her, grabbing her leg and flattening her onto the ground. She turned face up, just as he knelt down on top of her.

It was all too similar. Was this another dream?

No.

Perhaps this was the way she was destined to go out, the life being squeezed from her throat by Joe's hands. A drop of blood dripped from Joe's gashes onto her own face.

Jessica made two fists and began to pummel him in the chest.

'Fuckin' bitch!' he screamed, making his own fist and landing a heavy blow into her face.

Jessica's world turned on its axis and almost went black. She felt blood drip from her split and already swelling lip.

Bang! Bang!

Had she been hit again? Was it another gunshot?

No, it was something at the door, a heavy thumping.

Joe paused above her, looking towards the door, swaying as he sat on her legs. Jessica gasped in lungfuls of air, wheezing. Joe gave the smallest of nods, then gripped his hands around her throat again and squeezed.

Bang! Bang, bang!

Jessica tried to wrench his hands away as he bore down on her, screaming in her face like a man possessed, squeezing tightly, his rotten spittle dousing her cheeks.

Barely conscious, there was a final blistering bang, accompanied by a splintering of wood. Behind Joe's shoulders and still-screaming face, David Mercer appeared in the doorway as the door flung open, a fire extinguisher hanging down at his side. He tossed it down on the floor with ease and ran to her. David reached down and plucked Joe away from her like a rag doll. Jessica rolled onto her side, gasping for air. David held him for a moment in mid-air, before throwing him a few feet across the room like a discarded toy. He landed with a thud and a moan.

David's worried, pleading eyes looked down at her. She coughed, sitting up a little and gave a small thumbs-up. Joe began turning over on the floor. David fixed his eyes on him and walked the few steps slowly and stopped, standing over him.

Whatever expression he had, Joe returned his gaze with a look of terror.

Now David straddled Joe, twisting his arms helplessly beneath Joe's body. David flexed his arms, then sent a crushing punch into Joe's face. His head flipped to the side. Then he launched another with his left and Joe's head flipped the other way, blood flying across the floor. Then another... and another.

He was just getting started.

David kept punching until Joe's swollen eyes rolled in his head, then finally shut. He kept punching some more, now like kneading blood-soaked raw meat.

David reached his arm once more, his huge bicep sweating and trembling. Then he let his arm drop down.

'Not worth it.'

Exhausted, David rolled off him onto the floor.

'Jessica!' shouted Charlie, bursting into the room, running to her; his eyes darting over the scene in horror. Two cops ran in behind him.

'I'm okay,' Jessica croaked, as he bent down, running a hand over her face, kissing the top of her head frantically. Then he cradled her in his arms.

The larger of the cops drew his gun, his eyes moving between Joe's still body and David. Thankfully, he turned to David and said in a friendlier tone than expected, 'Is that him?'

'Yep,' David said, nodding as he sat spread out on the floor, panting.

'Jesus,' said the second cop.

Joe suddenly turned his bloodied and swollen face to the side, coughing up blood.

Everybody jolted. The second cop pulled his own weapon and almost fired off a round into Joe.

Jessica buried her face into Charlie as he held her, stroking her hair. In the background one of the cops called for back-up and a paramedic team.

The first cop holstered his gun and pulled out his cuffs, standing over Joe as he wheezed and coughed up more blood, unable to open his battered eyes.

'Not sure I'm gonna need these,' he said, glancing towards David with a sideways smile.

'He tried to kill her... he tried to kill Jessica,' David offered.

'Don't you worry none.' The cop took in David's raw, bloodied knuckles. 'I'd say you're a damn hero then. Son-of-a-bitch had it comin'.'

218

Chapter 69

Nine Months Later

The courtroom was silent, save for the two voices exchanging the information regarding the verdict. Joe stared down at the floor impassively. His hearing had been irreversibly damaged in the events at The Waldorf. He had to concentrate hard to hear, even with the artificial aid in his ear.

'And count five?' asked a voice.

'Also guilty,' came the response.

'Count six?'

'Guilty.'

There was a flurry of shouts from the gallery, from bereaved family members.

The judge asked for silence and then declared in a solemn voice that Joe had been convicted unanimously on all charges. Joe continued to stare at the floor, his expression flat. The judge outlined exactly what he thought of Joe, which in so many words said that he considered him a real piece of shit.

After the judge had finished and asked for Joe to be led away to commence his life sentence with no chance of parole, Joe shrugged, then looked out into the court room for the first time. Seated towards the front together were Jessica, Charlie, Bev and the newly remarried Mercers.

Jessica locked eyes with him, Joe stared back. Jessica squinted her eyes, her face hard, giving him a defiant nod. A cop took Joe by his handcuffed arms and turned him around and led him towards the steps.

Joe's tongue flitted around the inside of his mouth. It found the little pin, wedged between his gum and back molars. He pushed it back further, resisting the urge to gag.

Not yet.

There would be plenty of time to decide when best to use it.

Author's Note

Firstly, thank you for buying my book, I hope you enjoyed it. If you didn't; to hell with you. Just kidding. But if you didn't, I'll try even harder with the next one. I always love to hear from readers- feel free to get in touch. I'm on all the usual social media, dear help me, even Tok-Tok.

All the best,

Simon.

Printed by Amazon Italia Logistica S.r.l.
Torrazza Piemonte (TO), Italy

56888716R00127